ALEX CANNA

The South Tower

First edition

Cover art by Philip Brook

This book was professionally typeset on Reedsy.
Find out more at reedsy.com

To every victim and hero of 9/11—and the many who were both.

I

Part One

Chapter 1

Eight more blocks to go and Nick could feel the first prickles of sweat form under his carefully ironed shirt. He was already carrying his jacket in one hand. The thinnest he had. The only one he had. Briefcase in the other hand. If only everyone would just get the hell out of his way. It's not like you're on a field trip, guys. This is Manhattan, for God's sake—empires to build, universes to master!

Nick edged his way through a sprawling line at a bus stop. For a moment he considered joining it, but a glance at the stationary traffic was enough. He'd already abandoned a yellow cab five blocks north. Past the bus stop, he accelerated again. And almost collided with a large man crossing the sidewalk with a bucket-sized cup of coffee.

"Watch yourself, man!" the coffee drinker growled.

"You watch yourself," Nick muttered, then quickly stepped back as a kid on a skateboard clattered past, school bag over his shoulder.

Another street. Another block. He looked up for the hundredth time. Up, up, and up. Even for Manhattan, they were breathtaking, so tall his brain simply refused to compute their scale or distance.

"You got eyes?"

Nick tore them from the towers. A woman had wheeled a baby stroller in front of him and he'd almost collided with it.

"My apologies." He dodged the stroller and hurried past. She looked at him strangely. Did New Yorkers not apologize? Was it his accent? How much of the Midwest was left in his accent anyway? Would the Big Swinging Dicks of the insurance industry mark him as a bumpkin, or was his accent as far beneath their notice as his sales pitch had so far proved to be?

Nick checked his watch. Again. He was okay. Unless . . .

The green man turned red. Nick squinted in a stripe of dazzling sunlight as a crowd gathered around him. A bus half turned the corner and got stuck with nowhere to go. A cacophony of horns blasted from every direction. The bus driver flung up his hands. The traffic was going nowhere, but did that mean he could cross the street? Did people take jaywalking seriously in Manhattan?

The other pedestrians stood there, griping. No one stepped out. Finally Nick dashed across, a zigzag route taking him to the next sidewalk, horns and invective ringing in his ears.

The first trickle of sweat ran down his back. He should have brought a spare shirt. He should have bought an extra shirt when he got this one. He'd just have to wear his jacket throughout the meeting. Hopefully the AC would be set to chilly. Damn the weather. It was beautiful, a clear, sunny September morning with barely a breeze. In the far distance, behind the improbably skyscraping majesty of the towers, a passenger jet arced lazily, drawing its white curves across the blue.

Hopefully New York would respond to him better than Boston had. In meeting room after meeting room, they'd listened to him politely, told him in old-money tones how thought-provoking his ideas were, shaken his hand with warm promises of future cooperation . . . and brushed him off like dandruff.

New York, he prayed, would be different. At least this was a town where people said what they felt, or so it seemed as he rushed past another cab driver confrontation.

"Where you get your license, man? Up your pimp's ass?" A local, Nick guessed. By his tone, it could have been a pleasantry. Maybe it was.

"Up your girlfriend's ass, half hour ago. Putting it back tonight too." Iranian? Turkish? But equally good natured, although a nearby cop on a motorcycle gave them a warning glance.

The traffic cleared, the two drivers saluted each other with their middle fingers, and the jostling commuters seethed onward.

4

CHAPTER 1

Nick looked up again. Had he left enough time for the elevator ride? He hadn't considered it, but it looked as if it might take some time to get to the ninety-third floor—and how long would the wait be at the bottom? Finding some clear sidewalk, Nick started to jog.

He'd pushed hard to get this meeting, and it had been put off twice already. Nick wasn't sure if he could afford another brush-off—another month and he'd probably have to go back to a quiet underwriting job, probably back in the Midwest. Underwriter. Could there be a drearier job title? He looked at the throng with envy—they all seemed to know just who they were, where they were going, and what they'd do when they got there, up on their thirty-second or sixty-sixth or one hundredth floor.

Another two blocks. Sirens. Nick rushed the last yards of the crossing as a fire engine accelerated toward it, blaring at him. Nick sniffed the air for smoke but there was nothing. Well, nothing but diesel, sweat, baking, and fermenting street gunk. Probably one of the most invigorating smells in the world, Nick realized.

And there he was, in the towers' courtyard. Limos and yellow cabs disgorged handsome men and women, talking into flip phones, eyes invisible behind mirrored sunglasses, egos on full display. Fountains gushed holy water, encircling a gleaming metal sculpture that reminded Nick of RoboCop. Another twisted piece of giant metal art looked the way Nick's stomach felt. To the left of the artwork was the South Tower entrance, below 110 dizzying stories of improbably soaring silver. His adrenaline seethed. He'd soon be up there. In the land of the gods. Where they'd be eating from the palm of his hand.

Yeah, right. Either that or feeding him to RoboCop.

Inside, the AC was blissfully refreshing. Nick lined up for security. A phone was operated, a quiet voice inquired, and Nick was ushered to a bank of elevators. Lights blazed above the doors. Whirrs and hums and muffled clanks. Doors opened and nicotine-starved capitalists spilled out, already pulling cigarette packs from shirt pockets, some with their cigarettes and lighters already in their hands.

Nick shuffled into the elevator with twenty or so work-dressed, briefcased

5

people. The doors pinged shut; gravity gnawed at his stomach, then released it, leaving him with a feeling of going nowhere while he anxiously watched the numbers, then a few seconds of ear-popping semiweightlessness as the numbers slowed and stopped.

The seventy-eighth floor. Nick followed the little crowd to another bank of elevators. Quiet lighting and muted conversations, the smallest of prework small talk. The weather was popular and could stay. The Giants were less popular.

"Lost thirty-one to twenty, yeah. Guess they just can't take the altitude in Denver."

"You watched the whole thing? I called it a night at halftime, you couldn't have gotten much sleep."

Another elevator arrived. They got in. They pushed buttons. Nick lit up 93. The doors closed and the two businessmen carried on discussing the prospects—or lack of them—of the New York Giants and their star defensive end. Nick tried to memorize details, hopefully useful for a watercooler moment in the very near future. If things got that far.

The 93 went dim. The doors opened and Nick waved at Tash, chic in black skirt and turquoise blouse. She was looking down at her watch, biting her lip.

"Tash, great to see you again!"

She looked up, relieved, smiling. "Nii-ick. Here you are!"

They shook hands. "Get you a coffee?" asked Tash, glancing at her watch again.

Yes please, thought Nick. "No thanks, I'm fine. Raring to go." The butterflies in his stomach certainly were.

"Great, our meeting room's just down this way."

Desks and offices passed in a blur. "Staying anywhere nice?"

In a fleapit over a strip bar, thought Nick. "Staying with friends in Connecticut," he said. "Connections were a bit touch-and-go this morning. Ended up doing quite a bit of walking—but I've got to say, it's the perfect day for it." Oh God, stop babbling.

"Yes, isn't it? Well, here we are." She ushered Nick into a meeting room.

Table and four chairs. On one side, a series of narrow louvre blinds separated by vertical aluminum columns. At one end, a whiteboard. And oh, yes please, a water jug and glasses. "Settle in, I'll fetch Gareth and Uday." She put down the notebook she'd been carrying and hurried off.

Nick downed two glasses of water in a row, then refilled his glass. He took his jacket off and inspected his shirt as well as he could. No sweat marks, phew. He opened his briefcase and got out his notes. On a fresh page of his notebook, he wrote, "Tash, Gareth, Uday" in a scrawl illegible enough that no one else would be able to read it. But hopefully it would save him the embarrassment of getting one of their names wrong later.

Then Tash was back with a young Asian man in gray silk trousers and a baggy white shirt. "Nick, Uday." They shook hands. Uday looked a little awkward, uncomfortable with eye contact. His eyes roamed to the wall and Nick followed his glance.

Tash noticed. "What am I thinking?" she exclaimed. She pulled a cord and one of the louvre blinds rolled itself up. "May I present . . ."

"Wow." Nick felt a giddy wash of awe and vertigo.

"Manhattan. Or some of it, anyway. Not often as clear as this, actually, you're in luck."

Sunlight burst through the narrow floor-to-ceiling window. They were looking east, over the stiletto towers and canyons of Lower Manhattan, the East River, and further away Nick could just see Lady Liberty. Far below, antlike people milled. Tiny, colorful cars, buses, and trucks crawled along the grid of streets. Boats left shining Vs on the water. Another jet glinted in the sky. Islands and high-rises sprawled into the distance.

"Do you ever get used to it?" Nick asked.

"Not really. Every day's different. Snow, fog, sun . . . so you haven't been up in the towers before?"

"Years ago, sightseeing. The weather was a disappointment though—you could barely see across the river."

"Well, when we're done here you should go up to the observation deck. You won't get a better view than today. This isn't bad, but the view to the north puts this to shame. Uh, Uday?"

Uday had sat down, facing away from the window. He smiled unconvincingly at Nick and Tash. "I'm not really a fan of heights. But please, go ahead."

"Oh, I'm sorry," said Tash. "Mind if we close the blind again, Nick?"

"No problem, it's letting in a lot of glare anyway."

As Tash closed the blind again, a man with slicked-down blond hair, pink tie, and cold eyes strode in and dumped himself in a chair opposite the window, stretching his arms out for a moment to leave his multiknobbed watch visible.

"Sorry, been on the phone with Grendan," he announced in a way that implied some respect was due.

Uday lifted his eyebrows. Tash tensed. Gareth looked at Tash as she and Nick sat down. "You have the floor."

"Okay, let's do the introductions quickly," said Tash. "Gareth here is head of risk strategy, North America. Uday is one of our top risk analysts. And this is Nick Sandini, independent risk consultant. As you know, I was recently at the Boston Risk Strategies Conference, where I caught Nick's presentation. I thought he raised some compelling points, which is why I've invited him to talk to us today."

"Ah yes, Boston." Gareth turned to Nick. "You had one of the lunchtime sessions, I recall. Get a good attendance?" Uday's lips twitched. Tash narrowed her eyes.

"Reasonable for a nonmainstream topic," said Nick, relaxed. "I'm aware I've got less time today though, so if we're ready, I'll get straight to it?" Everyone nodded. "In fact, I'll even spare you the laptop slides." Smiles. So far so good. Not that he had a laptop.

"Going to draw you a quick picture though." Uncapping one of the marker pens lying on a ledge below the whiteboard, he slashed a flat line across the space. To the left of his line, he drew a rudimentary ship with four raked-back funnels heading for an iceberg on the right. The iceberg had a small tip above the line and a large jagged mass below it.

He pointed at the tip of the iceberg. "The essence of my argument can be broken down to this one point: both in the real world and in the insurance

8

world, a perceived absence of risk actually creates risk. I call it the Titanic effect, after the ship that was famously designed and built to be impossible to sink. Which is why her captain steered her into an iceberg, why nearby ships couldn't understand why she was setting off distress flares, and why she didn't have enough lifeboats to go around. And, of course, why she was hopelessly underinsured—a disaster for her insurers, Lloyd's of London."

"All a long time ago." Gareth looked at his watch.

"Precisely. So we'd naturally expect things to be completely different today. But perhaps not. In apparent total contrast to the supposedly ultrasafe *Titanic*, we now have air travel. It was always perceived as a high-risk form of travel; to begin with, it was literally suicidal. Which is why today, trainee pilots have such a high washout rate, why the flight deck is jam-packed with every conceivable kind of double-redundant gauge, why passenger jets with Panamanian flags aren't popular—and why, amazingly, air travel is now considered extremely safe by both insurers and the airlines themselves."

On the whiteboard, Nick drew a pair of wings and a tail fin on the ship. "Which is why airliners are now flying with less spare fuel and airports have less spare landing capacity."

He jabbed the marker pen at the underwater bulk of the iceberg. "Operating on the edge of the safety margin has become standard practice. But on paper, it's still perfectly safe and within regulations.

"Now let's move on to trains."

Gareth yawned and Nick grinned. "Thank you, you've proved my point already. Boring. But boring creates risk. The safer trains appear to be, the more boring driving them becomes, the less concentration the driver can maintain, the more risk builds. And unlike air travel, where you can usually spot a looming disaster before it becomes fatal—and clear a runway or land on a motorway—errors of judgment in rail control rooms happen in moments, and once two trains are heading for each other on the same rails, there's probably nowhere else to go. But trains are so unglamorous and un–media worthy, they get away with being five times less safe than planes. They literally bore people to death.

"But the Titanic effect doesn't just apply to physical safety. Let's turn from passenger vehicles to financial ones. And yes, financial markets show the same warning signs. The difference is, traders aren't trying to minimize risk, they're trying to exploit it. The better the algorithms get at doing that, the greater the resulting appetite for risk. He—or she—who can exploit ever-larger risks wins. But, as we know, when it goes wrong—"

"LTCM," Tash said, nodding.

"Long-Term Capital Mismanagement." Uday smiled.

Gareth frowned. "Surely we've all learned the lesson from LTCM."

"Sure. So we get initial caution, followed by more complex algorithms, followed by a mentality of 'it can't happen again.' The problem is that the algorithms can only factor in data—the stuff that's known. The unknowns—and unknowables—end up as 'margins of error.' But, as I'm sure we all know, management hates margins of error: what use is a forecast with a twenty-five percent margin of error? So, under management pressure, the margin gets shrunk—and as time goes by and nothing goes wrong, it's shrunk still further, right?"

Uday chuckled, attracting a quick glare from Gareth.

"So," Gareth interrupted, "your argument . . . is that the longer nothing goes wrong, the more chance of disaster?"

Nick couldn't help smiling. "Well, no, that would be the classic gambler's fallacy, as you're well aware. Rolling nothing but sixes or having a catastrophic fire isn't more likely today because it didn't happen yesterday, or even last year. No, what changes over time—as nothing goes wrong—is people's perception of the risk, so the people whose job it is to minimize that risk start to cut corners or become negligent. Security briefings and training get deprioritized, bad habits creep in, guards sleep on the job, warning signs aren't taken seriously.

"Three Mile Island—the nuclear power station that almost went into meltdown just a couple of hundred miles away? The first sign of trouble was a little warning light everyone should have noticed, except one of the ops room staff had developed the habit of hanging his keys over it. Now, you could say he wasn't following the correct procedure. But a better procedure would have predicted complacency and prevented it.

"Those are just a few examples of how unquestioned reliance on routine creates overconfidence, leading to increased risk. But that still doesn't take into account all the people who're actively increasing risk, intentionally or unintentionally. Employees who break protocol on purpose, either because their remuneration scheme rewards risk—in the case of LTCM—or simply because they have a grudge against their employer.

"And then you've got the people who're actively looking for targets to destroy. They love routine: they can research it and plan a way around it. So an iconic target, with a highly structured security routine, is what excites them most."

"Courageous of you to visit us up here then," deadpanned Gareth.

Along with Tash and Uday, Nick laughed politely. "I was going to get back to air travel but, yeah, the World Trade Center is actually a great example. So far, it's had one major attempt to bring it down: the car bomb in the underground parking lot, back in 'ninety-three. The obvious reaction to that was heightened security. And that obviously makes everyone who works here feel safe enough to stay around. But there's another response to the bombing that has actually increased risk for everybody here."

Nick paused for a sip of water. Uday's eyes twitched toward the still-open blind. "Well, don't keep us in suspense," said Gareth, and Nick noticed a tiny smile from Tash. He put his glass back on the table.

"So we're in the World Trade Center back in 1993. A rented van is driven into the underground parking garage. It's loaded with a twelve-hundred-pound homemade bomb, a mixture of nitroglycerine and dynamite surrounded by hydrogen cylinders. There are two people in the van. They light a twelve-minute fuse and get the hell out. The blast is supposed to topple the North Tower into the South Tower. Instead, it opens up a six-story underground crater. Five port authority workers are killed, plus the child one of them is pregnant with, but amazingly just one car driver dies. About a thousand people are injured though, mostly from smoke inhalation in the stairwells and elevator shafts. The fire burns for two hours. Twenty-four people are rescued from the rooftops by helicopter."

"And that fucking Arab terrorist escapes to Pakistan," said Gareth.

Uday studied his hands, his mouth a thin line.

Nick continued. "Straight after the blast, the human error factor starts to mount. At first, some authorities decide the explosion was caused by a malfunctioning transformer. Even after they realize it was a bomb, the experts still have wildly different theories about what kind of bomb it was. There's even a theory, with no evidence, that it released cyanide.

"Then a piece of the van is discovered, and they trace the van to a rental outlet in Jersey City. To which, incredibly, one of the conspirators returns to collect his deposit, claiming the van's been stolen."

"Unbelievable," said Tash, shaking her head.

"So he's arrested, followed by his coconspirators. More or less. One of the two guys in the van's already fled to Pakistan, as you said. The other guy in the van is arrested and then, guess what, he's released. He flees to Iraq.

"But the biggest error? That would be the one made by the FBI before the bombing. An Egyptian informant warned them about the plan a whole year earlier. Turns out the FBI considered using the guy in a sting operation, but they abandoned the idea and did nothing further with their intel. But instead of the FBI taking some responsibility, the victims are still trying to sue the NY Port Authority—the WTC's operators—for damages, claiming they were negligent in letting the car into the parking lot."

"And I'll bet my Rolex that'll be laughed right out of court," sneered Gareth.

"But in the meantime, it's a distraction from the real causes of risk. The FBI wasn't forced to learn their lesson. While, under threat of legal action, the port authority is now checking parcels, for God's sake. *Parcels.* That bomb weighed twelve hundred pounds."

"Exactly. Having them vet our stationery supplies makes us all feel better," Tash said, smiling.

"No paperclip bombs," laughed Uday.

"And perhaps the most crucial result, the port authority got into a turf war with the police and fire departments and now dictates its own policies on what should happen if there's another bomb or fire. Which has very little chance of meshing with what the emergency service personnel are trained for. But that's still not what concerns me most. While the official view is that it can't happen again, the guy who built the bomb is still out there. And he and his followers have got an age-old grudge to settle and all the time in the world to figure out how they're going to do it, and they now know why their first attempt didn't work the way they wanted it to."

"What do you mean?" asked Tash.

"Well, the investigation showed that if the car had been parked just a few yards from where it was, the explosion would have undermined the North Tower's support and toppled it onto this one. Like dominoes."

Uday looked a little ill.

"Okay . . . but do you really think they'd risk using the same tactics a second time?" asked Tash.

"Probably not. But there's a fanatic out there who's had eight more years to study these buildings. If there's a vulnerability, and there always is, he'll have figured it out. Getting it wrong is a sore point with him, and he wants to make amends. For us, it's abstract. For him, it's deeply personal."

"So . . ." Uday rubbed his face. "You're saying the risk management procedure becomes the risk?"

"Yes. The procedure creates a sense of security. Security creates complacency. Complacency creates risk. Either because people start thinking it's safe to take the occasional shortcut or flaunt procedure—like Three Mile Island—or because the chain of command loses sight of risk and makes bad decisions—like with the *Challenger* disaster, where management overruled the people who understood the dangers.

"Or, finally, because the procedure becomes visible to an outsider—or insider—with their own agenda. Someone who actively studies the procedure to figure out its weakest point and exploit it. So the mail room may be scanning for explosives—but what about nerve gas or anthrax? You don't have to destroy the building to cause a disaster."

"So here's the thing," Gareth interrupted. "According to your interpretation, everything develops an unquantified additional risk over time. Fine. Maybe you're right. But if we slap an escalating premium onto everything we insure, how many clients do we end up with? They'll just go somewhere else."

Tash raised a finger. "That's not what Nick's proposing though. And I'm guessing he's just about to get to that." She smiled at Nick.

Nick grinned. "Thanks for the segue. Yes, here's where it gets interesting. At the moment, insurance premiums are based on averaged risk—so I might pay the same premium on my car as my neighbor does, because we both drive about the same distance each year and we both park on the same street at night. But the insurer can't see my neighbor has started taking a shortcut through the local gangland with his doors unlocked, while I'm sticking to the freeway.

"Obviously it's not worth the insurer's time to investigate our car usage to that level. But on the level of jumbo jets and office buildings? Absolutely. So what I'm offering you is sophisticated modeling that can show you how one airline's risk is increasing over time, or how much riskier this world-famous building we're in right now is compared to that shorter one nobody's heard of outside the window."

For the tiniest fraction of a second, Gareth's eyes narrowed in what was almost a flinch.

Nick continued. "When you've modeled the dynamic risk profile, you can sell the client a risk reduction program—which they pay for upfront—followed by lower premiums. A unique competitive offering you can use to attract more clients. And at the same time, you end up with less risk on your books. More business. Less risk. Everybody wins."

Tash leaned forward. "That's what attracted me to this idea, Gareth. More income upfront, less risk on our books—plus the prospect of actually reducing risk in the real world. Which, after all, is what insurance is all about. Not just picking up the pieces after the Three Mile Islands and the *Challengers*, but keeping the pieces together. And that's what clients will buy into."

Gareth was silent. Nick waited. He didn't know it, but he was holding his breath.

Then Uday piped up. "The dynamic risk profile, as you call it . . . would you show it to the client upfront? As a basis for negotiation?"

"It all depends—"

14

"Because I was thinking if you do, and the client says no, they don't want the risk reduction program, they just want to carry on as they were, do we increase their premiums and maybe chase them away? Do we buy reinsurance? And if we do, do we show the reinsurers the new risk profile? Are we legally required to? In which case . . ."

Gareth started to smile, leaning back with arms folded across his chest.

Nick returned his smile, reached into his briefcase, and brought out a slim folder. "I was kind of hoping you'd bring up those issues, because this is where it gets really interesting. But also a little more technical. What I'd like to—"

Then the world rocked on its foundations.

* * *

"What in the name of fuck was that?" said Gareth.

They all looked at each other. The water in the glass jug was still rippling gently. They could dimly hear car alarms, what sounded like hundreds of them.

"A demolition, maybe?" suggested Nick. Tash and Gareth opened two of the blinds and they looked out, Uday standing well back.

At first it didn't look any different; perhaps more birds were flying about. "The traffic's completely stopped," said Tash.

They all peered down, except for Uday. "They're getting out of their cars," Nick pointed out.

"That boat, look! It's turning around," said Tash. What looked like a tour boat that had been heading eastward, probably to the Statue of Liberty, was doing a tight U-turn.

Tash caught Nick's eye. I have a very bad feeling about this, he almost said but didn't.

Someone stuck their head inside the door. "We've just heard from someone in the North Tower," he said breathlessly. "Some kind of explosion."

Gareth whipped around from the window, looking like he'd been punched. He turned to Nick. "This isn't some kind of sales stunt?"

Nick shook his head, confused. Gareth had begun to sweat, pulling at his tie and pushing back his hair.

Uday had backed away from the window to stand by the door. "I think we should . . . I think we should maybe get out of the building."

Damn fine idea, thought Nick. "I'm with you. Coming, Tash?"

"I think that's probably wise. Gareth?"

Gareth reacted as if he'd been slapped in the face. "The North Tower will be fine," he said vehemently. "And so will this one."

A wide-eyed young female admin appeared in the doorway. "Gareth? Grendan is asking for you in his office. Really urgently."

Gareth downed his glass of water. He looked as if he wished it were neat alcohol. "Right," he said to nobody. "Let's go see what Grendan wants." And he lurched out of the room.

"I think the rest of us had better just head downstairs," said Tash. "Let's go." The admin looked uncertain. "Kendra? You too, you're coming with us."

On the way to the elevators, the place was buzzing. No one even pretended to work. Some were heading to the elevators. The rest were either uncertain whether they were allowed to or simply scorned the idea.

As the four of them stood waiting for an elevator, a rumor leapt through the workers like a bolt of lightning.

"A what?"

"A plane?"

The elevator doors opened and they stumbled in, shocked. An uneasy silence enveloped them as they descended. Too soon, the doors pinged open again. Nick tensed, then realized he was back at the seventy-eighth floor Sky Lobby.

They got out and joined a confused mob waiting for an elevator to ground level. A uniformed security guard arrived, wearing a port authority badge. They turned to her, clamoring for information.

"Do you know what's going on?"

"Can you tell us—"

"Folks," she said in a commanding voice. "I need to ask you all to please return to your workplaces. Things are a little confused on the ground right now and we need to keep things calm down there to let the emergency personnel do their jobs. Please return to your workplaces. We will keep you informed. No, I have no further information right now."

By sheer force of a badge and personality, she herded most of them away from the bank of Down elevators. Still, many persisted and as soon as an elevator's doors opened, they packed their way in, pleading unmissable appointments.

"Die-hard smokers," commented Tash.

"Should we follow them?" suggested Nick. He looked at Uday, who looked extremely uncomfortable.

"I'm fine," said Uday. "We can go back upstairs."

Bravado, thought Nick. Probably one of the most common causes of death. He turned to Tash.

She shrugged. "I guess we go back up again."

"Um, to be honest, I think our meeting might be over," said Nick.

Tash gave him a glance. "Are you kidding? After your risk analysis just proved one hundred percent accurate? This may just be your moment. Come on."

"Sure, but what about Gareth? He looked like he's in some kind of situation—it certainly didn't look like I was going to be his priority anymore."

"Let's just see, shall we? I have no idea what's going on, but maybe it's something you can help with."

As they waited for their elevator, more and more people began to defy the port authority's advice. Then Tash noticed Kendra standing awkwardly between the two elevator banks.

"Kendra, what are you doing? I thought you were heading downstairs. Go on, get in that elevator over there."

As Kendra paused in indecision, the open elevator quickly filled up with people squeezing and shoving their way in.

"Space for one more?" called Tash.

"We'll barely get the doors closed," someone replied.

"And we can already hardly breathe in here," grumbled another, making a face at another woman worming her way in sideways.

The doors closed.

"Okay, Kendra, you stay here and just make sure you're on the next one down," said Tash, heading across to the other elevator bank with Nick and Uday.

* * *

Back on the ninety-third floor, the place was seething.

"Come on," said Tash. "Let's just take a minute to see what we can from the windows on the other side."

They joined the crowd pressed to the north-facing windows, watching the black smoke gushing from the top floors of the North Tower just fifty yards away, driven by massive gouts of flame.

"My God, you can feel the heat right through the windows."

"Imagine what it's like for those people."

"I've just heard the top floors are totally cut off."

"With all that smoke up there? How can they breathe?"

"Not so sure they can."

"What kind of plane was it?"

"They're saying it was a private plane."

"Like a Cessna?"

"If that's fuel that's burning, it must have been a mighty big Cessna."

"Why aren't there helicopters trying to rescue them?"

"You think they can land in that smoke?"

"Hey, there's a TV in one of the meeting rooms. Let's go see what they're saying."

Some of the crowd moved off. Tash and Nick followed.

Tash spotted a colleague. "Rico! Have you seen Gareth anywhere? We were just in a meeting."

Rico blew out air, shaking his head. "You haven't heard?"

"Heard what?"

"He just insured the World Trade Center."

18

"No!" Tash looked shaken, hardly able to breathe. "Please say you're joking."

Rico shook his head. "Wish I was."

"You are fucking joking."

"Seriously. He made us liable for"—he pointed—"that."

"When?"

"Emailed them a commitment first thing this morning, apparently. Been negotiating confidentially for weeks."

"That's insane. Sure it's a great contract to win, but who insures the building they work in themselves? It's insane."

"Well, he's with Grendan now. They're trying to see if they can back out of the deal."

"Well, that's honorable."

"Right now, it's survival. The reinsurance deals aren't all agreed on yet. Actually, I don't know if any are."

"So this whole company . . ."

"Might not be here come lunchtime. It all depends on how bad the fire is and how many people are trapped up there—and who was in control of that plane."

"Jesus, this is awful. There are people dead, people burning alive, and here we are worrying about our fucking jobs." Tash looked around. "Keep quiet about this, OK? Less panic, the better."

"No sweat. Well, I'm off to see what the TV's saying," said Rico. "Find out whether I need to get my résumé out."

They followed. The room with the TV was so crowded they could only stand outside, where they couldn't hear the commentary properly, just the people around them.

"Guy on the TV's saying there's been an explosion in the South Tower."

"*Our* tower? Holy shit!"

"Where? What floor?"

"Didn't say. And you can't see the South Tower in the footage, just the North Tower."

"Think both towers got hit at once?"

"By planes?"

"No, by bombs."

"Makes sense. It sounded like more than one explosion."

"I heard three explosions."

"Me too."

"So you think we're on fire too?"

"Don't think so, I guess they just got it wrong."

"Who would even do this?"

"Same guys who tried to blow up the North Tower in 'ninety-three. Arab terrorists."

"Didn't they catch all those guys?"

"The actual bomber got away."

"What do those loonies even want?"

"Looking for a war, I think."

"They're going to get one."

"Anyone know who owns the WTC?"

"Isn't it a consortium?"

"I heard the insurance policy was due for renewal recently."

"As long as we didn't get it."

"Guys, is that all you can think about?"

"Uh, are you suggesting the owners sabotaged their own building?"

"Hey, guy on the TV's corrected himself, it's just the North Tower."

"Thank God."

"So what were the other explosions?"

"Three bombs, I guess."

"What about the plane?"

"*Tash!*" A shout from down the way.

"Oh shit, it's Grendan. Our boss. Follow me."

Tash hurried down the corridor to where a bear of a man stood, short red hair in tufts, shirt trailing over his trousers, tie pulled loose.

"Tash," he roared. "How does Head of Risk North America appeal to you?"

"But . . . Gareth?"

"But Gareth what? That cocksucker doesn't work here anymore. So look—I know you're wondering if the job actually has a future beyond five minutes ago, but you've got more brains in your tiny little butt than that fucker had in his entire gene pool. Christ, the short-dicked prick couldn't satisfy a donut, yet still he manages to screw us?"

"Grendan!"

"What?"

"I'm honored. I accept the job."

"Excellent. Well, let's go sit down and figure out what to do with this mess your predessfucker just shat on us. Did I tell you I'm pissed off?"

"Grendan."

"Yes, what?"

"I'd like you to meet my first hire, Nick. Grendan, meet Nick Sandini. Uh, we're still working on his exact title."

"Congratulations. Wouldn't stress about the title just yet though. Right, I'll see you in a meeting room on the south side in one minute. I'm going to round up a legal or two. And bring him, looks like he's the only person not losing it this morning. Myself included."

Grendan stomped off in one direction, Tash and Nick in the other.

"What the hell was that?" asked Nick.

"That was Grendan, force of nature. You'll get used to him. You were going to meet with him if Gareth gave you the okay. No longer necessary. I thought I'd short-circuit things."

"I noticed. Thanks."

"You're welcome. Okay, let's try this meeting room. Everyone's over on the north side, we should be fine here."

There were glasses and a water jug on the table, obviously left over from an abandoned meeting. Nick poured out two glasses, gave one to Tash, and clinked his glass against hers. "Thanks very much for the job offer."

"Offer? You mean you're still thinking about it?"

"I accept."

"Congratulations." She smiled. "I think. I hope. Wait, what's that now?"

An announcement was being made over the PA system: ". . . if the conditions warrant on your floor, you may wish to start an orderly evacuation."

"Now they tell us. Can't they make up their damned minds?"

* * *

"Bitch!"

They spun around to the door. Gareth stood there, cardboard box in his arms. He flung it down and miscellaneous desk drawer junk flew out over the floor. Nick noted a nasal hair shaver, a couple of ties, and a copy of *The Art of the Deal*.

"You fucking scheming bitch! You couldn't wait to tell Grendan, could you?"

"What? That's nonsense, I—"

"And you!" Gareth grabbed Nick by the tie and shoved him up against the wall. "You and your bullshit theory. I'll show you an increased-risk scenario!"

The blinds were open, and with the window facing south, Nick had a perfect view. His eyes went wide, his mouth open.

"What the fuck . . ."

A big passenger jet, missile gray, flying lower than their own window, was hurtling northward into Manhattan like a monstrous metal shark.

". . . is that plane . . ."

As if it had spotted its prey, the plane swung left to plunge straight toward them. Its engines screamed louder and louder and they all turned to look as its cockpit filled their field of vision, its windows like mad, malevolent eyes.

". . . doing!"

And they were all thrown across the room.

* * *

It sounded like the end of the world.

First was the sound of two jet engines, just yards away, screaming like they were about to burst. Then was the sound of God knows how many tons of

22

airliner smashing straight through the steel and glass frame of the tower, followed by the now-mangled plane being ripped to pieces by the concrete floors of the tower, which acted like a giant cheese grater. The sound of those separate pieces of airliner scraping at high velocity between the floors of the tower, smashing, tumbling, and ricocheting into and through walls, office furniture, and people, while its tons of jet fuel erupted. Followed by the sound of whatever was left of the airliner smashing into the far side of the tower. And the sound of tons of detonating jet fuel bursting out through the smashed north and west windows and exploding into giant balls of flame. All of this noise compressed into less than a second. Followed by a moment of comparative silence as people, office partitions, furniture, computers, and printers tumbled and fell to the floor.

It looked like Tash was screaming as she tried to stand, and Nick had a feeling he was shouting too, but his sensory system seemed to have shut down. He stopped moving his mouth. Then the screams of scores of people hit him all at once, like hell's volume knob had been given a twist.

He crawled over and hugged Tash, but she'd already stopped screaming. He looked around to see how Gareth was and found him staring contemptuously from the corner of the room, somehow still standing, back against the wall. "Oh, look, Mr. Boy Scout fell down," Gareth sneered.

Nick stood. The impact and noise had somehow affected his balance and he had to lean on the table for support. The tabletop was slippery with water, and he almost went down but recovered. He reached down for Tash and helped her up.

"We've got to get out of here!" Nick heard himself shout, transfixed by the boiling black smoke that had blotted out the view outside.

"Follow me!" Tash shouted back at him.

They staggered out through the meeting room door. It was as if they'd walked into a different world. Dust billowed. Ceiling panels hung haphazardly. Office partitions leaned crazily. The floor was a tumbled sea of furniture, paper, folders, computers, and monitors—and people, struggling to sit, stand, or simply wipe the blood off their faces.

"Gareth!" shouted Tash. She went back into the meeting room, where

Gareth still leaned against the wall staring vacantly out the window. She walked over to him and put a hand on his shoulder.

"Oh, fuck off," he snarled, brushing her hand away.

"For God's sake, get your shit together. Come on!" She gave him another second, then shook her head and turned back to the door. Outside, people were drifting to the stairwell doors. Others were packing their briefcases or changing their shoes.

"Come on, nearest stairwell is this way," said Tash, leading.

They followed a group of other people. Run! Run! thought Nick. It was as if they were so determined not to panic and lose control they were intentionally moving extra slowly. Or were they just dazed?

"Pull your thumbs out!" shouted someone from behind them. "Last one out of the building gets fired. Let's move!"

The pace quickened, and Nick breathed out with relief. Still, there was a bottleneck in front of them as people held the stairwell door open for each other. Nick grabbed a loose sheet of paper off the nearest desk and folded and refolded it into a wedge. As he and Tash got to the door, he rammed the folded edge underneath it and kicked it tight. Now the door could stay open on its own.

"Nice work," said the person behind Nick.

They hit the dimly lit stairs and began the downward trudge. Smoke was already trickling up the stairwell, getting thicker all the time. It smelled like nothing Nick had ever smelled before: a mixture of burning fuel, chemicals, meat, fabric, and who knows what. He needed something to put over his mouth and nose. Damn, he'd left his jacket in the meeting room. He wrenched at his left shirtsleeve, just below the shoulder. He got a tear going and ripped. He undid the cuff and kept ripping until he had the sleeve completely loose, then, holding both ends, pulled it tight over his mouth and nose and tied the ends behind his head.

He started on the right sleeve. It was more difficult this time using his left hand, but finally he got it off. Tash was a few stairs ahead of him. She looked around in surprise when he tapped her on the shoulder, then took the sleeve and tied it around her own face. Below them, people were already

24

coughing from the smoke, but so far, nobody was panicking.

"I chose a helluva day to wear stilettos," said a woman to general laughter.

A man was trying his cell phone. "No signal," he said, snapping it shut.

A heavily built woman was struggling to keep up the pace. She stopped, panting heavily. "You go on ahead," she said to her colleagues. "I'll catch up with you in a bit."

As they squashed past her, someone grumbled, "They could have made these stairs wider, you can barely fit two people next to each other."

Then they all stopped dead. "What's going on?" people muttered. Below them, they could see people turning around.

"Stairwell's blocked," someone shouted. "Completely disintegrated and on fire. We're going to have to go back up or find another stairwell."

They joined a patient huddle of people trying to get back out of the stairwell and emerged into an unknown business, everyone looking just as confused and anxious as back on the ninety-third floor.

Someone gave them a curious look and they pulled down their makeshift bandit bandannas.

Nick turned to Tash. "Just trying to figure this out. The plane hit us on the south side of the building, just below us, and it was pitched over at an angle like this." He tipped his right hand, thumb down, little finger stretched out. "So—"

"You saw it flying toward us?"

"Yeah. It was flying crazy low, heading north, then it just tipped over and swung right into us. So what I'm saying is, let's try a stairwell on the other side of the building."

"Got it. Follow me."

Tash led the way through the debris. "What's going on here?" she whispered. "Why are so few people trying to get out? They're mostly just hanging around their desks."

At that moment, the PA system boomed out. "Please remain at your desks while we investigate the situation. Please remain—"

"Well, screw that," said Tash as they reached the fire door. "Stairwell A" read the eyelevel sign. Nick pushed it open and they joined another ragged stream of people trudging down the stairs. The smoke wasn't quite as bad as before, but Nick and Tash kept their bandannas around their necks.

"Looking good," said Nick. "Depending on how high the plane hit, we might even be able to catch an elevator from the Sky Lobby."

"That would be a relief," said Tash over her shoulder. "I'm not looking forward to ninety floors of this."

Once again, the stream of descending people concertinaed to a halt. "Can't get down," they heard a woman's echoing call from below. "It's completely blocked."

"You sure?" someone responded.

"I'm sure. It's all blocked up with rubble. No way through."

Around them, people swore and muttered.

"What should we do?" said Tash.

"Is there another stairwell?"

They went down one flight to the nearest door, the sound of a fire alarm wailing behind it. The man in front of Nick opened it toward them. A blast of heat and smoke gushed out, and the man cried out and slammed it shut again, coughing and touching his burned face.

"You okay?" said Nick.

"Just about. Glad I don't work on this floor."

They looked at each other in horror as the implication sank in.

"You can say that again," someone agreed, and they hurried higher up the stairs.

"Let's give it another couple of floors," said Nick. "We need to get a bit farther above the fire."

As they climbed, more smoke followed them from below, and Nick and Tash put their bandannas back on. Two floors up, the straggling crowd was met by a group of people coming out of a fire door. The conversation wasn't promising.

"Why are you guys coming back up? Can't you get through?"

"No, this stairwell's blocked and on fire."

"Shit. The others are no good either."

"Oh God no. You've tried them all?"

26

"That's what they say."

"So what now?"

"We're gonna head for the roof. Maybe they'll organize an airlift."

"What? Like they organized our evacuation when the other tower got hit?"

"Can't see how we have much choice, really."

"Guess you're right there. Okay guys, up we go."

* * *

At the eighty-eighth floor, they could all hear the frenzied banging on the other side of the shut fire door.

Nick twisted the handle and pulled. It was either stuck solid or locked. But now muffled shouts came through the door. "Hey! Help us! The door's jammed shut!"

Nick looked up. The wall above the door looked profoundly cracked and the doorjamb was warped.

"Even if they get the door open, it looks like the ceiling's going to come down on top of them," said Tash.

The people around them looked at each other, helpless, and climbed on.

"Can you get to another stairwell?" Nick shouted at the door.

"Too much rubble!"

"You're going to have to try and move it!"

The muffled sound of an argument came through the door.

Then: "Okay! We'll give it a try!"

"Good luck!" shouted Nick.

There was a double tap on the other side of the door and then silence.

As Nick and Tash followed the crowd higher, they heard a crash from above. Seconds later, dust billowed down onto them.

Two floors higher, they found the fire door open with rubble all around it. Inside, roof beams and cabling hung in a haze of dust. A man sat on the stairs, mummified with dust, blood soaking down one side of his face and into his shirt.

"All right, buddy?" said one of the climbers.

"Fine, fine, I'll follow you guys in just a minute."

Finally, just below the 105th floor, the migration came to a halt. "What now?" grumbled Nick.

A man a few stairs up from Nick and Tash turned around and broadcasted the news. "They're saying the roof door is locked. And the indoor observation deck isn't open yet either."

The news was greeted with a mixture of swearing, despair, and resignation. A few people simply sat down and sobbed. Then, with no explanation, the crowd started moving upstairs again.

"What's happening? Has someone unlocked it?"

"God, please, please, please."

But at the 105th floor, the door stood open, and they crowded through it into the now-familiar debris-strewn chaos. "Is this as high as we can go?" asked Nick.

"I guess so," said Tash. "There's no tenant on one-oh-six right now. They moved out a while back. The indoor observation deck's on one-oh-seven but usually only opens later."

Nick was puzzled. "Aren't there floors higher than that?"

Tash explained. "Two more floors. But they're just for machinery. AC, elevator winches, whatever. They'll be locked too, and besides, they don't have roof access. There's an escalator from one-oh-seven that goes right through them to the roof."

"Well, at this point the observation deck door sounds like our most promising option," said Nick. "How do we get there?"

"Stairwell B. At least, that's what someone told me the last time we had a fire drill. Can't take—*cough*—much more of this though."

They found Stairwell B and trudged upward, squeezing past a line of people coming down in defeat. Two floors up, a knot of people pounded and kicked at the solid fire door. A keyhole looked impassively back at them.

"Anyone in there?" shouted a tall black man. "Open the door!"

"When does it usually open?" asked Nick.

"Nine thirty, I think," Tash replied.

"Would the people who work up here have arrived yet?"

"Doubt it."

Another man turned to them. "If nobody's in there yet, they're quite likely stuck in an elevator right now. With the key."

"What about the other stairwells?" asked Nick. "How high do they go?"

"All the way up," said the tall black man, "But the doors are solid steel and locked." He shook his head. "I've tried them both. This one's our best bet. Anybody want to charge it with me?"

Nick nodded. "Let's do it. I'm Nick, by the way."

"Jerome. On three?" He and Nick shoulder-charged the door. It was like charging a boulder. "That's one solid door," said Jerome, staggering back.

Nick agreed, rubbing his shoulder. "Damn. My shoulder feels half broken."

"Unlike the door," said Tash. "Look, we can barely breathe up here, let's go back down to 105."

On 105, the smoke was growing thicker by the minute. With few chairs available, most people sat on the floor in small groups. Nick and Tash sat by a north-facing window with a relatively clear view of Manhattan. Looking west, they had a direct but smoke-obstructed view of the North Tower. At a nearby desk, a woman was on the phone. "We need to open the door to the roof. No, you don't understand, there's too much smoke inside and it's getting worse." She shook her head and replaced the phone. "Nine-one-one. All they do is tell us to sit tight and wait."

Everyone else with a cell phone was trying to get a signal. A few were lucky.

"Honey? There's an accordion file up in the study—yeah, that one. It's got all our insurance policies in it, plus our other admin stuff. I've been meaning to sort out our home insurance—I think it might be overdue. Honey? Honey? Shit, cut off."

"Babe it's me. No, there's no fire on our floor, just this smoke. No, they say there's no way down. Babe, you'll have to fetch Amelie tonight. Remember her favorite book is *Green Eggs and Ham*. I love you, babe."

A Blackberry was being passed around. "This thing's getting a signal if anyone wants to make a call."

A large, bald man staggered past, coughing, red-faced, eyes streaming. He almost tripped over a trio of Asian women sitting on the floor, and he stopped and jabbed a finger at them.

"It's always your people causing this shit," he said loudly.

The women looked up at him, startled. "Our people? What do you mean?" one replied. "We're Indian."

"Ignore him," said one of her colleagues. "He's just frightened." They continued their conversation in what Nick presumed was Hindi, with an occasional contemptuous glance at their accuser.

The bald man glared around, ready for more confrontation. A bearded man, leaning against the wall and wearing thick glasses and a camouflage-patterned flak jacket, obliged.

"You think this is caused by Arabs? I assure you this has nothing to do with them. This is Bush and Cheney, engineering an excuse to go back and finish off Iraq."

"Ah, bullshit, man, you mean to tell me the American government is behind this?"

"George Bush, his dad, and the CIA. They want to finish what they started in Iraq—and Dick Cheney wants to get his hands on all those oil fields. Him and his oil industry buddies."

"Bullshit."

Flak Jacket spread his hands. "Of course you don't believe me. That's what they're counting on. But did you hear the news guy? Saying the South Tower got hit five minutes before it did? He already had the script, man—but the plane was late, so he had to apologize and change his story. All preplanned, man. You'll see."

Tash turned to Nick and said quietly, "I don't know which of them is stupider. Or more offensive."

"Barely half an hour and there's already a conspiracy theory. These guys are unbelievable," agreed Nick.

The smoke grew thicker, coming in through the air vents below the windows. People laid jackets over the vents. Most of the crowd improvised their own bandannas from shirtsleeves.

"Unbelievable," said Tash. "First they tell us to go back to our desks when we could have all evacuated, then they lock us into a death zone. What next?"

"There must be a way out. Somehow, we have to get through that door."

"We tried. It's a fire door, after all."

"And meanwhile, the smoke's getting thicker. Stay here, I'm going to find a window opener."

"What do you mean?"

"Hang on, I'll show you."

Nick came back less than a minute later, dragging a heavy square planter. There was a hole in the soil where he'd ripped out whatever had been growing in it.

"Hope nobody arrests me, but I think we need this more than the ficus did."

Nick dragged the planter to a window, picked it up and swung it at the glass. The planter bounced back, the window still intact.

"What are you doing?" yelled a man. "You'll just give the fire more oxygen."

"The fire's twenty stories below us, and it's got all the oxygen it wants," replied Nick reasonably, but the man wasn't ready to listen.

"Don't break the window, you'll just make it worse."

Someone else took Nick's side. "Look, dude, we won't be able to breathe in a few minutes anyway. Do you want us all to asphyxiate?"

Nick swung the planter again, aiming one of its bottom corners at the window. At the moment of impact, the entire window burst into pebble-sized crumbs of glass, with Nick and the planter almost following them into space.

"Wow. Wasn't expecting that," said Nick, setting the planter down shakily.

"It's tempered glass," said Nick's ally. "Way stronger than the normal stuff, but when it does break, it's instant. And harmless." He picked up a small chunk and rubbed it between his fingers to demonstrate. "See? No sharp edges."

Nick put his head through the now-clear window and took a massive breath of nearly fresh air. Luckily, the window was just below the dense blanket of smoke coming from the North Tower. Immediately a crowd formed around him, all desperate for air.

"Let me take that from you," said Jerome. "I'll open a few more windows."

"Thanks," said Nick. "It looks like this side of the building has got the least smoke outside."

"Well," Nick said after more windows had been smashed out, "at least it's a bit cooler now. Not sure if it's much less smoky though."

"At least we can get an occasional clean breath," said Tash. "It's just a waiting game now, it all depends on the fire department."

Behind them, a woman was pleading into a phone. "We're stuck up here and the smoke's real bad, real bad. You've got to get us some help, fast. I don't know how long we can last." She listened, then put the phone down.

"Was that the fire department?" someone asked.

"Nine-one-one. They say the firemen are in the building, we just have to sit tight. But I've got to say that woman didn't sound too confident."

"I don't want to come across all negative," growled Jerome, "but the fire department has two buildings with massive fires more than eighty floors up to deal with. I'm not sure there's much they can do."

Flak Jacket sidled closer. "Take it from me, they're not interested in saving us. They'll have been instructed to stay out of the way."

"And I'm instructing you to stay the fuck away from me," replied Jerome. "Any more of your horseshit theories and you're going straight out a window." He looked around. "I suggest y'all give your families a call, if you can."

Nick exhaled slowly. His eyes stung. Must be the smoke. He leaned out a window, not wanting to face anyone for a minute. That was when he saw it. Except his brain refused to make any sense of it at all.

A bundle of fabric, falling from one of the North Tower windows, flapping faster and faster as it accelerated. It was only the screams from a woman at the next window that forced him to accept what he was seeing. "Someone's jumped! Oh my God! Someone's jumped!" It seemed to fall forever, long enough for everyone nearby to turn and see. Then the bundle – a living *woman* – hit the plaza far below and was still.

A wave of horror swept through the onlookers: shrieking, gasping, sobbing. Then the horror slowly turned to fear. And all around Nick, people pulled out their cell phones and started to dial.

Nick turned from the view to look for Tash. She was sitting two windows away, her head bowed between her knees, shoulders shaking.

He took a deep breath and went over to her. Kneeling down, he put a hand on her shoulder. She looked up, face wet and streaked with grime. Nick dug in a pocket and produced a clean tissue. She wiped her eyes and blew her nose.

"Your family?" asked Nick.

She shook her head. More tears, a gasping moan. Nick waited a few seconds. "You don't have any family? Anywhere?"

She shook her head. "Back in India. In Bangalore. I didn't marry the worthless piece of shit they chose for me, I didn't become a housewife, or a mother, or even a doctor. I was basically a total disaster for them. At some point they stopped recognizing my existence. My brothers too. Last time I tried to call my mother, there was just a message saying the number had changed."

"Jesus, that's rough. I'm sorry," said Nick. He sat next to her, arm around her. She leaned her head on his shoulder.

"You?" she said.

"Me?" he replied, avoiding the issue.

"Your family."

Nick took a deep breath and coughed convulsively for a few seconds, eyes streaming. "Sorry. Car crash. I was seventeen. I was driving." He felt her tense up, and took his arm off her shoulder. She took his hand and looked into his eyes. He looked down. "I pulled out in front of a truck," he continued haltingly. "It was signaling a turn, but it . . . it just kept coming."

"God, that's awful. Who was in the car?"

"My parents. My brother. I barely got a scratch."

"That's a lot for a seventeen-year-old to handle."

"Tell me about it. Anyway, years later, that's why I became a risk consultant. It's not a career, it's more like compensation. My deal with the world, trying to even the numbers. And now, today . . . I haven't made the slightest difference. Not one goddamn bit." He looked into Tash's eyes, then lost control in an eruption of guilt, self-pity, and grief. Tash held his hand until he turned away to wipe his eyes and nose.

* * *

Back under control, Nick found himself watching a helicopter hovering in the distance. Safety, so near, yet so hopelessly distant. Did they feel as helpless as he did? As if to taunt him, the floor shook, and the whole building rumbled ominously.

"Guys, does it feel like the floor's just tilted slightly?" It was Jerome.

"Can't be sure, but now that you mention it . . . if we had a ball bearing, or just a ball, we could see if it rolls."

"What else is round?"

"A water glass?"

Jerome looked around and found a glass that hadn't been broken when the plane hit. It looked perfectly cylindrical. He placed it on its side on top of a desk and let go.

Slowly but steadily it began to roll. It gathered speed, rolling right off the desk into Nick's waiting hand.

"Try another desk," said Jerome.

It rolled on two other desks.

"Doesn't look good," said Nick. "If—"

They felt the floor shake again for a couple of seconds. There may have been a distant crash somewhere below them; Nick wasn't sure with all the other noise going on.

"Try it again?"

Nick put the glass on its side again and it seemed to run faster this time. Jerome shook his head, grimacing hopelessly.

Nick went over to Tash, sitting by a smashed-out window and hanging out for the occasional breath. She was shaking, sobbing quietly. She looked up as Nick sat down next to her.

"I don't know how many people I've watched jumping from the North

Tower," she said. "Men. Women. I know you saw the danger, but how did we all get this so wrong?"

Nick put his arm around her. "I don't want to have to jump," Tash continued. "I have to have hope. No matter what."

Nick was silent for a moment, then said, "If the ceiling were to fall down . . . where would the safest place for us be?"

"Jesus, really? Ah, top of the stairs?"

They walked to the nearest Exit sign and pushed the door open. "Can barely breathe here," coughed Tash.

"I know, but let's just give it a couple of minutes, okay?"

They climbed as high as they could. It was smokier and dustier than before, but breathing was still possible through their bandannas. They sat down, leaning against the locked steel door, eyes closed. There was a constant noise of cracking, grinding, and distant crashing. It felt like being in a cave inside a slowly disintegrating glacier.

"Pretty sure there was some sort of collapse a few stories down, just a few minutes ago," said Nick.

"Can't . . . stay here . . . for long," wheezed Tash. "Smoke's getting worse."

"I don't think we have long," said Nick as the floor shook beneath them again. "I think the safest thing for us to do is sit in this doorway."

"Not if it's for more . . . than a minute or two," gasped Tash. "Can barely breathe—oh my God! Oh my God!"

The floor tipped over and the lights went out. Then they were falling through a deafening crescendo of chaos. Nick reached blindly for Tash but missed. Careening chunks of concrete and metal pummeled them. Flames erupted around them.

In the hell-like glow, their eyes met. Then there was just pain and panic, darkness and deafening noise, and then it was over.

Chapter 2

When he was fourteen, Nick had had a tormentor, a taller, greasy-haired kid who sat behind him in history and seemed to exist purely to trip and tease Nick, hide his books, and put the occasional thumbtack on his seat.

One day, the young Nick was walking into the classroom—the teacher wasn't there yet—when an ankle tap from behind made him stumble. He whirled around to see the greasy-haired kid looking innocently away. Without thinking, Nick punched upward with all his strength, hitting the kid's jaw hard enough to snap his head back and provoke a satisfying expression of shock and pain.

A moment later, as the other kid's fist had lashed into Nick's forehead, Nick left the ground and flew backward to hit the corner of a desk with the back of his head. There was a gap in time after that—a few seconds at least—then Nick had come to, a couple of other boys dragging him upright moments before the teacher breezed in obliviously and silenced the excited class.

That missing chunk of time, followed by a sense of dazed displacement, was what he felt now. He'd just lurched through the air, his vision blurred, ears deafened by a monstrous noise, with a recollection of blinding pain. Then he'd crashed down on some kind of solid surface, striking his head on it as he went down.

But where was the pain? Was this what it felt like to die? Memory of intense pain, followed by . . . nothing?

Moments later, it was quiet enough that he could hear individual people shouting. He looked around and his vision slowly cleared. He was lying on a floor, in a room, with a half memory of being hit by something massive—concrete? No, something flying—a jet plane flying right at him from nowhere, from right out of the blue sky. And he'd been crushed by the impact—except he could feel sensation return to his legs and arms, and they looked like they were still where they should be and the right lengths and shapes. So everything must have been just some weird hallucination.

Moments ago, it had been so dark. But now the light was powerfully bright—the sun was actually in his eyes when he opened them fearfully. He raised a hand to shield his eyes and say, "What the fuck?" but it came out as just a groan.

There were other people in the room, Nick realized. One, a man with rumpled blond hair, was standing, shoulders against a wall, sneering down at him. The other, a woman using the table to pull herself up, looked like she was coming out of her own nightmare. But then she looked at Nick and he remembered. His meeting. His presentation, his big chance. But what kind of ghastly disaster was this—how had a meeting gone so horribly wrong?

He met the woman's eyes. God, she's beautiful. God, I'm so ashamed. What did I do? "I'm . . . I'm so sorry," he said, climbing to his feet. There were water glasses and sodden areas of carpet on the floor, as well as an assortment of office junk scattered around an overturned cardboard box. The blond man was staring at him like he was a discolored and odorous form of cheese.

"Nick!" said the woman, looking into his face with concern. "You all right? Can you get up?"

"What . . . what did I do?"

"You fell over. The building's been hit."

"Yes, I think the plane collapsed," slurred Nick, blinking, turning his head carefully. No pain.

"You hired this guy? What a fucking joke," said the blond man.

"Go screw yourself," said the woman. "Oh wait, I remember, you've already screwed the company."

I was hired? "Tash?"

"Come on, we need to get out of here. Let's go." Tash straightened herself and reached down for him. He took her hand and levered himself up. Still no pain, just utter disorientation. He looked out the window and it got worse. What was all that paper flying about? Wait, of course—the plane crash.

"Did you see it hit?" asked Tash. "You were standing right here with that ass." She gestured at the blond man—Gareth, that was his name. "Surely you saw it."

Of course he had, but what were they doing in the North Tower? Hadn't the meeting been in WTC2, the South Tower? "Yeah, I saw it. It had . . . it had a blue and red tailfin. It came from . . . there, from nowhere."

"Come on," said Tash, ushering Nick out the door and into the wreckage and milling confusion outside. "I think we're all in shock to some extent. Particularly Gareth. In a way, I almost feel some kind of sympathy for him. Or might if I wasn't so freaking terrified."

Fortunately, other people seemed to have a plan, and Nick and Tash followed them to one of the stairwells. As they started the long, slow descent, the strong smell of smoke jolted his memory. "We've done this before," he said.

"What do you mean?" Tash gave him a quick glance. "We took the elevator down to the seventy-eighth floor, is that what you mean?"

Nick shook his head slowly, still trying to clear his mind. He looked around. A sense of déjà vu was pulling his brain apart.

"I chose a helluva day to wear stilettos," he heard a woman say from somewhere below them.

"We *have* done this before," Nick said, just loudly enough for Tash to hear. "See the guy in the glasses? He's going to complain about cell phone reception, just about . . ."

"No signal," said the man, snapping his cell phone shut.

"And that woman? She's about to stop for a rest."

The woman stopped, panting heavily. "You go on ahead," she said to her colleagues. "I'll catch up with you in a bit," she and Nick said together.

Tash looked at him sharply. "Do you get this a lot?" she said quietly. "Wish

38

you'd forecast the plane flying into us."

"Into *us*? What do you mean? How did we get to the North Tower?"

"Huh? You're confused. The North Tower got hit by a plane about twenty minutes ago. We tried to evacuate the South Tower but were turned back. Then the South Tower got hit just below us. Got it?"

"Okay, got it. But we're wasting our time walking down this staircase—in a minute or so, someone's going to tell us the stairwell's completely disintegrated further down."

"Are you saying you know that for a fact?"

"Hundred percent."

"Well, let's try another staircase."

"No use, they're all cut off."

"This is crazy—you know what's about to happen, but not what happened just two minutes ago?"

Nick leaned against the wall and people pushed past him. "Let's just stop a second while I figure this out."

"Keep moving. Let's figure this out when we find out for sure the stairwell's blocked. I want to believe you, but—"

"Sure. Of course. I can barely believe this myself."

They continued their descent. For Nick, it was like watching a replay of an awful movie.

"Okay, here it comes."

Moments later, they heard the bad news from below. The crowd shuffled to a stop in a miasma of smoke and fear.

"Shit," said Tash. "So what now?"

Nick spoke quietly. "All three stairwells are blocked, and the doors to the roof are locked."

"You mean we're trapped? We'll just have to hope they put this fire out before we all asphyxiate."

"We need to get off the staircase for a minute."

They followed the crowd up again and Tash reached for the next fire door, but Nick stopped her with a hand on her arm. "Not here, that floor's on fire."

They took the next door out of the stairwell into a smoky, open plan expanse of desks. A few confused people looked at them hopefully.

"Stairwell's impassable," Tash told them.

"They all are," said Nick.

"Shit," said one of the office workers. "What's plan B?"

"Let's see if we can get on the roof, wait for a chopper," said another. His colleagues shrugged and agreed. "You coming?"

"After you," said Tash. She waited till they'd gotten past, then turned back to Nick. "So really, what is plan B?"

Nick was silent for a moment. "I don't know anymore. We didn't find a way out before."

"Before? Before what?"

"Before . . . before I woke up in the meeting room. It's like I'm in a time loop or something. Yeah, look, I know it's insane, but—"

"That doesn't begin to describe it," said Tash. "I'm only going along with your . . . I don't know, your ESP . . . because what's one more unbelievable thing on a day like this, right?"

"Well, okay. I'm not saying we're in a time loop, just that it's the best way I can describe what I know."

"But can you remember what happened before the plane hit us? Gareth's meltdown? Him being fired? No? You being hired?"

Nick turned away. What did he remember?

"It's a strange sort of memory that only works forward," said Tash. A jagged laugh quickly turned into head-in-hands sobbing. Nick made to hug her and she backed away.

"So what next?" she cried. "Aliens? Bigfoot?"

Nick couldn't reply.

"No, seriously," Tash continued. "You didn't tell me—how does this end?"

"You really want to know?"

"Oh God, no, please, no." She sagged to the floor and curled up in a ball.

Nick gave her a minute. "We've got to try and escape," he said. "We don't have much time."

"Why?"

"The building's going to collapse—in about forty minutes."

"Collapse?"

"The plane's impact must have weakened the building, smashed right through some of the core support columns."

Tash sat up again. "The other tower doesn't look like it's falling down."

Nick turned. They made their way through the debris to the windows on the west side of the floor. From there they had a grandstand view of the North Tower, still consuming itself in a torrent of fire and smoke.

Like being kicked in the stomach, his memory returned.

"Okay, I'm back," he said.

"Back? You look like you're about to—"

Nick found a planter just in time, a big stainless steel cube with some kind of large-leafed plant in it. He retched into it and felt his breakfast gush out. Luckily, the plant hid his face and most of the mess from Tash.

When he was finished, he helped himself to a tissue from a nearby desk and cleaned his face, then crumpled the tissue and threw it in a trash basket.

"You said . . . you're back?"

"I can remember everything now. Backward—and forward. Thanks for the job, by the way."

"For what it's worth at this point, you're welcome."

"Yeah, well, sorry for making a mess of the place."

"I believe that used to be a Delicious Monster." Tash indicated the plant.

Nick snorted with laughter and grabbed another tissue.

"So does the North Tower collapse too?"

"I don't know. I don't think so. Certainly not before . . . before this one. But it was hit much higher up, so there's less weight pressing down on the impact zone."

"So we just wait . . . or asphyxiate?"

"I can't—"

"Oh my God!" screamed Tash.

Nick followed her horrified gaze to see, through the blizzard of paper, a woman falling down the length of the North Tower, faster and faster, her dress flapping. They watched, hypnotized, until she fell out of their line of sight.

Tash had her hands over her face, as if to blot out the sight. "Oh my God! I—I guess the smoke or the heat just got too much for—oh my God, there's another one!"

This time it was a man, clutching what looked like a door. As he picked up speed he began to tumble out of control, veering left and right as the door caught the breeze, before he too swooped out of sight.

Tash was crying again. "Is that us in forty minutes? Because I don't know if I can wait till I can't breathe any more—or till I get crushed by twenty floors of concrete."

"Who says we should just give up?" said Nick, handing her another tissue. "We've got forty minutes to figure out how to get out of here. That guy—the guy clinging to the door—at least he had a plan. Not a great plan, but a plan. We just need a better one. We can do this."

"Look, I don't want to be the one to break it to you, but I haven't seen many parachutes lying around up here."

"I'm thinking of going up instead. Onto the roof."

"You think they'll send helicopters to rescue us?"

"It's all I can think of. Problem is, the doors to the roof are locked."

"Then . . . ?"

"We'll just have to open one. Come on, we need to find some tools."

* * *

Feeling like thieves, Nick and Tash clambered through the shattered expanses of desks and cubicles, opening cabinets at random, giving each a quick search. Mostly it was just folders, files, and stationery. Strangely, the few people around just let them get on with it, too stunned with shock to object or get involved themselves.

Finally, one woman challenged them. "So just what are you two doing?"

"Looking for some tools. The door to the observation deck's locked and we need to open it somehow."

The woman pointed down a row of desks. "You want the kitchen. There should be a toolbox under the sink in there."

Nick and Tash made their way to what was left of the kitchen. The door and sheetrock walls were leaning in different directions. Nick wrenched the door open and a wall fell in, spewing cabinets, fittings, glasses, mugs, and who knows what. Dragging another wall out of the way, Nick spotted a metal sink. A broken pipe trickled water into the mess. Cables dangled from the ceiling, some loose, some stretched tight between shattered bits of sheetrock.

A refrigerator lay on its front. "Help me with this," said Nick, and together they hauled it upright. As they did, the door fell open and the contents crashed out onto his feet. Soda bottles, milk, lunch leftovers, and a plain white cake box. Through the box's transparent lid, Nick saw chocolate icing with a message in pink: "Happy Birthday, Jann!"

There was a cabinet crushed under the sink and Nick heaved and shoved until he could reach inside it. Among bottles and cans, he felt a plastic case about the size of a briefcase and dragged it out, wrenching his back as it got caught again and again.

Finally he had it out, a blue toolbox with a translucent lid. He popped it open to see a jumble of tools: screwdrivers and wrenches, compartments filled with screws, bolts and other fittings, a small flashlight, a wire cutter, and—digging down—a claw hammer.

"Great." He put the flashlight in a pocket, fastened the case again, and picked it up. They rushed back to the stairs, the unbalanced weight tearing at Nick's back. Stumbling on a loose piece of debris, his back clenched up in agony.

Tash steadied him with an arm. "You okay?"

"I'll be fine."

Tash sighed.

Just outside the stairwell, a metal fire extinguisher hung on the wall. Nick picked it up with his spare hand, grimacing.

"What's that for? The fire's downstairs."

"It's to balance the weight of the toolbox. Better for my back. Let's go."

* * *

By the time they reached floor 107, the pain had Nick in a vice-like grip. Jerome was attacking the fire door with an office chair. Nick clattered the toolbox and fire extinguisher onto the landing floor, gasping with relief. He glanced at his left wrist: just twenty-two minutes left.

"Anyone else wanna try?" said Jerome, coughing uncontrollably. Someone else took the chair from him and took a swing. All that happened was that the chair broke, plastic and metal flopping uselessly to the floor.

"Got a toolbox here," panted Nick. "We could unscrew the hinges"—he looked more closely—"if they weren't on the other side of the goddamn door."

"How about this?" said a big man with a vowel-crushing South African accent from just behind Nick, offering the fire extinguisher Nick had just put down.

"Hand it over," said Jerome, "let's give it a go."

They made space for Jerome. Nick retreated a few steps down the stairwell and collided with Tash, who was doubled over, coughing and gasping for breath. Holding the fire extinguisher by the handle, Jerome took a mighty swing at the door. It barely made a dent. He put the fire extinguisher down and coughed uncontrollably.

"Let me take a swing at it," said the South African. He grabbed the handle in both hands, wound up like an Olympic hammer thrower, spun around, and slammed the base of the fire extinguisher into the door, just as Tash got far enough up the stairs to see what was happening and scream, "No!"

The impact was too much for the highly pressurized fire extinguisher, which blew apart in two opposite directions. The handle burst off the canister, shot through the man's hands, and glanced off his cheek, sending blood and bone flying, then buried itself in the wall behind him.

At the same time, the canister—blasting foam from its open neck—rocketed off in the opposite direction, bounced off the tiled floor, and smashed through the side of Nick's head.

44

Chapter 3

The impact sent Nick tumbling to the floor, a howling roar surging through his brain. He lay still, eyes closed, waiting for the pain to hit him. The roar subsided. He took a gasping breath, lifting a hand experimentally.

"We've been hit! We've been hit!" screamed a woman. Tash.

Moving carefully, Nick bent his arm to touch the side of his head, expecting to find blood and splintered bone. Instead, it felt dry and fibrous. Was that what brains felt like?

"Nick! You all right?"

Surely they could see for themselves. He opened his eyes a fraction. The pain still hadn't hit him. Why was he in this meeting room again? Had they moved him, given him an anesthetic and brought him downstairs? He examined his injury with his fingers. All he could feel was his hair.

"Nick! Can you get up?"

He looked around. Tash was kneeling over him, Gareth looking down at him with contempt.

"My . . . head," said Nick weakly.

"You hit your head?" Tash looked concerned. "I can't see anything. Can you sit up?"

Of course not, thought Nick.

"He's pathetic," said Gareth. "Don't waste your time."

Nick lifted his head and shook it slowly. Still no pain. Gently, he tried pushing himself upright and found that he could. He got to his knees. His back pain had gone too. Through the door, he could hear people screaming.

Outside the window, paper swirled in snow-like flurries. The sense of dislocation crashed through his brain.

"Oh God," he said, "not again." He crawled over to the trash can and was violently ill into it.

"Nick!"

"I'm fine, I'm fine. We need to get that toolbox! Follow me."

"What are you talking about? We need to go down the stairs."

"I'll explain as we go. Come on, I've done this before."

* * *

"Anyone know what these—*cough*—walls are made of?" asked Tash through her shirtsleeve bandanna.

Around them, people shrugged. Nick drew back the hammer. "Okay, give me some room. Let's find out."

The hammer's head buried itself two inches deep in the wall. Nick stood back and looked at it. "Now that's interesting," he said, coughing.

Jerome wiggled the hammer back out of the wall and poked the hole with a finger. "It's just plasterboard. Sheetrock." He turned to Tash. "Nice thinking. Name's Jerome, by the way."

"Tash, hi. And this is Nick."

"And I'm Obie," said the South African. "You want to give me that hammer? I've got a helicopter to catch."

Just a few minutes later, they'd created a perforated rectangle in the wall about a yard on each side, the bottom edge just below knee height.

"I know how to punch that out," said Obie, setting off down the stairs. He came back seconds later carrying a fire extinguisher.

"Whoa, better not hit the wall with that," said Nick. "I've seen one explode. Real ugly." His hand went to the side of his head. Not a dent, not a twinge. This time loop thing certainly took some getting used to.

The others looked at him curiously. "He's right," said Jerome. "You could do yourself an injury with that."

Obie put the extinguisher down as if it were made of wasps. Nick exhaled quietly.

"Okay, who's going to help me kick this sucker in?" asked Jerome.

Together, he and Obie attacked the rectangle with a backward mule kick. The piece of sheetrock caved in with a crunch. Behind the hole was darkness and dust.

Nick quickly climbed in and found himself fumbling around among poles, buckets, boxes, and shelves. "Looks like a utility room," he shouted. "Let's see if I can find a door." He felt the walls and found a handle. A second later he was in a corridor. "All right, we're in business! Come on!"

Tash, Obie, and Jerome clambered through the newly created door into the utility room and then into the corridor. Nick could hear more people following behind them.

They hurried along the corridor and found themselves in the Top of the World Observatory, dominated by its wraparound view of Manhattan. The last time Nick was up here, the view had been marred by gray, low-hanging clouds and drizzle. Today, a storm of smoke and flying paper greeted the panting, coughing viewers.

The black-and-white tiled floor was surprisingly free of debris. Moving quickly, they walked past unmanned souvenir stalls and fast-food outlets. "The escalator's around the corner here," said Tash.

But the escalator wasn't running, so they ran up the stairs next to it. At the top of the stairs was a revolving door. They pushed through and ran up another flight of stairs, next to another stationary escalator. The stairs ended in an enclosed space facing a metal roller door with a lock and keyhole at knee height on the left. On the wall to the left of the door were a metal box and an intercom phone.

They looked at the phone. Tash raised her eyebrows. Nick shrugged and picked it up, and they listened to it ring unanswered, far, far away in another world where disaster followed a stricter script.

"This is not looking good," said Obie. He grabbed one of the slats of the roller door and pulled upward. "Shit! Fuck!" He kicked the door and fell back, barely keeping his balance, then hopped about on one foot, wincing in pain. "Sorry about the language, lady," he said to Tash.

Tash shrugged and caught him by the elbow to steady him. "Let's just fucking hope the other door's unlocked," she said.

As they came back down the stairs, their news was greeted with shocked disbelief by one would-be escapee after another. Unsurprisingly, everyone insisted on going to see the roller door for themselves. "I guess they all think they'll be the one to discover the magic Open Sesame button," said Tash.

They were almost at the bottom of the stairs when they heard banging and shouting from above.

"Stop! Stop!"

"Are you out of your mind? Stop it!"

A ripple of fear ran through the people on the stairs as everyone craned their necks to see better. The news reached them seconds later. "Some crazy asshole just smashed up the phone."

"Great," breathed Nick.

At the bottom of the stairs to the other rooftop door, a few people were already coming down, angry and dejected.

"Doesn't look promising," said Nick.

"Damn door's locked," came the response. "And nobody's answering the phone. They probably evacuated the control room. Although we'd still need a key anyway."

"What if we phone nine-one-one?" someone asked.

"Someone tried, they say they can't deactivate the lock. Sounds like they don't want us on the roof. Just like they didn't want us to evacuate in the first place."

"Well, let's find out just how strong the door really is," said Nick. He strode off and came back with another metal fire extinguisher.

Tash looked at him in horror. "You're not going to hit the door with that, are you? It'll probably explode."

"Not if I empty it first," said Nick. "Wait here." He jogged down a corridor, found a bathroom, walked in, yanked out the fire extinguisher's security pin, and let it rip, instantly filling the room with a roar and a cloud of vapor. A minute later he was back with Tash. "Right, let's head up."

Tash shook her head. "I just hope the fire doesn't get up here."

This door was just like the other: phone on one side, lock near the floor. Tash rattled the security door. "Can't fucking believe it."

"We just need to apply enough force to break these slats apart," said Nick. "How hard can it be?"

He gave the fire extinguisher a test swing and the people around him stood back. Tash looked at him, biting her lower lip. He wound up and took a massive swing at the center of the door. The impact rattled the door with an impressive noise but, apart from a scrape, made no impression.

Nick stepped back, dazed and coughing. "That was embarrassing," he muttered.

"Better to be embarrassed than . . ." But Tash stopped and blinked, and a tear ran down her cheek. She shook her head angrily, turning away.

"Let's have a turn, buddy?" It was Jerome. He slammed the fire extinguisher against the door and grimaced from the jolt. "Rattles your brains, don't it?"

He tried again, then handed the fire extinguisher to someone else. "Head hurts like hell already. Sorry."

"I'm going back down the escalator," said Tash. Nick followed her awkwardly. He'd expected to fail, but that didn't make it any better.

* * *

"Nick, admit it, you know something the rest of us don't."

"Yes, I do. But—"

"It's classified, I get it, and you can't tell me who you work for. But I'm guessing you had warning about all this."

"It's not like that at all."

"Then tell me."

"If I told you, you would think I was making fun of you. Or just deranged."

"Okay. But this knowledge of yours . . . could it help us get rescued?"

"I think it could. I just don't know how."

"Talk to me."

"I'm trying. The thing is, I believe I can rescue not just us but a lot more people besides. But I need you to trust me."

"Are you saying this"—she gestured at the stairs, where they could still hear someone pounding away with the fire extinguisher—"isn't going to work? Because it's the only hope I've got."

"It might. But I need a backup plan. And that plan's going to need your help."

"Okay . . ."

"You know when the plane hit our building? And I said, 'Not again'?"

"I remember."

"I didn't mean 'not our building as well.' I meant 'not our building again.'"

"I don't understand."

"This is not the first time I've been in this building as it gets hit by that plane."

"I'm sorry, you're freaking me out."

"I don't blame you. It's totally freaked me out too. It's fucking crazy. But if you imagine for a minute that it was true, how could I make somebody believe me?"

"I don't—"

"Because if we don't make it through the next few minutes, I'm going to be back in that meeting room, back with you and Gareth, back at the moment the plane hits."

She shook her head in despair.

"The problem," he continued, "is that the next time it all starts over again, I have to try and get someone, like you, to help me all over again. Without them thinking I'm just crazy. Or misunderstanding me and organizing a lynch mob."

"So . . . ?"

"Maybe if you tell me something nobody else can possibly know, about yourself, it would help save time if we have to do this over again."

She stared at him, blinking.

"Something personal, but not incriminating," he said, smiling.

"So that's how you knew about the door? Because you've been here before?"

"Exactly. But this time, you came up with the idea to go through the wall. So next time, if we need a next time, we can try that right away. But I'll still need your support to get other people to go along with my suggestions."

"So you need a . . . trigger fact that'll convince me to trust you?"

He nodded.

She thought for a moment. "Okay, here's something I've never told a living soul. When I was a little kid, we went to England on one of my father's business trips. My mother took me and my brothers to a playground and I was going down the slide. A bigger boy had climbed halfway up and he spat on me as I went under him. Called me a filthy coolie. So I climbed the slide again, and he was waiting for me again. And as I got to him, I shoved him right off the slide. The piece of shit broke his collarbone, howled like crazy. He blamed me, but I denied it, and luckily no one believed him."

"That's perfect. And good on you too."

"So what now, Mister Time Traveler?"

"Want to check out another stairwell with me? There's one we haven't tried yet."

"Let's go."

Fifteen floors down, overcome by coughing, they left the stairwell to find an open window. Leaning out into the comparatively clean air, Nick had an idea. "Tash? Let me try something out on you. Imagine . . . imagine today's events led to a major global conflict."

"Okay."

"A conflict that turns out really bad for everyone."

"Okay . . ."

"And at some point in the future, there's a huge scientific project to somehow go back in time to change the outcome of today."

"That's crazy, but okay . . ."

"Okay. And so this project—they somehow manage to send somebody back in time to try to get everyone to safety."

"Why not just try and stop the people flying the planes?"

"Exactly, that would make a lot more sense. But suppose for some technical reason they can only send someone back to the moment of impact."

"Well, no offense, but why not find someone with more experience with the building—or some training with planning a rescue?"

"Yeah, I'm struggling with that one too."

"Nick?"

"Yeah?"

"Don't beat yourself up. You're not doing so bad, you know?" Tash punched Nick on the shoulder. "Come on, we'll find a way out. I know we will."

They returned to the stairwell. They made it down to the eighty-ninth floor before the stairs dropped away from under them.

Chapter 4

H e was free-falling again. Down the staircase. Surrounded by fire. No he wasn't, he was in a room somewhere. In sunlight. He hit the floor. There was Tash. She was dead. No, she was on the floor, screaming. And that—

"The fuck you looking at?"

That was Gareth.

They had to get out of the building. He and Tash picked themselves up off the floor. Outside, someone was shouting about fire escapes.

"Tash?"

"Come on, we need to get out of here!"

"Damn right we do. But first I need a quiet word with you." While Gareth sneered, he leaned closer so he could talk directly into Tash's ear. "About a kid on a slide. And his broken collarbone."

Tash stared at him, dumbstruck, then steered him out into the chaos outside the meeting room, where she stared aghast at the dust-covered and bleeding people picking their way slowly through the wreckage.

"Tash?"

"Okay, talk. Quickly."

A minute later, Tash was still trying to keep her jaw from hanging open. "Okay, so what now?"

"How many stairwells are there?" asked Nick.

"Three—why?"

"Because we've only explored two so far. It's time to make sure about the last one."

"I've just called 911," said someone loudly. "The woman said to stay where we are."

Tash looked at Nick. "Did you hear that?"

"They're confused," said Nick. "They haven't realized yet that we've been hit by a second plane. And they certainly don't know that the building will collapse in less than an hour."

"Huh," sneered Gareth, from the meeting room door. "Or not. This building's designed to withstand a Boeing 707 at full speed. I'm staying here."

"Your funeral," said Nick. "Tash, you coming?"

She gave it a moment. "Let's go."

"Enjoy the walk," said Gareth. "I'm staying."

They walked briskly out of the meeting room. "Let's try the stairwell closest to the side the plane hit," said Nick. "The plane was tilted over so it might have escaped the impact—and the fuel explosion."

"This way then," Tash said, pointing. "I'll lead."

Smoke was already filling the air. "It's going to be unbreathable soon," said Nick. "Need to move fast."

Nick opened the staircase door and smoke billowed out. They coughed. "Sure this is a good idea?" said Tash.

"Only one way to find out. Follow me."

Down they went, floor after floor. At some of the doorways stood small groups of people debating whether to go down or up or stay put.

"There'll be firemen coming up," said a man loudly. "If we block up the stairs, they're not going to be able to control the fire."

"That's not a fire you can control," shouted Nick as they went past. "And if you wait up here, you soon won't be able to breathe."

Some followed. Some stayed.

Soon they met people coming up the stairs. "Smoke's bad down there," panted one. "Real bad."

"Going to get worse if we stay in the building," replied Nick.

"I—I think I'm going to turn back," said Tash, wheezing.

"Come on," said Nick. "Trust me. Just another few flights of stairs. Then

54

we'll know, one way or another."

Tash dithered. "Okay," she relented and followed Nick down.

Passing the eighty-fifth floor, they could hear the inferno raging just feet away from them on the other side of the stairwell wall. With no lights working, they followed fluorescent strips on the stairs. It felt like a descent into hell.

As they passed the eighty-third floor, they met a group of people coming up the stairs toward them, gasping and coughing. A man held out his arms to block their way. "Ain't no way down," he said, shaking his head. "Ain't no way down."

"What's it like down there?" asked Nick.

"Stairwell's completely collapsed," said the man. "Only way is up."

He climbed on past them. They looked at each other.

"What now?" asked Tash. "Should we go up?"

"Let's get up on the roof," said someone else. "If things get bad, they'll rescue us from up there."

"Only one problem with that. The doors to the roof are locked."

"Surely someone has a key?"

"No, it's too early in the morning," said Nick. "But the doors also need to be released from the control room downstairs via an intercom system. And the control room's been evacuated."

They stared at him. "How do you know that?" one asked.

"Uh . . . I heard someone mention it as we were coming down the stairs. Didn't want to draw your attention to it at the time though."

"Yes, but . . . surely someone has the keys? A janitor or someone?"

"Yeah, exactly," said one of the others. "It's a safety thing, they have to have keys."

"I know. I agree. It's just that . . . they don't."

"What do you mean?" Tash said quietly. "Is this one of the things . . . you just know?"

Nick nodded. The others had already started the long climb back up.

"Well, we can't stay here," said Tash, coughing. "Coming or not?"

"Yeah, all right, let's go up. I'll stop along the way and get some tools though. I have a feeling we'll need them."

* * *

Nick put the hammer back in the toolbox. They ducked through the newly smashed-out entrance to floor 107 and made their way up to the solid-as-ever roller door.

"This is terrible," shouted Tash. "Fucking unbelievable."

People shook the doors, pounded on them, and shouted into the intercom system, pushing buttons at random.

"Can't we phone somebody?" shouted Tash.

"We've tried," answered a man, waving his cell in frustration. "No one can help."

Tash looked at Nick, who shrugged. "So what now?" Tash asked him.

The man with the cell phone was looking at Nick curiously. "Why am I getting the feeling that you're not surprised by any of this?" he said.

Nick shook his head and turned away.

The man shouted after him. "It's like . . . it's like you *know* something."

Nick looked around. He stayed silent. Too many people around.

The man continued, "I just get this feeling about you. It's weird."

A nearby man in a camouflage-patterned flak jacket turned to them. "You know what, I don't think they want us to get out of here. Something really strange is going on."

"What—who do you mean?" said the man with the cell.

Flak Jacket puffed up his chest as others turned toward them. "I think there's more to this than a navigation disaster. I think those planes were diverted into the towers on purpose."

A woman shook her head. "I think we'll find it was the Taliban, or that bin Laden guy."

"And I'm thinking the CIA, or someone, put them up to it. They've been itching for a war in the Middle East and now they've staged their own Pearl Harbor. We're just collateral damage."

A thin, balding man with glasses joined in. "Like when Woodrow Wilson wanted us in the First World War, he sailed the *Lusitania* straight into a trap. A thousand lives sacrificed to rile up America."

"Now that's just horseshit," someone else retorted. "And do you think they could cover up a crime like this? The CIA is leakier than a colander, you think they could keep this a secret?"

Flak Jacket fixed his eyes on Nick. "You, sir. You seem to know something. Am I right?"

"If I knew this was going to happen, I certainly wouldn't have hung around waiting to be trapped up here. No goddamn way. And we can't afford to waste time arguing, we need to get through this door."

"And how do you propose we're going to do that?"

Someone else spoke up, pointing at Nick. "That man there? He was trying mighty hard to get down stairwell three. I seen him trying to convince this lady here. He didn't want to come up here, no sir. Seems like it turned out real unlucky for him the staircase was blocked. Not according to plan, is what I'm thinking."

Flak Jacket folded his arms and stood squarely in front of Nick. "Got anything to say?"

Then Uday appeared, looking sly. "He was in a meeting with us on the ninety-third floor earlier. When the North Tower got hit, he was real keen to get out of the building already. Like he knew something was going on."

"Seriously?" replied Nick. "Why would I even be in this building if I'd had any idea what would happen?"

"Maybe you were just making sure it would happen," said flak jacket. "Like planting the navigation beacon. And you were just making noises about getting out. Because you thought you'd still be able to get out later."

"Because those stairs weren't supposed to have been blocked, were they?" said Uday. "That wasn't the plan!"

"Would you all shut up already!" shouted Tash, glaringly furiously at Uday, who took a step back, cowed. "Talking isn't going to get us through those doors!"

"Well, what is?" asked the thin balding man.

"Okay, okay. I don't have an answer. But we're not a mindless rabble. We can think our way through this."

This got the attention of an expensively suited, gray-haired man. He lifted his wrist and tapped on a wafer thin watch. Patek Philippe, Nick thought. Whatever, it seemed to command instant respect. The man spoke, equally commanding. "Okay everyone, I have a suggestion. We all take five minutes to think up some solutions. And let's form small groups, three or four in each group, and tackle the problem. What do you say?"

Without comment, everyone agreed. As they started to separate into groups, the Patek owner pointed at Nick and Tash. "And you two are with me, if you're agreed?"

With a sigh of relief, Nick stepped over to join him, Tash following.

Flak Jacket jabbed Nick in the chest as he passed. "Ain't over, pal. Ain't over."

The Patek owner walked Nick and Tash over to a more private corner. "Thanks for the intervention," said Nick. "That could have gone any way at all."

Their new ally snorted. "CIA couldn't execute a plan like this without it leaking like a burst water main. Damn fool conspiracy theorists. Anyway, enough of that—how do we get out of here? Let's get some ideas on the table. I'm Malcolm, by the way. Good to meet you. Or it would be, in other circumstances."

After quick introductions, they got into it. "Here's a few options," began Nick. "One, we cook up some explosive and blow out the door. Tricky, I agree. Two, we hack the electrics and send some current through the locking system. We probably just have to complete a circuit somewhere. But where? Three, we find an oxyacetylene torch and melt through it. Yeah, as if. If only I had some mechanically-minded brain cells. Okay, someone else's turn."

Malcolm stepped in. "You seem to have covered the obvious solutions. Okay, how about we chisel out the hinges . . . ahh . . . heck, we hit the locks with a pneumatic drill . . . ahh . . . use some sound oscillation gizmo to shatter the locks . . . no, I've got nothing. Tash? Your turn."

Tash frowned. "You know, when you mentioned a pneumatic drill, I thought, why go through the door? Why not just go through the wall? Or the ceiling?"

"Good thinking," agreed Malcolm. "Those doors are probably twice as sturdy as the walls. But what could we use to knock out a wall? Where could we find a ten-pound hammer?"

"Plenty of cutlery in the kitchen," said Tash. "How about, I don't know, a butcher's cleaver? Or a steak tenderizer? A rolling pin? A long-handled saucepan?"

"Something with a bit more weight," said Malcolm.

"We could try fire extinguishers again," suggested Nick. "As long as they're emptied first."

"That's at least a ten-pound hammer," agreed Malcolm, his eyes shining. "Good thinking! Right," he clapped his hands, "I think our five minutes are up."

In a lower voice, he said to Nick, "Considering the political atmosphere in the room, I'll head this one up, if I may?"

Nick agreed with a quick nod, and Malcolm called for quiet.

Nobody else had any better ideas, and the fire extinguisher idea met instant agreement. Nick and another man each grabbed a fire extinguisher from the wall. "Follow me!" shouted Nick. "We need to dump the gas first or they'll explode."

They blasted the contents of the fire extinguishers into the small room, then ran back upstairs, where Jerome and Obie—the two beefiest men among them—were waiting.

Facing each other, they each held a fire extinguisher by its handle and swung, alternately, at the same spot on the wall. Immediately, plaster ricocheted around the small space. The two men kept up a steady rhythm for half a minute before surrendering to coughing spasms.

They'd cleared a patch of plaster, but the brick below was barely chipped. "Can't—*cough*—get good leverage by just holding the handles," said Jerome.

"And—*cough*—the fire extinguishers aren't long enough to build up enough of an impact," added Obie.

"Never mind, let's keep on trying," said Malcolm, and another two men stepped in. As the first took a mighty swing, the neck of the handle simply snapped off. Everyone scattered as the canister bounced off the wall, luckily without hitting anyone.

"Whoa, just had a thought," said Nick. "Malcolm, you talked about a bomb earlier. What if we aimed a full fire extinguisher at the wall and blew it up?"

"Interesting. How would we get it to explode?"

"Well, okay, not a full-on explosion, more of a bursting apart. If you bash the full canister hard enough, the handle and the canister will fly apart in opposite directions."

"Sounds crazy, but it's worth a try. How will you contain the burst?"

"We can block in the fire extinguisher with a couple of filing cabinets," said Obie.

Obie and a few others went back to the 105th floor to fetch the filing cabinets and two fresh fire extinguishers. Back up at the roller door, they placed the filing cabinets in an L shape in the corner. Then Nick placed one of the full fire extinguishers with its handle against one filing cabinet and its base pointing at the left-hand wall.

Standing back, he picked up one of the empty fire extinguishers. "If you all want to stand back, I'll take it from here."

"You're sure about this, man?" said Jerome. "You did use the word 'bomb' just now, you know."

"Under control," said Nick with a confidence he didn't remotely feel.

"Just a second," said Obie. "I think one of us should sit backed up against the other side of the filing cabinet—to keep it jammed in place."

"Don't look at me," said Jerome. "I may be the black man, but, no, man."

"Just thinking out loud," said Obie. "I'm volunteering." He sat down with his back to the filing cabinet. "Okay, go for it."

Everyone else retreated down the stairs. Nick stood over his "missile" and raised an empty fire extinguisher as high as he could, then flung it down with a massive clatter, leaping back at the same time to shelter behind the filing cabinet with Obie. No response. He picked up the empty canister again.

Obie looked around apprehensively. "It's not like this is nerve-racking or anything," he said.

"You got that right," said Nick. He tried again. No luck. A quick look at his watch. "Fuck it," he said, picking up the other full fire extinguisher, lifting it high and flinging it down onto the other. They erupted simultaneously, the canisters smashing into the wall and back into the filing cabinets, the handles spinning and bouncing out of control between walls, filing cabinets, and roof almost too fast to see. Obie grunted with pain.

The wall was barely damaged. Obie staggered upright with blood pouring from his head.

"Oh Christ, not again," said Nick. "Sorry, Obie, I really am sorry, I just didn't—"

"You fuckin' crazy fuck. What you mean 'not again'? And how did you even know my name?" Obie's fist hit Nick squarely in the nose, knocking his head back against the wall.

Quite the routine, thought Nick, darkness descending once again.

Chapter 5

"Tash, step through this door a second?"

They'd come down one flight of stairs and Nick was anxious not to waste any more time. Tash followed him through the ninety-second-floor fire door. For some reason, this floor didn't look quite as damaged as their own. They stood aside to let the evacuees past, then Nick spotted an empty meeting room. He pointed Tash toward it.

"Nick, what's going on?"

"Sorry, I know we can't afford to waste time, but the stairwells are all blocked, destroyed or on fire."

"How would you know? We were only hit a minute ago."

"I just do, like I know about the kid on the slide—the one who's collarbone you broke?"

Pause. "What. The. Fuck?"

"We've got to get some tools together, then head up to the roof. It's locked, but I'm hoping we can open the door with the right tools."

"What tools? Where?"

"Back on your floor. Come, we'll go up one of the other stairwells."

"I'm . . . I'm having some kind of out-of-body experience. You lead, I'll follow."

* * *

They'd both spent the last few minutes looking for something useful, but Nick hadn't found anything besides the toolbox. Frustrated, he gave up and returned to their agreed meeting point. Tash was already waiting for him, holding a small canister to her face.

"Beautiful cool fresh air," said Tash, holding the can's straw-like nozzle to her lips and sending a blast into her mouth. "Mmm."

"Whoa, Tash, not such a good idea."

"What do you mean? It's just air." She shot more into her mouth and breathed in deeply. "God, I feel better already."

"Yes, because it's not pure air. It's got propellant in it—it's like sniffing glue. Give it here before you addle your brain."

"Seriously?"

"Seriously. I used to abuse this stuff all the time before I reached drinking age."

"What? Was that on your résumé?"

"Actually, it's one of a few things I left off my résumé. The thing is, this gas is an extremely efficient vice—you not only get a high from it, but you could also use it to score your next high."

"What do you mean?"

"You just have to leave some gas left over and spray it on somebody's bicycle lock—it makes the toughest steel as brittle as a breadstick—then you smash the lock with a hammer, fence the bike, and buy more gas. Simple."

"You . . . what?"

"Just one thing I'm not proud of. I've got a bit of a list. I was pretty messed up at the time, and, yeah, I'm the only one to blame. In fact, I—"

"Shut up."

"Huh? I mean, I know it's not what you were—"

"Shut up." She held the canister up and shook it. "You said there's a lock upstairs that needs smashing. Come on!"

* * *

"Okay, Tash, you keep the button down and I'll get ready with the hammer."

The two of them knelt down at the roller door lock. Tash shook the can, directed its nozzle at the lock, and pushed the button. A film of gray-white liquid, almost a paste, grew over the steel.

Nick silently counted to ten. "Okay, let's wreck this thing." He lashed the hammer down with a perfectly aimed blow and they clearly heard the lock snap. Nick put the hammer aside, grabbed the lock and twisted it right off, dropping it quickly and blowing warmth onto his hand. Shouts of triumph erupted from the small crowd around them.

"Tash, you utter genius."

She grinned with delight. "Well, pardner, we're not outta these hee-yar woods yet," she said in a mangled Texan accent. Nick laughed, then erupted in a coughing fit.

"No . . . more . . . of the funnies," he gasped. "Right, let's get this door open."

Multiple hands gripped the roller door wherever they could.

"Okay! One, two, three, pull!"

They heaved upward, straining, coughing painfully. The door didn't budge. One by one, they stood back in disappointment.

"We obviously need to switch on the electric motor somehow," said Obie, pointing at the box above their heads.

"If they would only answer the goddamn phone," said Jerome.

Nick looked at the other box, the one to the left of the door, next to the intercom phone. "So what's in there then?" he mused. Everyone shrugged. "No idea? Well, let's find out," he said, reaching for the toolbox.

A couple of minutes later, he had the box's metal cover off, exposing some simple wiring. "I'm guessing there's a switch downstairs that completes a circuit and starts the motor above our heads," he said. "But I'm damn sure there must be a way for a technician to hot-wire the system here as well."

"Don't look at me," said Jerome. "I've never hotwired anything in my life."

"While on the other hand . . ." said Nick with a devilish smile, and Tash sighed and rolled her eyes.

* * *

"Nope," said Nick, after a while. "There's not a volt of current in any of these wires." To make his point absolutely clear, he held all the now-naked ends of wiring in his bare fingers.

"Shit!" shouted Tash. She shook her head. "I really thought we were on the way out of here." She looked around at her crestfallen conspirators. "So what's our next option?"

Everyone looked at Nick. Then the floor started to tilt.

Chapter 6

"If we want to stay alive, we need to move fast! The building's support columns are made of metal. And right now, they're melting. The building will collapse in under an hour."

Tash looked horrified. Gareth looked contemptuous.

"Listen! The floors below us will be an inferno—just like Tower One. Our only option is to get past them somehow."

Nick and Tash stood at the windows, looking out at the billowing black smoke and airborne litter.

Tash looked at Nick. "Do you mean you want us to climb down the outside of the building? We're ninety-three floors up!"

"Yes. We start just above the fire, go through a window, drop four or five stories, climb in again, and carry on down the stairs. Guys! We need to get moving! We need to find ropes, cables, cords!"

"Knot some sheets! That'll do it!" Gareth rocked back on his heels, laughing, thumbs in his belt. "I knew you were a Boy Scout!"

Nick turned to him. "You want to stay here? There are no ladders that can reach us. We save ourselves or die."

Gareth pointed at the nearest ceiling speaker and sneered. "You two can run around in a fucking panic. I'm staying here until they put the fire out."

Then the door burst open and Uday rushed in, near panic. "It's getting smoky in here, guys. And I can't see anyone putting out the fire over in the North Tower."

Nick nodded. "No one's putting out any fires. Those planes were full of jet fuel. Help me round up every phone cord on the floor."

66

Gareth headed for the meeting room door. "I'm going to head up a few floors. There'll be cleaner air up there. Might even get up on the roof, catch the first helicopter. You can play Boy Scouts all you like. Phone cords—what a fucking joke!"

He walked out. Uday looked lost, then followed him.

There were two phones in the room. Nick detached their cords from their bases and handsets and stretched out one of the coiled lengths. "Hopefully these'll provide some shock absorption when we join enough together. Want to help me?"

Tash followed. "Are you serious? You think we can get past the fire by hanging on phone cords?"

"I know what the alternatives are: death by smoke inhalation or, if you escape that, being crushed when the building collapses. Don't believe me? I've been here before. Over and over again. That's how I know about your racist bully with the broken collarbone."

Tash's eyes went wide. She shook her head, in shock.

"Come on, Tash. Whether you believe me or not, there's no time to waste."

Nick headed into the office's open plan area, where most of the workers were milling around at the windows. Working furiously, he started to disconnect one phone cord after another. Tash followed doubtfully.

"Hey!" A hand landed on Nick's shoulder and he was spun around. A man in a blue-and-white striped shirt shouted into his face. "What the hell do you think you're doing with our phones? This is a fucking business, we've got people to call!"

"This is a goddamn emergency! These phone cords can help us escape!"

"No, they're going to help us do our jobs! Which, right now, means selling more stocks!"

"Don't you even understand? No, you don't. Oh, for God's sake." Nick shoved the phone cord into his arms in disgust. "Go ahead, die, be my guest." He turned away and shrugged.

Tash grabbed his arm. "Follow me!" she said. They got to a large, double-doored office cabinet and she flung it open. Among an assortment of office junk were two shelves of old desk phones, neatly wound up in their cords.

"How many do we need?" she shouted.

"Five floors, three yards per floor, fifteen yards, plus a good safety margin . . ."

"Fuck it, we'll take them all." She grabbed one of the phones and tried to disconnect the cord. "Damn! These cords don't come out."

"We'll have to take them as they are—just need to grab wire cutters from the kitchen. Need something to carry the phones in though." He looked around desperately.

"I'm on it! See you back here!"

When Nick got back with the toolbox, Tash was waiting with a double-decker mail room cart. Nick tipped it over and an assortment of post cascaded to the floor.

"Hey!" came a shout. "Who do you think you are?"

Nick rolled his eyes at Tash and turned to a small man striding toward them. "Fuck off!" he yelled, and the man backed away. "Sorry," said Nick, shrugging, "but we just don't have time for this."

"Never liked him," shrugged Tash, as she packed phones onto the cart. "Okay, done, let's go."

"Stairs?"

"This way."

With Nick holding the toolbox in his free hand, they dragged the cart around and over debris, past the elevators, lights all showing 78.

"Seventy-eight's where the fire is. I hope no one's in those things," said Nick as they charged on to the stairway doors. Tash shuddered.

They barged through the doors and paused at the stairs. People were streaming upward, coughing from the smoke.

"How do we get the cart down?" shouted Tash.

"Pick it up. I'll take the front, you take the back."

They made it down one flight of stairs before Tash shouted "Stop!" and put her end down. "No way can I do that all the way down!" she shouted. "I'll trip and kill you! And it's too goddamn heavy anyway."

"Okay. It'll just have to come down on its back wheels."

Nick pulled the cart from the front and it bounced down step after step on

68

its back wheels. A phone bounced off with a crash, and the people heading up the stairs past them gave them filthy looks. Tash picked up the phone and replaced it on the cart.

"This won't work," she shouted.

"Got a plan! Let's get this back up on the landing!"

Back on the landing, Nick used one phone cord on each deck of the cart to fasten down the phones. He grabbed the front with one hand, picked up the toolbox with the other, and headed on down. The cart clattered down behind him, but the phones stayed on.

The smoke grew thicker as they descended. Their eyes streamed and they coughed continuously.

"You sure about this?" shouted Tash between coughs.

"Just two more floors to go!" Nick yelled back.

Seconds later they emerged onto the eighty-fifth floor. Deserted. It was seriously hot here. They raced toward the nearest windows.

"Too much smoke on this side! Wind's coming from the northwest, it should be better on that side."

It was. Reaching the north-facing windows, Nick rummaged in the toolbox, dragging out the pair of wire cutters.

"Right, I'll do the cutting, you tie them together!"

They got to work, Nick frantically cutting through the cables, Tash looping the ends and tying them together with reef knots.

"Looks like there's more than enough for two lengths," said Nick. "Hopefully that'll improve the shock absorption. And the strength."

"What are you going to attach them to?"

"Good point. Let me check something."

As Tash tied her last knots, Nick shoved the cart up against the window. There was no way it would fit through. Excellent. He tied one end of each of Tash's bastardized phone-cord ropes to the midpoint of the cart.

"Okay, stand back!"

He pulled the hammer out of his belt and swung it at a window, claw end first. The glass burst outward like a shower of hail. "Hope no one's below that," he shouted, using the hammer to clear the frame of any remaining granules of glass.

He wrapped the other ends of the ropes around both ankles before knotting them. "Let's hope that works."

He stuck his head out the window and immediately pulled it back again. "It's an oven out there! I'm going to have to be quick. After I drop, I'll break through a window below the fire. Then I'll untie myself and yank the ropes three times. You pull them up, tie them around your ankles, and out you go. I'll be waiting for you!"

"How will you break in through the window down there?"

"I'll use the hammer again, it's in my belt."

"No it's not, it fell out!"

Tash handed him the hammer and he rammed it through his belt, then crouched on the window frame, his back facing the void.

"Wish me luck!" he shouted.

Tash barely had time to shout, "Break a leg!" before Nick tipped over backward. Blasts of intense heat seared his face as he fell past four or five floors of inferno, then he was yanked to a stop as the cords yanked on his ankles, slamming his head into a steel column. A moment later a scream came from above and he plunged back into freefall, followed by the phone cord rope and the shattered remains of the mail cart.

Chapter 7

"Tash! Can you fetch a double-decker cart from the mail room?"

"What?"

"No time to explain. I'll meet you at that big cabinet—the one with all the old phones in!"

Seconds later, Nick was tipping over the cart, shedding its cargo with a crash. He turned toward an indignant man and glared him into silence.

"Right. Tash, we need to put all these phones on the cart, then secure them tight with one phone cord on each deck."

With the phones onboard and secure, they rushed to the stairs, Nick carrying a toolbox in his free hand. "Follow me!" shouted Nick, dragging the cart clattering down behind him as people scattered out of his way.

On the eighty-fifth floor, they charged for the north-facing windows.

"I'm going to cut off these phone cords, you tie them into two ropes," Nick said.

"Oh my God! What are we doing?"

"We're going to drop below the fire, smash our way back in, and go down the stairs. Trust me, I've done this before."

Tash looked at him like he was crazy.

"Don't worry," said Nick. "I'll go first. You'll see."

Tash shook her head, then got to work as Nick handed her the first two cords.

As she completed the ropes, Nick smashed through the window and cleared the edges. Then he dragged the nearest desk—a big, heavy piece—into place a couple of yards from the window. It was all he could do to tug it across the carpeted floor. Perfect. "Right. Just need to tie these ends to the desk legs . . . like that. Now these ends to our ankles—don't move!"

"No! No! We're on the eighty-fifth floor! We'll kill ourselves!"

Nick put his hands on her shoulders and looked into her eyes. "I'll go down first, I'll show you."

She said nothing. Nick tied the spare cord around the neck of the hammer and stuffed it into his belt. "Quick, tie this end to my wrist."

"No!"

"You have to trust me! I know what I'm doing."

Dubiously, she wrapped the cord around his wrist and tied it off.

"Great! I'll go first, then you can follow."

Tash cried with fear as Nick hugged her shaking body.

"Wish me luck!" he said.

As she gave him a final desperate hug, he held her tight and threw himself backward before she realized what he was doing. They tipped out into space together, Tash thrashing in terror.

They separated as they shot through the flames below. The phone cords stretched and went taught, smashing Tash's forehead into the back of Nick's head, then relaxed slightly as, above them, the desk's drag took effect.

Dazed, the two of them bounced once more as the desk hit the window frame. Moments later, the cords burned through. Tash recovered enough to scream all the way down.

Chapter 8

"**N**o!"

"I'll go down first! I'll show you. You have to trust me. I know what I'm doing!"

Dubiously, she wrapped the cord around his wrist and tied it off.

"Great! If I make it, you'll need that rope tied to your ankles for your turn. Come on!"

Tash cried with fear as Nick secured the cord to her ankles. He held her shaking body.

"Okay, help me sit on the window frame. Yes, like this. Now give me a hug and wish me luck!"

As she hugged him, he held her tight with both arms and threw his weight backward. They tipped out into space, Tash screaming in absolute terror, Nick hugging her as tight as he could. They shot through the flames below, and the phone cords stretched and went taught, the desk's drag absorbing the worst of the shock.

Instantly, Nick let go of Tash, pulled the hammer from his belt, and smashed it through a window at his eye level.

"Grab onto me!" he shouted and pulled himself through the window. At that moment, his rope went slack and he smacked the rough base of the window frame with his chest, losing most of his air, just as Tash grabbed him around the waist, a dead weight. Frantically he pulled himself through the window, granules of glass tearing his skin, dragging Tash in after him until she curled up on the floor, sobbing with terror and pain.

He sat with her, soothing her until he had his breath back and until she stopped shaking.

"Got to untie our legs now. We still have to get to the stairs!"

They fumbled at the knots in the thickening smoke, tearing the cords loose as their eyes seared and their breath choked. "Crawl! Crawl!"

They headed for the staircase. "Stay with me! Don't lose me!" But when he looked back, she wasn't there. He fled back and found her lying on the floor, spasming from lack of air. He grabbed her by the feet and spun her around and dragged. His lungs felt like they were tearing apart.

He couldn't see the way to the staircase. He pulled and pulled until the ceiling exploded with flame. And in the instant before Nick inhaled a lungful of ultraheated air, he remembered something.

Chapter 9

Early hours of the morning in Nick's community college dorm room. Stuck on page five of a psych essay. Only another two pages to go, he figured. If he could make his scanty material last that long. Two pages and probably another two mugs of coffee. Except he only had one spoonful of instant in the can.

But he'd worry about that in a couple of hours. In the meantime, what were the ethical ramifications of behavioral research?

The psychologists of the day had electrocuted people, bullied people, drugged people, imprisoned people, and more, all to prove people were capable of unspeakable behavior to other people under duress. And proving psychologists were capable of unspeakable behavior in their pursuit of fame, Nick decided.

He wondered how his tutor would respond to that accusation. She'd just done a landmark study where she'd arbitrarily classified people into demeaning, contrived categories and recorded the dysfunctional social interactions that followed. Oh well, possibly not the best way to get an A, Nick concluded wryly.

How about—

BOOM!

He put down his pen and opened his door to a heavy, acrid smell. Slowly, other people opened their doors. "The fuck was that?" asked his neighbor, Scott, in shorts, T-shirt, and sleepy hair.

"Better go look," Nick replied, and they headed down the passageway to where they thought the noise had come from.

The smell was stronger at the top of the stairs. Other students were peering up from below. "Sounded like it came from your floor," one said.

Nick and Scott looked at the storeroom door. It was where everyone stashed whatever they didn't have room for in their own rooms: sports kit, suitcases, bicycles, paint cans, and cleaning kit.

Nick reached carefully for the doorknob. "Hot," he said, putting his scalded fingers in his mouth.

The door was warm too. Smoke crept out from under it.

"Everybody out, now!" an older voice screamed, as the fire alarm howled into life. "Head for the fire assembly area! Out, out!"

They milled around on the dew-wet grass, complaining about the deepening chill and their overdue coursework while a team of firemen dashed up the stairs with big canisters on their backs. Minutes later, they were done, back in their fire engine, and gone.

"Seems like there was some kind of chemical reaction in the storeroom," explained their dorm warden. "Badly sealed cans leaking vapor into the air, and they reacted explosively with each other."

"Cool," the students agreed. "Like what chemicals?"

"Never mind. They've taken any intact containers away, so you can all go back to your rooms. And no, I'm not giving anyone any excuse notes."

Grumbling, they went back to their beds. Staring at his rambling essay again, Nick remembered a classic sleep-deprivation experiment and, with its help, padded out his efforts to a more or less okay conclusion.

After handing it in a few hours later, he couldn't resist peeking inside the storeroom. Even though there was hazard tape across the doorway, it had never had a lock, so Nick simply opened it and peered in. The smell bit deep into his sinuses, but before Nick jerked his head back, he clearly saw how the explosion had charred the walls, floor, and ceiling and destroyed one of the shelves running along the walls.

Now, pushing a mail cart in front of him, he and Tash charged down a very different passageway, opening every cupboard and pulling out anything that looked like it contained chemicals.

Minutes later, he parked the cart outside a meeting room and raced into the nearest kitchen, emerging with various bowls, cleaning liquids, and vinegar.

"Tash? You making breakfast?" someone asked, aghast. It was Rico.

"A bomb," Tash replied. "There's a door up there that needs shifting."

"How can I help?"

"Nick's the boss. Rico, meet Nick."

"Hi, Rico. Okay, um, I've never actually done this before, so I need to record everything I try. So a notepad and pen, for starters."

"I think you only get one chance to make a working bomb, you know."

"Yeah, I'm thinking I just mix tiny amounts of every combination I can and see what happens. If something reacts, then I'll figure out how to make a bigger version."

"Okay, got it, paper and pen coming up." He was back in seconds. "Notebook, pen . . . and reading glasses to protect your eyes."

"Thanks. Uh, if you can find anyone who knows any chemistry, that would be great."

"Hang on, I think I might have somebody." Rico dashed off.

In the meantime, Nick and Tash got to work in the meeting room, placing bowls at a distance from each other on the table. Then Nick selected two bottles from the cart outside the meeting room, tipped a drop of each into a single bowl, and waited to record the result.

"Bleach. And . . . ammonia."

"Oh God, that smells toxic."

Tash took the bowl outside and dumped it on a desk. Rico was coming back with a middle-aged woman in tow.

"This is Rosalyn, our chemist. Rosalyn, Nick. You probably know Tash."

"Hello. Oh my, what have you got there?"

"Bleach and ammonia?"

"Okay, you don't want to get that in your lungs."

"I'll get rid of it," muttered Rico, and hurried off with the bowl.

"Okay, next," said Nick. "Bleach and . . . vinegar?"

"Sounds bad," said Rosalyn. "But that's what you're looking for, right? You're trying to create an explosion?"

"Correct. We need to open one of the doors to the roof."

"Okay, bleach and vinegar rings a bell but I can't remember why. Let's give it a try."

Immediately, the bowl gave off a wisp of yellowish gas.

"Chlorine—you've just made chlorine gas. Good for trench warfare, no good for blowing doors off. Better lose that one too."

Rico came back and rushed off with the second bowl.

"Right, bleach and . . . drain cleaner?"

"What's in the drain cleaner?"

"Ahh . . . sodium hydroxide, it says."

"Too similar to bleach. No bang. Got any other kind of drain cleaner there?"

"Wait a second." Nick rummaged through his collection. "Got this one. Says it's got—um—sulfuric acid. Sounds nasty."

"Okay, that's more interesting. The first one, the sodium hydroxide, is a base, the opposite kind of chemical to this acid here."

"But won't they just neutralize each other?"

Rosalyn smiled wickedly. "Sure will. Plus anything nearby. Mix them and, if I remember correctly, you'll get salt water . . ."

"Great, so we can rust through the door?"

". . . and a whole lot of heat."

"That's more like it. As in blistered-finger heat or blow-a-hole-in-a-wall heat?"

"Depends on how much you have and how you use it."

Nick retrieved the sodium hydroxide and poured a spoonful into a bowl. "Better stand back." He gingerly poured a dash of the sulfuric acid and leapt back himself.

The bowl broke with a crack and a puff of steam. Nick felt a burning sensation on his cheek and dabbed at it quickly with his shirt.

"You okay?" asked Rico, standing by the door.

"Got hit by some spray. Nothing deadly. Glad I'm wearing these glasses though."

"Well, I think that mix is your best bet," said Rosalyn. "But how do you

78

intend to control the explosion? And be out of the way when it happens?"

"Never done this before in my life," said Nick. "You have any ideas?"

"Well, you have to contain the reaction somehow. Inside some kind of container that's hopefully sealed onto your door lock."

"A shopping bag?" said Rico.

"That would just burst away from the lock. Your container needs to be more solid, to push more of the force toward the lock."

"A smallish trash can? Taped to the wall?"

"Something like that. But how would you mix the drain cleaners once your container is in position? You can't premix them, they'd just explode in your face."

"Well, okay, how would you do that in a proper chemical laboratory?" asked Nick.

"We'd feed in the different chemicals through tubes that—"

"Tubes! Okay, where can we get ahold of some tubing? Long enough so we can be out of the way when the chemicals make contact with each other?"

"Plenty of cable around," said Rico. "What if we just drip the drain cleaner down the surface of the cable?"

"I think we'd need a bigger volume of drain cleaner than we'd get that way," said Rosalyn.

"Bigger tubing? Like a hose? Any hose around?" asked Nick.

"What about plumbing hose? Like from a kitchen sink?" said Rico.

"Two plumbing hoses taped to the nozzles of the drain cleaner bottles, both feeding into the same container taped against the door . . . hmmm . . ." Rosalyn bit her lip, thinking hard.

"Wait," Rico said, "here's a thought. If we can wedge some heavy furniture against whatever container we use, it'll not only keep the container in place, but it'll also contain the explosion—more impact on the door."

"Interesting. We'd have to get the furniture up the fire escape though—up to the door to the rooftop," said Nick.

"Okay, hopefully we can get it from the floor below—wait, that's probably locked too. So floor one-oh-five then. And hopefully we can get some muscle power from the people up there too. I'm sure they'll have plenty of these steel filing cabinets." Rico rapped on one of the ubiquitous cabinets surrounding them. "We can empty one to get it up the fire escape, then fill it with the heaviest stuff we can find."

"And if we raise the filing cabinet on one end and tilt it toward the door," said Tash, "we can just run the hoses down the top of it and gravity will do the rest."

An alarming cracking noise reverberated through the floor. Nick took a quick look at his watch. 9:58.

"Oh my God!" screamed Tash. "The ceiling's coming down—we've got to get off this floor!"

"Quick! Grab the drain cleaner!" shouted Rico.

"No! Forget it!" yelled Nick. He stopped, hands by his sides.

Tash, hurrying away, looked back and stopped in befuddlement.

Nick shrugged and sat down, leaning against a filing cabinet. "No use," he said, shaking his head.

Then the floor dropped away from them.

Chapter 10

"Rico, can you take this hammer up to the fire door at one-oh-seven? You'll need to smash through the sheetrock next to the door. Jerome and Obie should be up there, they'll help you. We'll follow in a few minutes."

* * *

"Rosalyn?"

"Hi Tash, what's up? I'm about to head down the fire escape."

"The word is they're all on fire or impassable."

"All three?"

"All three. But we have an alternative plan. Rosalyn, meet Nick."

"Hi, Rosalyn. Sorry for being so direct, but we have a door we need to get through, and could really use your chemical know-how."

"And you look like you mean business. Drain cleaner, drain cleaner, rubber hose . . ."

"Two rubber hoses. And I've also got tape, scissors, a box cutter . . . inside this aluminum coffee can."

"Which is . . . ?"

"Where drain cleaner A meets drain cleaner B."

"I take it you have one acid and one base drain cleaner?"

"Indeed I do."

"All right then! Where's the door?"

"It's the door to the rooftop. Well, one of them. We're hoping to get

81

evacuated by helicopter."

"Oh God, yes please. Let's go."

They hit the stairs, Nick and Rosalyn in front, Tash a few steps behind them.

"So, Rosalyn, have you always worked in insurance?"

"No, actually, I used to be a real chemist in another life."

Nick missed a step and stumbled.

"Nick? What did I just say?"

"Uh, it's nothing, sorry. As long as you're not suggesting that you live multiple lives."

"You're not familiar with the idiom?"

"Yes, it's just that I keep thinking I'll find someone besides me who does live multiple lives."

"Right. That's an interesting sense of humor you have, Nick. Where were we?"

"Your life as a chemist?"

"Sure. I used to be a research chemist. Doing cutting-edge work, for the time."

"What went wrong?"

"We got the wrong result on one experiment too many. Funding dried up on our project overnight."

"That's a bitch."

"Well, that wasn't why I got out though. We got new funding, you see. For a whole new project. From DARPA."

"Military R&D."

"Exactly. And . . . not that I necessarily have a problem with military R&D, but this particular project? Well, let's just say it wasn't something I felt comfortable about. Not that I'm allowed to tell you anything about it, of course. NDAs are forever, I think."

"What could possibly be wrong with working on nerve gas?"

"Ha, nice try. Anyway, I had to tell my boss I wasn't interested. And fortunately they were able to place me in another research team. But."

"You were the problem kid."

"Forget about promotion. And somehow my malcontent label followed me to every interview. That's why I diverted into insurance. It's my job to think unwelcome thoughts now."

"And it's all been good ever since . . . ?"

Rosalyn laughed and choked at the same time. "Well, let's just say both places sometimes feel equally toxic. In a purely metaphorical way, of course."

"Of course."

"And now we're nearly ready for our little science experiment. Hey, Rico, good work on the door."

They ducked through floor 107's ragged new doorway, coughing in the smokier air, and headed for the escalator to the roller door.

"Okay, now we need to get some furniture up to the door at the top of these stairs. I'll just have a word with these guys over here."

Minutes later, Jerome, Obie and Rico had wrestled a steel cabinet up to the roller door.

"What do you think, Rosalyn, door or wall?"

"Major disclaimer, I've never done this before. But I think you've got more chance of separating the door slats than getting through a wall."

A minute later, the cabinet was tipped against the roller door, squashing the coffee can against it. Nick had cut a hole in its plastic lid for the two hoses to go through. Rosalyn was taping down the hoses, leaving enough untaped hose at the higher end to attach the drain cleaner bottles.

"Almost there and still haven't slashed through any arteries. Okay, done!"

He rammed the lower ends of the hoses through the holes and taped them in place. Rosalyn opened the drain cleaner bottles and, holding them upright, taped the top ends of the hoses to their nozzles. Then she put a strip of tape across the belly of each bottle, leaving sticky ends protruding from each side.

"All I have to do now is tape down the bottles and get the hell down the stairs," she said grimly.

"No, you go down the stairs first, I'll do the bottles. Go on. This was my idea—if it goes badly, it's my problem."

Rosalyn shrugged and hurried down the stairs.

"Okay, here goes," said Nick, quickly lying the bottles down on the tilted cabinet, their nozzles pointed downward toward the door, and pushing down the sticky ends of the tape. With the hopefully explosive liquid flowing through the hoses, he turned and rushed down the stairs three at a time, stopping at the point where he could just see the cabinet. Everyone else was already safely down the stairs.

There was a hiss and a bang. The cabinet leapt back a foot, steaming liquid blasted in every direction, and the ripped-open coffee can spun through the air to tumble, clanging and banging, down the escalator. Whoops came up the stairs from below.

Nick ran up the stairs. The door now had an ugly scorch mark, but the slats were still in place. Soon, a small crowd had joined him. Obie, the South African, kicked the door in disgust.

"I think we're going to need a bigger bang," said Rico.

Chapter 11

"Hi, Rosalyn, I'm Nick. Do you have any idea how to make nitroglycerine?"

Rosalyn looked at Nick dubiously. "What? You're not satisfied with what the plane did to us?"

"I have a wall I need to get through and no time to do it in."

"O . . . kay. Might be able to help you. How long have we got?"

"Half an hour? Maybe forty minutes?"

She looked at him, wide-eyed. "You mean . . ."

"All fall down."

"Jesus." Rosalyn gulped and shook her head. "Even if I had all the ingredients and apparatus right here in front of me, I'd need well over an hour. Hours to do it properly."

"And to do it very, very badly? Just to make a really big bang?"

"You'd get a reaction but not the big bang you're after. But do you even have the ingredients? You'll need glycerin for starters."

"I don't even know what that is. Where would you find it?"

"Well, it's in a lot of pharmaceuticals and it's also used in foods. You get it in supermarkets and drugstores. Up here? I don't think so."

"Okay, you're the chemist. Any other thoughts?"

"How do you know—oh, never mind. Umm . . . there's some cleaning products that make a nice bang if you put them together wrongly . . . or rightly, you could say. Like, um, different drain cleaners, for instance?"

"We've tried that already, not powerful enough."

"*We've?* This is very, very weird. Okay, let me think. Forget gunpowder.

85

Takes days."

Tash piped up. "Hey, anything we could do with a battery, maybe? I've read about some kinds of batteries becoming unsafe."

"You must mean lithium ion batteries," said Rosalyn, nodding. "Like in this laptop." She pointed to the one on her desk.

"Sounds promising—must be plenty of those around," said Nick. "So how do you make one explode?"

"You cause a short circuit inside the battery and expose the insides to oxygen. That should cause a pretty impressive bang."

"A short circuit? How do you do that?"

"Simplest way is to just deform it somehow."

"What . . . could you just bash the battery with a hammer, for example?"

"Sure, want to try? I've got a fully charged battery right here in this laptop."

"Feel like climbing some stairs?"

Gasping for breath at the top of the escalator, Nick taped the more or less brick-shaped battery to the metal door's slats, watched by a small crowd of collaborators.

"So you're . . . going to have to wedge it there . . . real tight," warned Rosalyn between breaths. "As soon as you get a short circuit, the battery's going to expand rapidly before it actually explodes."

"Okay, so the moment I hit it with the hammer, we'll shove the cabinet up against it."

"Well, you'll get a couple of seconds warning when it short-circuits," said Rosalyn. "That'll give you time to get the cabinet in position and get out of the way. But you'd better wear safety glasses just in case. Uh, use these," she said, handing over her own glasses. "They're low-prescription, you should be able to see okay."

Nick put the glasses on and swung the hammer, smacking the battery with a mighty blow. The crowd flinched. Again. Again. And again. "God, my arm! I don't know if I can do this again!"

"Let me try," said Obie, taking the hammer. One mighty swing later, the battery began to vibrate and Jerome, Nick and Rico rammed the cabinet up against it and raced for the stairs. "It's going!"

Before they'd gotten even a few steps down, the battery exploded with a burst of bright flame, flinging the cabinet on its back, to the cheers of the collaborators.

"How's the door looking? How's the door?"

Nick climbed the escalator stairs again. The battery had settled down to a dull flame. The fumes smelled awful.

The door was fine. In fact, it lasted almost ten more minutes before the floor—and the building—fell out from under it.

Chapter 12

"You go on down, I just need to make sure no one's stuck under some rubble. I'll catch up with you in a minute or two." Nick dashed off before anyone could say anything, slipping past the flow of people, avoiding all eye contact, looking for . . . there.

He ducked inside the men's room, locked a stall door behind him, and collapsed to the floor, nauseous and devastated, chills quaking through his body.

* * *

Minutes later he was still whimpering into his hands, fingers over his eyes. His stomach was boiling, his heart racing, brain whirling as if it was about to burst apart. Panic attack? Mental breakdown? He didn't know, but he did know that if he didn't get up and do something useful, he was going to die. Again. Along with everyone else.

He took a huge breath, stood up, slid open the bolt of the stall door, went to the sink, and coaxed a trickle out of a faucet, just enough to splash his face. Obviously the water supply downstairs had been severed. He guessed it wouldn't have much effect on burning jet fuel anyway.

Nick looked at his reflection over the basin and groaned. He looked like shit. Almost literally. The stress had done something to the muscles in his face and made him look gaunt and desperate.

Oh well. He felt a little better, functional at least. Time to get on with his search for the one thing that would help him escape. A jet pack, maybe. Or how about a—

As he opened the men's room door, a fortyish woman standing nearby looked up from her phone at him.

She put out her hand. "You must be Nicolas Sandini." She smiled like it was an afterthought.

Nick shook her hand automatically. "That's me, hi."

"I'm Ms. Morallis, pleased to meet you. I believe you've been offered a job with us."

Nick took a better look at her. Gray skirt, white blouse, severe hairdo. Piercing eyes aimed at him from under stiletto brows. Tread warily, he decided.

"Pleased to meet you. Yes, I've accepted the job offer. Starting today"—he smiled—"as of eight fifty-five or so."

Morallis cleared her throat and held up a navy-blue clipboard. "Well, there are a couple of formalities to complete first," she said. "As human resources director, of course it'll be my pleasure to help you with them."

"Is this actually a good time? I'd imagine everyone's priority right now would be—"

"It'll barely take a minute, just dotting the i's and crossing the t's."

Nick discovered he'd been herded into a meeting room. An internal room with no windows, as insulated from external reality as Morallis appeared to be.

"Would you like to take a seat?"

He didn't seem to have a choice. Nick sat down, with Morallis diagonally across the corner of the table. She extracted a multipage document from her clipboard and presented it to him like a treasured gift.

"This is your formal offer of contract. There are actually two copies here, you'll simply need to review it and sign them both, along with the signatures of two witnesses—not connected with our company of course—and return one copy to me, along with proof of your right to work in the United States. I presume you are a US citizen?"

With a growing sense of unreality, Nick scanned the front page, then the second, and the third. He was about to speak when the woman placed another sheet of paper in front of him, along with a pen. "You'll obviously need some time to review your contract, but if I may in the meantime get your signature on this?" A fingernail pointed at the bottom of the page, at a space above his name. "There's no witness signature required on this one."

Nick picked up the pen and Morallis took her finger away, the smile growing a fraction wider. Nick scanned the form and his grip on the pen grew tighter. Too tight. It snapped in two, a tiny piece of plastic flying off to bounce off Morallis's nose. She flinched, struggling to maintain her smile.

"Never mind. I'll fetch another pen," she said and left the room, returning seconds later.

Nick read the one-pager again, focusing on a couple of sentences halfway down, between wads of "insofar as" and "in the event that" verbiage. It read, "I accept that my presence at the company's offices was not to engage in an employment interview and that I neither was offered nor requested a meeting for the purposes of an employment interview."

Not exactly classic legalese, Nick noted, but there presumably hadn't been much time to spew this out.

He read the next section, then looked up at Morallis's bared teeth. "As you no doubt know, I was offered a job this morning, starting immediately, and I accepted it in front of witnesses. Including a director of this company."

"And I very much hope you have a long and happy career here," responded Morallis, pushing back her chair. "However, I do need you to sign this form now. If you can get the other back to me tomorrow, that will be excellent."

"You do obviously know there's a start date on this contract."

"Certainly. It wouldn't be much of an employment contract without one."

"And you do obviously know the start date on this contract is incorrect."

There was a tiny silence. "What do you mean, incorrect?"

"My employment began today: September eleventh. This has tomorrow's date on it. September twelfth."

"Of course, Mr. Sandini. I'm simply executing company policy. Due process may not always be convenient or welcome, but it's in place for a reason and I am not able to make exceptions for one person."

"Ms. Morallis. I am assuming this is simply an ass-covering exercise to avoid liability for my injury or death in case I die in your company's care."

"Mr. Sandini, when you read your employment contract more thoroughly, you will discover inappropriate language may constitute grounds for dismissal. On which basis I am moved to retract this offer until further consultation with your line management."

Morallis reached for the documents, her teeth substantially more radiant.

"Let me help you," said Nick and tore them neatly in two. "In the unlikely event that you and I survive the next half hour, I look forward to meeting in an employment tribunal. I presume this meeting is adjourned?"

Morallis's mouth snapped shut. She seized the torn documents and walked out without a further word.

Nick shrugged and looked at his watch. Another wasted life, he concluded. Still, he presumably had plenty more. Strangely, he felt a lot calmer after the confrontation. It was almost therapeutic to find that in the midst of horror, petty bureaucracy and corporate callousness could simply go on as normal.

He stood up and drifted slowly out of the meeting room. Morallis had disappeared, but Tash was standing in the middle distance looking around. She spotted Nick and hurried over.

"Nick! You didn't get ambushed by that Morallis vampire, did you?"

"I'm afraid I tore up all her paperwork." Nick sighed. "Listen, I had an idea . . . do you know of any large safes in the building?"

"You want to lock her in one? I heard she has a coffin under her desk."

"No, actually, I was thinking . . ."

* * *

"The whole building? Collapse? Just . . . just . . . fall over?"

"Straight down. Like a house of cards." Nick demonstrated with his hands.

Tash gaped at him. "With us all inside?"

"Plus all the firemen still trying to reach us."

"There must be a way out! There must be!"

"There's no way down. It's one giant inferno down there. And the door to the roof is locked and no, nobody has the key."

Tash shook her head. "But can't we—"

"No. Solid security door."

"So what do we do?"

"We find a place where we can survive the collapse."

"And you . . . we . . . have tried before?"

"Yes."

"How many times?"

"Seriously? I've lost count."

"Oh my God. So we need . . . what?"

"A stronger place. Strong enough to survive fifteen floors landing on it."

"Like a steel vault?"

"Sure. Got one?"

"I might have. Follow me."

As they climbed the stairs, Tash explained. "We used to be on the hundred and third floor. Then we needed more space, so we moved down to our current two floors. There was a big old vault up there. And I'm thinking it might still be around."

"And you have the combination?"

"If they haven't changed it. Long after we moved, someone in finance told me one day that he'd set the combination to the date we moved in there."

"And you remember the date?"

"Sure do. It just happened to be exactly a month after my birthday."

"Surely they would have changed it."

"But that's the thing. The finance guy said the new company never asked for the safe combination. He suspected they didn't even know they had a safe."

"You're kidding."

"You'll see."

Up on the 103rd floor, the reception was deserted. Just as well, as an I-beam had torn through the ceiling to smash through the desk.

"Ummm . . . this way."

Nick followed Tash down a smoke-filled corridor, heading for a T-junction. Someone blundered up to them and carried on going, shouting into the distance. Then a woman in a wheelchair came out of an office, a bulky cast over one ankle. She stopped, blocking their way, looking up at them hopefully.

Nick improvised. "We're doing a headcount," he said.

The woman looked doubtful. "Stay here, I'll see what I can do," she replied, and wheeled herself off down the left-hand corridor.

"Quick, let's go," said Tash, and they rushed off in the opposite direction.

A moment later, Tash opened a door to a storage room and closed the door behind them again. "Those shelves there. They swing right out."

Nick grabbed one end and pulled. Nothing.

"Other end, other end!"

This time, the shelves swung out as if they were on ball bearings, revealing a thumb-width hole in the wall paneling behind. Tash put a finger through the hole and pulled the panel open. Right behind it was a six-foot-high safe door, with a big five-spoked wheel facing them.

"Holy fucking moley. You're right, they obviously never realized it was here."

Tash grabbed the wheel and pulled. "It would be just crazy if . . . oh my God!"

The safe door swung open.

Nick shone his flashlight inside, revealing a three-foot deep space with five equally spaced shelves, all empty. The steel looked, and felt, inches thick.

"Damn! Pity about those shelves!" said Nick. He wiggled one and it popped straight out. "Thank God, they come out! Grab this?" He passed them one by one to Tash, who leaned them up against the wall.

"How much time do we have?" asked Tash.

Nick checked his watch. "About . . . twelve minutes."

"Well, I don't know about you, but I think I'll just go to the bathroom first."

"Good idea. I think we passed them along the way."

They walked back toward reception. The woman in the wheelchair was waiting for them. "I've taken a head count," she said. "We have thirty-four people up here at the moment. It would have been more, but—"

"That's great, thanks," said Nick. "We just need to use your bathrooms quickly if that's all right."

"Oh, of course," said the woman. "Do you have any more information though? People are getting very worried."

"We really don't know any more than anyone else," Nick replied. "Best just to stay calm and wait."

They left her behind as they got to the bathroom doors. "See you in a few minutes, don't be too long," said Nick.

A minute later, he was pacing up and down in the corridor. Tash came out a couple of minutes later. They walked back to the storeroom and got there just as the wheelchair woman came out brandishing a key.

"Something very odd's going on in there," she said. "I thought I should check the storage room in case anyone was in there too. Only . . . there seems to be a safe in there, and it's standing open."

Tash looked at Nick, a glance noted by the woman.

"We'll have to take a look," said Nick.

The woman parked her wheelchair firmly in his way. "Can you show me any identification?" she asked.

"Sure," said Nick, pretending to look in his pockets. He took a quick look at his watch. "Three minutes," he said to Tash.

"Three minutes? To show me your identification? I don't think so." And the woman closed the storeroom door firmly and locked it.

"I'm afraid we're going to have to take that key, ma'am," said Tash. "All doors must stay unlocked until this emergency is over. In case anyone gets trapped."

"But I don't even know who you are."

"You don't really think that if we looted your safe, we'd be trying to take another look at it, do you?" asked Tash.

The woman looked undecided.

"There have been reports of looting on other floors. We need to look into this," Tash insisted.

"Well, okay," said the woman, reopening the door. They trooped in.

Nick stepped halfway into the safe. "You'd better take a look at this," he said, switching on his flashlight.

Tash squashed in after him, pretending to examine the wall of the safe.

Half standing in her wheelchair, the woman peered into the tiny space.

"No, no, this is an investigation now, please step back."

Visibly affronted, the woman pulled her head back. Nick quickly slammed the door shut from inside. Fortunately, he could cling to the handle while the woman jiggled it from the outside.

"What are you doing?" came her muffled voice. "Open the door!"

"God, I feel awful about this," said Tash. "The poor woman."

"There's barely enough room for us," said Nick. "And not much air either."

There was a monstrous roar and they lurched downward. "Brace yourself!" shouted Nick.

The fall ended with an almighty impact that slammed the two of them into the floor of the safe. The noise crescendoed as floor after floor after floor smashed down onto the safe's roof. Then there was silence.

* * *

Nick woke to a world of agony. He tried to sit up and screamed. It felt like he'd broken his right wrist and his nose. Ow. And a couple of ribs on his right hand side. It was pitch black. The safe was lying tipped over to the right, so he was lying partially on Tash, partially on the safe door. Tash wasn't moving. He felt around with his left hand and found his flashlight at his feet. He tried the switch and, amazingly, it worked. Harsh light and grotesque shadows complemented his pain. He pulled his head back to see better. The door of the safe was red with wet liquid. Wincing, he watched a string of blood drip from his nose onto the door's inside handle. He figured he'd probably broken his ribs on it.

Nick shook Tash gently. She didn't move. He felt her wrist for a pulse. "Please, please, please," he whispered.

She shook his hand off and groaned. "My head, oh, my head."

"I think I broke my nose on it. Oh God. I could've brought some painkillers if I'd been thinking," Nick said.

"We're alive, anyway. I think. Let's get out of here. Can you open the door?"

"Let's wait a little while. If we open it now, we'll just let a ton of dust in—at least we can breathe for the moment. We're probably under tons of rubble, remember?"

"Better turn the flashlight off then."

They lay quietly, each in their own stew of pain.

"How long do we wait?" she asked.

"A few more minutes to let the dust settle a little. Then we see if we can even open the door. But . . . if we're under a whole lot of rubble, realistically it'll take hours before people start to poke around. There's probably fires and flooding going on right now and they'll need to sort that out first."

"Great. How much air do we think we have?"

"I suspect we've got at least a few hours. But as long as we can open the door . . ."

"Oh my God, try the handle now!"

"But . . ."

"Just try the handle! You don't have to open it all the way."

"You're right, you're right. Ouch. Ow. Hang on."

Nick twisted himself around to get his left hand on the blood-sticky handle, putting weight on Tash.

"Ow!"

"Sorry. Wait. Okay." He pulled the handle. It moved an inch before it met resistance. He pulled again. It wasn't easy using just one arm, but it felt like the handle moved a bit further. He heard rubble moving and settling outside. This was good.

He kept working at the handle, moving it backward and forward.

"Are we stuck?" gasped Tash.

"Can't tell yet. But I'm hoping we can get some fresh air through this door, even if we can't actually crawl out."

"Keep trying, I'm not sure I like it in here."

"Maybe I can use my knee to push against the handle. Ouch. Okay. Let's try this."

96

The handle moved a little further. He rammed his shoulder against the door but it stayed firmly shut.

"Here, shine the flashlight on the door."

He contorted himself so he could kick against the door with his right knee.

"See any dust?" he said.

"Nothing."

"Well, the door's not budging. But hopefully, if the handle's open, the door isn't airtight anymore, if it even was to begin with. We're just going to have to sit tight and wait until the search operation starts."

"Right. You can break out the milk and cookies now."

"Cookies, milk, flashlight, and scary stories. It's been a while. Sorry, nothing doing. But I might just have some gum on the bottom of my shoe."

"Seriously, I'll take it."

They laughed, both grunting with pain, and laughed again.

"We'll need something to bang against the metal with, to attract attention," she said.

"My head."

"You think that'll work?"

"No. It just hurts, is all."

"What about the batteries in the flashlight?"

"Yeah, better switch it off, I guess."

"No, I meant we could take them out of the flashlight and bash them on the side of the safe."

"Good idea." Tash twisted the flashlight apart and the light went out.

"Aha . . . three batteries."

"One for each unbroken wrist. Okay, pass mine over."

She handed him a battery. Together, they pounded their three batteries against the side of the safe.

"I'm worried we'll just sound like random noise," said Nick. "Let's try a recognizable melody."

"Okay. Ahh . . . tequila?"

"You've found a bottle of tequila?"

"No, the tune. 'Tequila.'"

"Of course. 'Tequila' it is."

Together they hammered out the rhythm, yelling out "Tequila!" at the appropriate moments. After a couple of minutes, they paused to listen for a response. Nothing.

"If I wasn't in so much pain, and if we weren't maybe about to suffocate, this would almost be fun." Nick winced. "Come to think of it, I vaguely remember reading somewhere how long someone would be able to survive on the air inside a coffin, you know, if they'd been buried by mistake."

"And?"

"Something like five hours, apparently. I think that was based on using half a liter of air every minute."

"Sounds hopeful. This is pretty large for a coffin."

"Two of us, about four coffins' worth of space? Could survive a day, no problem."

"Well, let's take it easy anyway. Better give me your battery back, I'll keep them all in the torch, I'm not sure I could reach it if it dropped down into the corner. Thanks. Try and sleep, save our air. Could you set your watch for two hours or so? In case the carbon dioxide makes us too sleepy?"

"Good idea. Nighty-night." Using his watch's illumination, he set an alarm for two hours. "Set. Two hours."

* * *

His watch's peeping woke Nick up.

"Ohhhh . . . ouch. Can't believe I slept. You awake?"

"Huh? Wha . . . ? Oh God, oh God, oh God. Was having nightmares. Then woke up to this. Ow. My legs are spasming with cramp. If only I could stretch them out. Ow-ow-ow. How's your nose feel?"

"Like my wrist. Still broken."

"Well, at least we haven't asphyxiated yet. Can you hear anything?"

They listened.

"Not sure," said Nick. "I think I can hear some kind of vibration, I don't know."

"Should we try banging on the steel?"

"Let's wait, we'll use up oxygen faster if we get energetic."

"Just a few seconds."

"Okay, let's do it."

She took the flashlight apart again and handed Nick one of the batteries. Together, they improvised a noisy off-the-cuff melody.

"Whoo! Whoo! Here we are!"

Silence.

They tried again.

Silence.

"Here's my battery. Let's switch the flashlight on again. Just for a while."

Tash sniffled. "All those firefighters we saw coming into the building."

"Jesus. Hope some of them made it out in time."

"I can't imagine how brave those guys are. Absolute heroes. They must have suspected they might never make it out alive. And . . . I'm just thinking about their families now."

"I doubt if most of their families even know yet."

"This . . . this must be on every TV in the world right now. Surely."

"Yeah, you're right. All those families waiting to find out if their husbands and wives and parents are coming home."

"What about yours?"

"Died in a car crash. Long time ago."

"Jesus, I'm so sorry."

"Well, as I said, all a long time ago. And your family's back in Bangalore, you told me."

"I did? Well, they don't even know—or care—where I work at this point."

"When we get out . . . we are going to be so famous."

"Hold the front page. Just hope I get an opportunity to wash off the bloodstains first."

"Although they would make you look more heroic. Um . . . so who'll get your role?"

"What, in the movie? Oh, that girl from *Speed*, of course."

"Sandra Bullock? Good choice. So does that make me Keanu Reeves?"

"Hmmm . . . I'd insist on Matt Damon if I were you."

"Good call, thanks. Hey, didn't he come back from the dead in one of his movies?"

"You're thinking of Brad Pitt in *Meet Joe Black*. He played a dead guy who'd become the Grim Reaper or something. Seen it?"

"Yeah. Don't remember it too well though. Although I definitely feel like the Grim Reaper."

"So how many times have you, uh, *reaped*?"

"Just the ten or so. I can only think that I must be on some kind of quest, or mission . . . to . . . I don't know."

"Not to be rude or anything, but I'm still kind of assuming you're having some sort of delusion . . . like an advanced form of déjà vu."

"Yeah, but every time I come back, I learn something new. About the building, about the people in it, about what won't get us out in time. So how does that fit with your theory?"

"I don't know . . . maybe you're remembering some movie or novel? Has this happened anywhere else—a plane flying into a skyscraper? Maybe you remembered the details without consciously being aware of it."

"Okay, that sounds possible. But then how do I know about your grandma and how she sang to you when you were recovering from having your tonsils out?"

"What!?"

"And how you wanted to be a pilot?"

"Wow. So we've had these kinds of conversations before?"

"Well, not like this, but yeah."

"And . . . have we ever survived this long before? I mean, after the collapse?"

"No. This is new. The collapse is as far as I've ever gotten."

"So when you . . . go back . . . does anyone else ever remember what happened, or—"

"No, just me. As far as I know, anyway. I mean, it doesn't always help, telling people. They just think I'm crazy. But I've told quite a few and

100

nobody's said, like, 'Yeah, me too.'"

"So why you?"

"I don't know. All I can think is that somehow it's my role to get out of this alive . . . and maybe get someone else out too. Like it's important somehow in some big way. A way that maybe I'll never even understand."

"Like the universe is self-correcting somehow?"

"That sounds so over the top, but I don't have another suggestion."

Tash shifted her weight under Nick and bumped his nose with the back of her head, making him yelp reflexively. "Sorry," she said, "just trying to stretch my legs. You know, I used to work with these quants who ran stock market simulations. They'd imagine there was a drought or an earthquake, and the computer would come up with different results—these stocks would crash, those stocks would surge, that sort of thing—so they could have all these strategies up their sleeves in case that sort of disaster really did happen. And they could run the same simulation over and over but with slightly different inputs. A bigger earthquake, in a different place, whatever."

"So we're code . . . in a simulation? Or like in the *Matrix*?"

"Okay, so that *Matrix*-type stuff is fantasy, sure. But maybe we've been hypnotized or something and we're really just lying on beds somewhere with electrodes stuck all over our heads. And maybe the simulation has just gone a bit crazy."

"Pretty cruel simulation, I'd say."

"Yes, I suspect we can sue the bastards. Hey! Whoever's running this bullshit! Wake us the fuck up, now! We are in serious pain here!"

"Doesn't seem like they're listening."

"How're you feeling? Looks like you've stopped bleeding anyway."

"Soon as I think about it I feel worse. Let's keep talking."

"Okay, back to the real world. In a steel safe, buried under God knows how much rubble. Time for another battery symphony, I think."

"'La Bamba'?"

"Sure."

They kept it up for a minute or so before stopping to listen.

"Not a sound."

"Imagine if you were standing right on top of us and heard 'La Bamba.'"

"Ha. Uh, let's check for a phone signal."

"Nothing. You?"

"Nothing. It might help if I could poke my phone out the door. Dammit."

"I'm almost out of battery anyway." Tash was quiet for a moment. "Hey."

"What?"

"In any of your other . . . lives . . . do we ever get, you know, closer?"

"Uh, no, afraid not. All the smoke and panic . . . kind of kills the mood, I guess. But I tell you what, when we get out of here? I think we owe each other a date."

"Somewhere that's not in a tall building."

"Hotdogs on Coney Island Beach?"

"Sold. Want to snuggle?"

"Yes. But I'm too sore to move."

"Me too. You can hold my hand though. Ow! Sorry, it hurts."

"Mine too." Silence. "We'll get out of here, I promise."

Tash bumped her head against Nick's nose again. "Sorry! I'm just thinking . . ."

"Do you know that you bash my nose every time you think?"

"Mm. I went to a talk once about quantum theory. And that damned cat."

"Ha, yes, Schrödinger's cat. The cat in the box. Is it alive or dead? You don't know until you open the box."

"Well, yeah, but it's not dead or alive, it's dead *and* alive. Because in our world it may be dead when we open the box, but in a parallel world it's still alive."

"And we're Schrödinger's cats."

"Meow."

"And we're still in the box?"

"Exactly. And that's the point. I think. The point is, in Schrödinger's theory, every time there's a choice of possible outcomes, a new reality splits off."

"And?"

"And every time you die, another reality splits off, where you come back

102

and try another way to escape from the tower."

"Okay . . ."

"But why are you the only one to take your memories to each new reality? And . . . why are the other realities waiting for you at the moment the plane hits the building? It's like they're all frozen, waiting for you to get free."

"That's some theory."

"But why you? Why is it all about you?"

"Ha-ha. Here's another theory."

"Try me," said Tash.

"You know about the Big Bang, when the universe got started, like thirteen billion years ago?"

"Sure."

"And before that there was no time, no space, no matter, no . . . laws of gravity and stuff. No nothing."

"Ri-ight . . ."

"So the universe had to begin all at once. In its very first moment of existence, it had to get everything exactly right to survive. Because if there wasn't the right amount of matter or if the atomic forces or gravity had been the slightest bit more or less powerful, it wouldn't have worked. It would have just fizzled or imploded or something."

"Okay . . . Sorry, hit your nose again, didn't I? It just sounds extremely unlikely."

"Ow. Exactly. But the fact that we're here means the universe did get every single factor dead right. Unless . . ."

"Unless it didn't get it all right the first time," said Tash. "Unless it got it wrong, over and over and over again."

"Hundreds and millions and billions of times where it left out a particle or some decimal was in the wrong place. Until finally it got it right. But the point is that somehow, it carried on trying, and trying, and trying."

"Okay . . ."

"But now . . ."

"It's all gone wrong again. And the universe is trying to find a way forward."

"But rather than go right back to the beginning, it's trying to just change one small thing."

"Because going back thirteen billion years would be a waste."

"Exactly. But why, in the whole freaking universe, would this be such a big deal?"

"Well, what if it's a crux point for life in the universe? What if Earth is the first place to produce life or the last place left with life still on it?"

"Okay . . . and unless I escape the collapse or help other people escape the collapse, someone somewhere starts a . . . situation . . . that snuffs out life on Earth."

"Shit. So those two planes—"

"Were an act of war. Had to have been. I mean, how could navigation go so bad, on two planes, in that time frame?"

"Still. I'm a lot happier believing you're simply suffering from some crazy delusion. Or that I am."

"In your delusion, do you feel like making some more music?"

"Sure, why not? How about 'La Cucaracha'?"

They beat out the rhythm, singing along.

"What comes after 'duh-bah-duh-bah-duh-bah-dum'?"

"Tired now. Let's listen."

They listened. Nothing.

Nick whacked his battery against the steel wall in frustration. "Maybe there's just so much dust and smoke they can't get close yet."

"Maybe. I feel like I could sleep now. Just for a few minutes. Okay?"

"I'll wake you up soon."

He fell asleep too not long after.

Neither woke up.

Chapter 13

Nick had often wondered what happened to disaster movie characters after the closing titles. Their families would have been ripped apart, their homes destroyed, they'd have survived traumatic plane and train crashes—and then, once they'd plunged a knife, harpoon, or bullet into the chief villain's vital organs, they'd dust themselves down, turn to their costar, and say those immortal words, "Let's go home."

And that, apparently, would be the end of the matter. No years of PTSD and screaming nightmares. No seeing monsters and villains in every shadow, no being followed down every dark street by phantom footsteps. No $400-an-hour therapy. Had a fictional character ever seen a therapist's bill? Nick had often wished he could afford counseling—he sure as hell needed it, he knew—but in the end he'd usually settled for the comfort of his old friends Jack Daniels and Jim Beam. Or whatever else was behind the bar. And, if he got lucky, whoever.

Right now, he was groping his way, heart pounding and body trembling, to a desk drawer he'd opened while hunting for tools and chemicals, lives ago, back when the only deaths he'd experienced were being crushed to death in an instant, before he'd suffered the horrors of slow asphyxiation or burning to death. Sure, the physical pain never lingered into the next life, no matter how agonizing each death was, but mentally, each fresh trauma accumulated with grim toxicity.

Finally, the poisonous stew was bursting out of the psychic bottle. Nick knew a few places in the upper floors where he could find some scotch or vodka—his recons had been thorough—but right now he needed something stronger. And soon. The way his mind was unraveling, it felt like a full-blown, call-for-a-straitjacket, basket-case episode was just minutes away.

He looked around. There was no one else on this side of the floor. He opened a desk drawer and rummaged right to the back, past all the bits and pieces a high-powered executive collected without trying—notebooks and business cards and bulldog clips and champagne corks and a tie, plus a pack of condoms and a pair of panties—Nick looked up; there was still no one around—and finally a tiny, squat bottle with a prescription label.

Xanax, thank God. The label said 2 mg, no more than one per day. Anti-anxiety, anti-consciousness, and the best antidote to bad memories Nick had yet found. He took three, gagging them down dry.

As his senses grew number, Nick sat first on an office chair, then on the floor under the desk. He wept until he was overcome with coughing, then lay down to get the cleanest air he could. He still had the medicine bottle in his hand. He counted six tablets in the bottle. He considered swallowing them all at once, but slowly, slowly decided it would simply plunge him back into the same traumatized state he'd been in on awakening. No—what he needed now, he decided, was as long a period of stress-free semiconsciousness as he could sustain.

He took one more Xanax and tried to think of nothing at all. Time telescoped out in an endless tunnel of near-nothingness and Nick slowly shed layer after layer of fear and pain, bathing in the gray numbness. Finally, he noticed even gravity had lost its power over him, and he free-fell into nothingness, a dull roar in his ears.

Chapter 14

One August, when Nick was around ten years old, the family had gone camping for a few days in a state park on the Illinois River. For Nick and his brother Joe, the biggest attraction was the rock cliffs lining the river, a paradise for two adventurous boys.

After they'd mastered the easier routes up and down the cliffs, they focused on a cleft in the rock face that formed a three-sided, twenty-foot-high chimney. But no matter how many times they tried, they couldn't find enough hand- and footholds to get them more than a third of the way up.

While Joe tried in vain to find a way up for probably the twentieth time, a couple of older kids sauntered up to the base of the chimney. "You lame-os want to see how it's done?" one of them asked.

Joe clambered carefully down, shrugged, and stood back.

Using the handholds, the kid pulled himself up for a couple of yards, positioned his feet against one side of the chimney, wedged his shoulders against the other side, and braced himself with his hands below. Then, by using his feet and hands alternately, he simply "walked" his way up the chimney until he was able to reach some protruding handholds again.

When it was the other kid's turn, he didn't even bother with the handholds, he simply wedged his feet, shoulders, and hands in the cleft and chimney-climbed the whole way up. Fifteen feet up, he took his hands away from the rock and ostentatiously picked his nose, continuing to inch his shoulders up one by one. At the top, he gave a brief wave, called, "See ya," and disappeared.

Nick and Joe were blown away. They'd just watched gravity become meaningless. "Whoa," said Nick. "That was cool. Let me—"

But Joe was already off, wedging his shoulders and feet into the opposite faces of the chimney. At first he pushed too hard with his legs, making heavy weather as he pushed back with his hands. "This is freaking difficult," he panted, shaking his head.

"Let me try," begged Nick, almost jumping up and down with impatience.

"Wait," said Joe, "just let me . . ." He readjusted his feet. Moments later, he'd climbed a whole foot. A few seconds later, he was five feet higher. "Wow. You hardly even have to push. Like magic."

He climbed a few more feet, then slid down. "You try."

For Nick, it was like being shown how to fly. After a few false starts, he was quickly whizzing up and down the bottom half of the rock cleft. "Right, let's do this," he challenged his brother.

Minutes later, they were high-fiving each other at the top. By the time they left for the drive home, they could both ascend the chimney almost without thinking.

Nearly two decades later, Nick looked carefully out a smashed-out window. This would be worth more than a high-five.

On either side of each floor-to-ceiling window was a vertical steel column that appeared to run all the way up the building from top to bottom. From where the glass windowpane used to be, the columns stuck outward about a foot.

"A three-sided chimney, all the way down," Nick breathed. With just a three-hundred-yard drop to worry about, he gulped, his testicles shrinking to the apparent size of the firemen on the plaza below.

"All right. This is for you, Joe."

Crouching sideways on the window ledge, he held his right hand against the column in front of him, pushing his shoulders against the column behind him, his right shoulder outside, his left shoulder still inside. He moved his shoulders up and down and felt his cotton shirt, sticky with his fear, clinging to the metal. He tried to get his right foot up below his right hand. Damn. The columns were too close together. There simply wasn't space to lift his feet into the usual chimney climbing position.

Back on that Illinois River cliff, he and Joe had mastered every trick possible for getting up—and down—the chimney. He knew he could work this out. It was simply a matter of trying another option.

With his right knee pointing down, he brought his right foot under his butt and wedged the sole of his shoe against the column behind him. Then he moved his left knee so it was pointing up and wedged it against the pillar in front of him. With his right foot tilting him forward and his left knee pushing him backward, he was effectively stuck. The only way he could descend was by loosening his left knee and his right foot alternately. With his left hand still in reach of the window frame, he gave it a try and slithered down a few inches.

The void on his right yawned magnetically at him and he closed his eyes for a few seconds to get his heart rate under control. He needed to wiggle himself a few more inches to the right to clear the window completely, but he was terrified of overbalancing. His hands were sweating so much he wasn't sure they'd be any use in guiding him down.

He wriggled back inside and collapsed on the floor. He stood up with legs like jelly and staggered to the nearby kitchen. First he threw up in the sink. Then he hunted under it and came up with a pair of plastic cleaning gloves. They were too small for him. Perfect. He dried his hands on a towel, over and over again, and finally forced them into the gloves.

Back to the window. The gloves gave him a far better grip against the steel, and no matter how much he sweated, they wouldn't come off.

He braced himself against the columns again and wriggled to his right. Oh God, there wasn't enough column width, he had to push his right shoulder out into space. Gasping with fear, he did, leaving just his spine, left shoulder and head pressing back against the metal. He didn't fall, and as long as he was ever so careful, he needn't overbalance. He now dangled over three hundred yards of nothing. He took all his weight off his hands, ready to grab the window frame again if he fell. Solid as a rock. Breathing in ragged gasps, he flattened his left hand on the opposite pillar, above his knee.

He slithered down as far as he could while still keeping his left hand near the window frame. Commitment time. He lowered his left hand to just above his left knee again. His heart rate was off the charts. He almost wished he'd fall right now, just to get it over with. He realized he was crying.

"Grow up, goddammit," he shouted. "Time to show this building who's boss."

He slithered down in two-inch gasps, keeping as close as he could to the physical solidity on his left. Minute by minute, he grew more comfortable. Even if his right foot slipped into the void, he knew his left knee would still brace him against his back.

He got into a rhythm: left knee, right foot, left knee, right foot, his back slipping awkwardly down the steel column. In his mind, Joe kept up a stream of encouragement. "Come on, Nicky, you've got it! Nicky, you're a hero! Keep going, keep going, you've got this!"

It was agonizingly slow though. He risked a glance at his watch—9:36. He'd been descending for five minutes, and he had just over twenty minutes left. And if he got below the fire and was able to get back inside the building, he still had to climb down seventy-something flights of stairs—he doubted the tower's lower elevators were still in operation.

How could he speed things up? He'd watched people sliding down ladders without even touching the rungs. Fast, but under control. But they weren't at risk of toppling off sideways; the ladder guided them straight down no matter what.

Still, he had to do something. He pulled in both his left knee and right foot at the same time and slid continuously for a foot before he panicked and put on the brakes again. Once he had his heart rate back down, he tried again. Another foot. And he hadn't moved sideways at all.

Foot by foot, he descended.

"Piece of . . . fucking . . . cake," he muttered, feeling his shirt and hands grow liquid with sweat. Fortunately, it didn't make any difference to his grip. In fact, his back was stickier than ever. But it still didn't slow his heart's frantic hammering. Never mind.

Six inches at a time, he lowered himself down the chimney. A steady rhythm was essential. "One. Two. Three. Four." Big breath. "One. Two. Three. Four." Breath. "Knee. Foot. Palm. Palm. Knee. Foot. Palm. Palm."

Goddammit, it worked. Gradually, his heart rate dropped and he felt more

110

solidly in control. Twenty-five yards to climb. Just twenty-five yards. And he'd already done—what? My God, I've dropped nearly two floors already! Only another six to go!

He descended another floor. He should be in the impact zone now. He looked to his left. This window was still intact. Inside it was burning, but out here it wasn't unbearably hot. The steel's conducting the heat away, he thought, all the way up and down the building. But what would the next floors be like?

Another floor. Oh God, how will I get back inside? He had the hammer in his belt, but how would he be able to swing it with enough force to smash through a window? Using it would hopelessly overbalance him—and take the weight off his shoulders. Maybe there'd be a burst-out window directly below him. If there wasn't, he'd have to carry on descending the chimney all the way to the bottom. Ten feet per story. At least 850 feet. And what would happen at the bottom floors? Did the columns go all the way down? He didn't think so. Maybe he could get someone's attention on the way down and they could smash out a window for him.

But below the burning floors, please, he hoped, heart rate accelerating again. Oh God, he thought, I need to pee.

Something whooshed down just inches away from his right shoulder and he almost lost his grip in fright. He caught a glimpse of a planter with a broken-off yucca still in it just as a rain of glass granules showered down on him. Someone had broken through a window somewhere upstairs. No, dammit, they were supposed to open one *below* him. Oh Jesus, what were the chances of anyone still being in one of the lower floors?

Nick shuddered and looked to his left again, bracing himself with all his might until he stopped shaking. He realized his crotch was wet. Least of my problems, he thought.

It was getting hotter. He couldn't see what was below him. He just had to carry on down the chute. He heard shouts from above. People in the windows of the North Tower were pointing at him and shouting encouragement.

"Go, man, go!"

"You can do it!"

He wanted to smile and shout back some cheerful banter. Instead, he felt bile rise in his throat and dribble down his shirt. Then people in the North Tower were pointing at something just below him and all shouting at once, he couldn't make out what.

He climbed lower and it grew hotter, wave after wave of heat. The metal was hotter too, like it had made up its mind to blister his skin. He didn't look to his left. He had to go faster, he couldn't take the scorching metal for much longer. No, he had to go up, now!

There was a roar as he felt the searing flame rush out and engulf him. As he tried to scream, the flame poured into his lungs and he curled up his legs in agony and plummeted past the explosion of fire.

Chapter 15

"Ms. Morallis, I was wondering if I could have a word."

"I'm afraid it's not a good time at the moment."

"Of course. It's a pleasure to meet you, I'm Nick Sandini, the company's latest recruit. In fact, I see you're busy fudging the date on my contract right now."

"Look, could you be so kind as to—"

"I'd save yourself the trouble, actually. The reason I dropped by is that I appear to have some kind of psychotic condition."

"Really."

"Yes. I appear to be able to predict or provoke people's behavior, and I think it's escalating out of control."

"People are upset today. I suspect it has less to do with you than you think."

"I wish you were right. But—like that man over there by the window? He's about to throw his little drawer unit through it."

"That's ridiculous. He's not going to do any such . . ." She fell silent.

"Ms. Morallis? You did see that? And that woman over there—she's about to throw her cell phone down on her desk and swear at it. Like that. But it's okay, she'll stop shouting in a moment and just sit down and tear at her hair. And that man, the older one over there—in a few seconds he's going to start laughing and empty his filing tray out the window, then just throw the tray out as well . . . yeah, like that."

"Mr. Sandini, would you please stop this juvenile prank immediately before you have cause to regret it."

"I wish I could, Ms. Morallis. I only wish I could. That woman over there?

113

Navy jacket? She's going to drop her mug on the floor and burst into tears .
. . there. You saw that? And now—I don't think I can help it—the lights are
about to start flickering. Right about . . . now. Can you make it stop, Ms.
Morallis? I'm worried what'll happen next."

". . ."

"Ms. Morallis?"

". . ."

"Don't move, Ms. Morallis, I'm just going to grab that man before he
throws himself out the window."

". . ."

"All right, I'm back, Ms. Morallis, that man's okay now. Ms. Morallis?
What are you doing under your desk? Can I get you anything, Ms. Morallis?"

Shrugging, Nick turned away. He wondered if the Xanax wasn't a little
too effective. He decided to lie down for a bit.

* * *

Nick shook off a fitful doze, becoming aware of a helicopter just yards beyond the nearest row of windows. In the wide-open fuselage, a cameraman
sat with his legs dangling out, panning his lens over the carnage. It was
an opportunity that wouldn't last more than a few seconds. Jumping to
his feet, Nick quickly backed away from the windows, then accelerated
through a twenty-yard runup, slammed a foot on the calf-high ledge below
a broken window, and leapt, instantly smashing his shoulders against the
vertical columns on either side of the window. Grunting in pain, he tumbled
through the window, lunged for a handhold, and missed.

* * *

Nick backed away from the windows, then accelerated through his twenty-
yard runup, slammed a foot on the ledge below the broken window, twisted
his shoulders and leapt, driving upward, pumping his arms and legs furiously,
reaching, stretching for the news helicopter churning the air just yards from

114

the tower. The lens of the news photographer's video camera turned lazily toward him, providing crystal clear focus to hundreds of millions of TV viewers around the world just as Nick's head met a rotor blade.

* * *

Nick leapt in a racing dive, arcing gracefully just inches below the churning rotors of the news helicopter, the video camera beaming his heroic lunge around the world as he reached for the open door. Then the frenzied downdraft of the blades battered Nick, plunging him into a flailing fall into the abyss.

* * *

Nick leapt in a low racing dive, aiming below the worst of the news helicopter's furious downdraft, stretching for the flexible rubber bungee cord dangling invitingly from it. As the camera followed his arc, the pilot made a tiny correction to allow for the violent updraft generated by the twin inferno, and the bungee twitched away from Nick's desperate fingertips.

* * *

Nick leapt in a racing dive, arching gracefully through the air as the pilot of the news helicopter rammed his joystick hard over to keep his churning rotors out of reach. The yawning door of the helicopter rushed toward Nick and he piled headfirst into the cameraman, breaking noses and jaws and ribs, skittling both of them toward the other, open door, bursting out into space an instant later.

* * *

Nick leapt, driving upward, focused on the net hanging out the side of the helicopter, reaching out with hands and feet, gravity piling on downward speed as he flew across the gap. Then the net rippled toward him in the wind and he seized its lowest rung with desperate hands and the nylon ripped across his hands like fire and he let go with a scream.

* * *

Nick leapt out the window, driving upward, and the helicopter was already in a vertical dive, matching speed with his acceleration. Tilted over, the rotor blades slashed harmlessly through the air just five feet to the right of Nick's arm as he reached for the open door and he wasn't going to make it and the cameraman leaned right and grabbed him by the elbow and swung him on board, not even stopping his filming, and said "Hey buddy, welcome aboard," and Nick crashed into the cabin as the helicopter swung its nose away from vertical, Nick's momentum carrying him between the pilots' seats, throwing him sideways and upside down across the knobs and buttons and levers and the pilot yelling, "Hey, you're going to kill us all," and trying to drag him off the controls but his stick was now trapped under one of Nick's limbs and the helicopter spun into a corkscrew and the Twin Towers whirled around and around and around with a blizzard of paper swirling inside the helicopter and every time the pilot decelerated, Nick got more entangled in the controls and then hundreds of millions of TV viewers watched their screens turn to fuzz.

* * *

Nick waved and shouted out of the window at the man in the harness and helmet standing calmly beside the cameraman seated in the back of the helicopter. The man in the harness pointed some gun-like contraption at Nick and a moment later a big lump crashed into Nick's chest and knocked him over backward. Nick got up, surprised not to be stunned or holed, and realized that the lump was another harness, attached to a rope, and the harness was already slipping toward the window, pulled by the rope, and Nick dived for it and clung on and got back up and stepped into the harness's two loops and held the rope in front of him at chest height and the helicopter rose, pulling the line taut and Nick gave a little hop and a moment later was swooping through the air below the helicopter. And the man in the helmet gave him a grin and a thumbs-up and Nick screamed with relief and joy. And then the man in the harness descended from another line, his flight overalls flapping violently in the buffeting wind from the thwopping rotors and then he was level with Nick and it wasn't a man but a woman with coffee-colored skin and she lifted her dragonfly goggles and she looked just like Tash and she said "Hey babe, just thinking about you," and she wrapped her arms around Nick and she smelled like jasmine and, no, she smelled like burning carpets and hot jet fuel and tar and burning flesh and hair, and her eyes were burning coals and her breath was roiling black smoke and Nick knew he had to wake up or die, wake up or die and he woke up with uncontrollable coughs tearing his chest apart and smoke too thick to see through and he got up and stumbled and fell down and he could still hear the helicopter, far away on the far side of the other tower and he coughed until he stopped.

Chapter 16

"What's your emergency?"

"I'm up in the South Tower of the World Trade Center—"

"Sir, we're taking a lot of calls right now. Our advice is to stay where you are. Help is on its way."

"I have information—"

"Good day, sir."

"God's sake."

Ringing.

"What's your emergency?"

"I'm in the World Trade Center. The support columns are buckling, you have to get the firemen out."

"The situation is being assessed, people are on the scene. Our advice is to stay where you are."

"You don't understand, it's about to collapse!"

"Good day, sir."

"Fuck."

Ringing.

"What's your emergency?"

"I'm in the World Trade Center, there's tons of explosives up here and a timer. It's—it's on forty-eight minutes and counting!"

"Sir, if you'll just stay where you are, help is on its way. Our information is that the plane strikes were due to a navigation error."

"No—"

"Good day. Sir."

Ringing.

"What's your emergency?"

Striving for a convincing Middle Eastern accent, Nick said, "I need to talk to someone in authority. I am man who activate navigation beacons in World Trade Center."

"Can I have your name, sir?"

"Never mind. I also plant enough high explosive in each tower to collapse both of them."

"Where are you, sir?"

"I am in South Tower on ninety-nine floor. I wish to speak to somebody in authority."

"Hold on, please."

"Hello?"

"Who am I speaking to?"

"Never mind. I order you to withdraw all security forces and firemen from both tower. Allah be praised."

"Where are you?"

"I am in South Tower on ninety-nine floor. Unless you withdraw your people, I will detonate enough explosive to collapse both tower."

"Sir, I don't think—"

"I am man who activate navigation beacons that cause the plane strikes, with the grace of Allah. I now need to talk to someone in authority. If you are not that person, I need you to connect me through to someone who is."

"Sir, I first need to establish you are who you say you are."

"Time is ticking, sir. Withdraw your people now."

"I will give that order, sir. Is there anything else?"

"I repeat, I have install five hundred kilograms of Semtex around the core supports of each tower. When I connect the detonator, both tower will collapse."

"What is it you want, sir?"

"I am not negotiating. Demolishing the towers is not negotiable, but I am giving you opportunity to evacuate everyone you can. We do not require those lives to be lost."

"You say you are in the North Tower?"

"The South Tower. I am in South Tower."

"How do I know that?"

"Can you not hear all the sirens?"

"You could be anywhere."

"I am in South Tower on ninety-nine floor and I am watching firemen running into both tower. They do not need to be martyred, that is why I call you."

"Wait. Hold the line. I am connecting you to somebody else."

"Thank you."

"Hello, who is this?"

"You do not need to know my name, I—"

"I need a name."

"You can call me Asif."

"Asif, you can call me Ron. Now tell me, Asif, where are you exactly?"

"Are you in helicopter? It sound like you are in helicopter."

"You've got it, Asif. I am in the helicopter standing off from the South Tower. Which floor are you on?"

"I am on ninety-nine floor, at window on north side. I can see you. I have detonator in my hand and I am ready to push button. But I will give you a few minutes to withdraw your firemen and evacuate."

"I need to see you to make sure you're not just stringing me along, Asif."

"Wait. All right. I am wearing a white shirt and I have a white bandanna over my face. I am waving to you. Do you see me?"

"Keep waving, Asif, keep waving, otherwise don't move. I'm still trying to locate you." *Muffled.* "Yes, we have visual confirmation." *Louder.* "Asif? Keep waving and stay where you are." *Muffled.* "Proceed." *Louder.* "Keep waving . . . Okay, when ready."

Too late, Nick saw the sunlight glint off the rifle's telescopic sights.

Chapter 17

"Join me for a drink?" invited a small, gray-haired man in a suit and bow tie, lifting a whisky bottle.

Nick wondered how he'd missed this office. It was hard keeping everything straight in his head. And the Xanax probably didn't help. Although at the moment, his mind was clearer than it had been for some time. Still, what the hell. He stopped in the man's office doorway.

"Twenty-year-old single malt," the man sighed. "Been saving it for a special occasion." He waved his other hand around, careful not to spill anything from the glass it held. "I guess this is it."

"Guess it is," agreed Nick with a tired smile.

"And you, sir, look like you could use a good stiff drink."

Goddamn, I could, thought Nick, walking into the office. "Twenty years old, you say?"

"Gift from a grateful client. A very grateful client. As he had every right to be. Shaved him millions. Saved him millions, I mean. Actually, shame—I mean, same thing." He poured an inch of whisky into a multifaceted crystal glass and handed it to Nick.

"Your health, sir," he smiled, and touched his own glass to Nick's.

Nick swirled it, watched the light twinkle in its amber depths, and inhaled the rich, complex odor, enticing even through the smoke. The hell with sobriety. He took a sip, felt the liquid play with his tongue and palate. "Sure isn't Canadian Club," he said.

"Laphroaig 1974. From one of Scotland's western islands," replied the man. "Always wanted to take my wife to Scotland. Never got the chance.

Or made the chance. Oh well." He tapped the bottle. "Priced this once. Somewhere in the thousands of dollars. So that means every sip costs . . . well, I do believe I'm through with doing arithmetic, don't you?" He took another sip and topped up their glasses.

Nick took another sip, or perhaps a gulp, then another. He thought he could sense the storm breezes and heather, peat smoke and time. "If I could get you out of this building safely, would you promise to take your wife to Scotland?"

The man raised his glass to Nick. "Well, well. Am I having a meeting with Mephistopheles? Or just the Grim Reaper tinkering with my mind?"

Nick held out his hand. "I'm Nick. I haven't quite fathomed the nature of my paranormal affliction yet though."

"Nick? Not Old Nick?" The man chuckled as they shook hands. "Please call me Quentin. Well met, sir. Or poorly met, but as good as it gets under the circumstances. So please tell me more. You do seem mildly detached from our immediate reality, if I may say so. And you don't even have my excuse of inebriation. A severe case of ennui is my guess."

"Ennui. Well yes, that makes sense. I do find myself in this sort of situation more often than I'd exactly like."

"This sort of situation?" said Quentin, looking around. "So you're presumably accustomed to escaping it? That is heartening."

"I haven't told you how I escape it yet."

"Well, I shook your hand and it felt perfectly firm, so I'm assuming you are not some form of spectral apparition."

"I hadn't actually considered that possibility." Nick smiled. "But if dying repeatedly makes me a ghost, perhaps I am."

They both turned as someone screamed from down the passageway, "Oh my God, she's just jumped!"

After a quiet moment, Quentin cleared his throat. "You profess to have died numerous times, but you hint at offering me life?"

"Actually, the more times I die, the more chance there is of that coming about," said Nick.

"Ah. So . . . do we get to repeat this pleasantly distracting conversation?"

"Potentially," said Nick, taking another large sip. "As a therapeutic exercise, I believe it's working quite effectively."

"So you do find your repeated death stressful?"

"It's the responsibility that comes with it."

"Responsibility? For . . ." Quentin looked around. "For us? The people who get caught up in your situations? The collateral damage, as it were?"

"Well, no. It's not that I'm responsible for their deaths, your deaths . . . that girl's death . . . it's that I feel responsible for trying to prevent them."

"Yes, I can see how stressful that would be. And do you ever . . . do you have any success preventing the deaths of others?"

"Well, almost, one person in particular, a couple of times. But in the end, I just help to get her killed."

"That must be traumatic. And I used to think I had a complicated love life. So, you simply materialize—powerlessly—in situations of disaster and doom?"

"Well, to be honest, it's just the one situation. This one."

Quentin refilled their glasses. Nick realized he'd been doing so repeatedly over the last few minutes.

Quentin sipped carefully. "So, if you don't mind me asking, how much longer do we have here?"

Nick looked at his watch equally carefully. It took a few seconds to make the calculation. "We seem to have . . . twenty-one minutes. And some odd seconds."

"Very odd, I'd imagine. Um. Couldn't resist that. So let me get this straight: in twenty-one minutes, everything goes up in smoke—"

"Down, to be precise."

"Down in smoke, but you come back for an encore?"

"We all do, in a completely relentless time loop."

"Yet you are the only one aware of each new loop?"

"That seems to be the way it works. Although my memory of each loop isn't exact."

"But the loop is set to the tower's implosion?"

"Actually, it seems to be set to my own death. Which sometimes precedes

123

the implosion and in one case followed it by quite some time."

"Yes, I see. So this is presumably not the first time we have had this conversation?"

Nick smiled. "Somehow, I've never noticed your office. But I'm not really a drinker. Not for the last few years, anyway. But I appear to have finished your rather excellent whisky. I'll definitely have to visit the distillery if this ever has a different ending."

"Well, if not, be sure to visit again, I've enjoyed your company. But if you'll excuse me, I have a phone call to make. May not have taken her to Scotland, but I can at least tell her I love her."

They shook hands and Nick stood up carefully, the room swaying around him. He walked carefully down the gently undulating passage. Through the gathering smoke, he saw a small group of men wrestling an elevator door open.

"Fantastic! Well done," he congratulated them. "The elevator! Why didn't I think of that? If you don't mind, I would like to pick up somebody on the nesht, nesht, next floor down." He swayed through the group and, before they could stop him, stepped into empty space.

This is a very, very fast elevator, he thought to himself.

Chapter 18

Prussicking. That's what it was called. But how you did it, Nick couldn't quite remember. Hell, he'd only ever seen it done on television.

Nick shone a flashlight into the eerie blackness of the elevator shaft and saw, within easy reach, six vertical steel cables gleaming with black grease.

Unclimbable without equipment, but in theory, you just needed a few loops of rope tied to the cables with some special knot that remained loose enough to slip freely—until you exerted just enough pressure, when it would tighten up and hold fast. Release the pressure, move the knot up or down with your foot in the loop, then stamp on it harder and it locks. Repeat until you've either climbed or descended the main rope. At least, that was the theory.

He shone the flashlight beam straight down, faintly illuminating a small part of the shaft's yawning chasm. Down there, cables gleamed like tendrils of cold fear. Unearthly noises gnashed and groaned in the deep, where metal was being tortured by pressure and fire, and 350 yards of pure nightmare beckoned.

Nick withdrew his head, stood up, and started experimenting with some electrical cord. First, he tied a six-foot extension cord into a loop. Then he wrapped it around a cylindrical desk leg and looped it through itself. He held the free end and pulled down hard. Down it came, juddering, grabbing, and slipping. By pulling in different directions, he figured he'd learned how to control the friction and could start and stop on demand. But what would it be like with a textured steel cable covered with grease?

Nick reached into the elevator shaft and rubbed his hand up and down the closest cable, then applied a coating of grease to the desk leg, glad nobody was watching. Now there was no resistance at all; the loop simply slid or fell straight down the table leg no matter how much Nick tried to tighten it. He gave it some thought, then looped the cable through itself again to create extra resistance. He tugged it up and down again. It seemed to work.

With his hammer, Nick bashed out enough sheetrock to make the gap in the elevator shaft's wall big enough for him to fit through with ease. Sitting in the gap, with his legs dangling over the abyss, he looped two cords to each of the two closest cables, one above the other. All four were joined together by a fifth loop connected to Nick's belt. Nick put his hands through the top two loops, grasped the greasy cables they were connected to, and, swinging himself out, leaned backward while he planted his feet firmly against the wall.

Even though his hands were clenched in tight fists, he could already feel them slipping on the cables. In desperate haste, he wriggled his feet through the lower loops, one by one. Thank God there was enough light coming through his hole, otherwise this would be impossible.

Moment of truth. Already slipping downward, he let go of the cables. As he accelerated, he thrust his arms through the upper cord loops in near panic and tried to cross his arms, throwing his upper body back and thrusting his feet forward at the same time. The cords caught and held on the cables. Momentarily. Then his torso bounced forward again, taking the pressure off all the loops at once—and he shot down in a blind panic.

Instinctively, he uncrossed his arms and flailed wildly for the cables again, now invisible in the darkness. He missed and fell back again, his feet kicking forward and creating another moment of resistance, flinging him back even harder. Instantly, his hands burst free of their loops and he tumbled upside down, bouncing for a moment, scrabbling for a hold, then one foot twisted free and his head rammed itself between the two greased cables, tearing agonizingly against his ears and he got his arms around them again and was jerked to a stop by the noose, now tight on his ankle.

Gasping in pain and panic, he wrenched his head back out from between

126

the cables and looked around in the darkness. Far above was a small beacon of light—his hole in the wall. He couldn't tell how far he'd fallen.

He pulled the hammer out of his belt. God knows how it was still there. He rubbed his hands on his shirt and trousers, wiping off as much grease as he could. He felt around with the hammer, trying to find—there. He swung and felt the hammer crunch into the side of the elevator shaft. Another blow—and the hammer hit something harder and bounced back, out of his still-too-slick hand, spinning away into the void. He shouted an animal howl after it until he heard it bounce off another wall and, seconds later, clatter on something below with an echo like the laugh of a demon.

He felt for his watch. It had torn almost completely loose from his wrist. Clinging on by a thread, just like him, upside down and impotent. The dial's faint luminescence said it wouldn't be long now. That was okay. He wasn't going anywhere.

Chapter 19

Working furiously, Nick and Tash stacked the old phones with their neatly rolled-up cords on the cart.

"You haven't explained why we're doing this," said Tash.

"Making a pair of parachutes," Nick answered grimly.

Tash paused, aghast. "You are fucking kidding me."

"Don't worry, I'm doing the test run."

"You've done this before?"

"Parachuting? Once. With phone cords and tablecloths? Not really."

"Tablecloths? Can't we just use umbrellas, or . . . or . . . handkerchiefs?"

"I'm deadly serious. Now where can we find some tablecloths?"

"Kitchen?"

"Show me."

Tash led the way to the kitchen and they quickly checked every cupboard and drawer. No luck.

"What else? Curtains?"

"Just blinds."

"Umm . . . couch covers? Drapes?"

"Wait. Roller blinds?"

"Show me. All I see are strip blinds."

"Follow me."

Sure enough, a row of meeting rooms all had narrow roller blinds, all of them fully rolled up. As Nick and Tash rushed into the first room, its two occupants looked up in surprise, then indignation, as Nick vaulted onto a spare chair and wrenched a blind away from its sockets.

"Removing fire hazards!" shouted Nick by way of explanation, moving on to the next windowsill.

"Good idea," said one of the office workers. The other just looked bemused.

A minute later, Nick and Tash had six rolled-up window blinds made of some kind of nylon fabric.

"Need an empty meeting room—and a bunch of staplers! And scissors!" shouted Nick.

"Meeting room on our left, and I'll round up the staplers and scissors," answered Tash.

Nick shoved the meeting room's single table to one side and piled chairs on it. Then he unrolled one of the blinds. The top edge was simply glued onto a cardboard tube and Nick ripped it off, throwing the tube aside. Stretched out, the blind was about eight feet long—but only two feet wide.

Tash burst into the room with an armful of staplers and two pairs of scissors. "That's not very big," she pointed out.

"You're right, dammit. It would take forever to staple enough of these together to be any use."

"What else is there? Carpeting?"

Nick pulled up a loose corner of carpet and wrenched it upward, straining against its glue. He pulled up a couple of feet of it, his back complaining bitterly. The rest was stuck under a heavy cabinet.

"Never going to get enough up in time. But it's way too heavy anyway."

"So what are parachutes normally made from anyway?"

"Used to be silk, must be some thin synthetic now, I guess."

"Um. What about flags?"

"Like those ones downstairs in the lobby? Are there any up here?"

"I'm sure I saw some up in the observation deck once, they could still be stored away somewhere up there."

"Sounds promising. How big were they?"

Tash held her arms wide. "About this big? Five feet maybe?"

"We'd need at least twenty of them. What are the chances?"

"Not sure. Wait, wait, I've got it!"

She rushed off, yelping with pain as she caught a shin on some debris, then grunted as she struggled with a cabinet door. "Ah, shit, come help me."

Nick clambered after her and cleared some space around the cabinet. Tash dragged it open. Inside were two large cans of paint sitting on a pile of folded sheets. "We had some repainting done earlier this year," she said. "I knew I'd seen these lying around."

"Beautiful," said Nick, dumping the paint cans to one side and grabbing the paint-stained sheets. "Four of them. We're in business."

* * *

"I am going to be able to walk away from this, right?"

"High expectations for a first date. Well, I'm the guinea pig, so you can see how I get on, okay? Anyway, if we're lucky, those firemen will catch us in one of those big nets of theirs."

While they were talking, Nick used a highlighter to draw long curved lines along one edge of each sheet. "This'll hopefully create a concave parachute when we join the sheets together. Can you cut along the lines with the scissors?"

Tash looked doubtful but got started with the larger pair. "Here's the other scissors," she said. "Catch!"

Just minutes later, Nick shouted, "Sheets are shaped!"

"Seriously, is this going to work?" Tash shouted back, face tight with fear.

"I'm feeling pretty confident," lied Nick, trying to keep his voice from shaking. "And remember, you're a lot lighter than I am, you'll fall a lot slower."

"Isn't there some trick to landing?"

"Yes. I'll get you to practice jumping off that table in a few minutes. Simple when you get the hang of it."

"Just how are we going to attach these to ourselves? We're not just holding on, are we?"

"A couple of backpacks should work as harnesses. See any around?"

"Backpacks? It's briefcase central up here."

"Damn. What about sports bags? We could wear them over our shoulders

130

with extra loops around our legs."

Tash looked dubious.

"We'll figure it out," said Nick. "Time for the stapling. If we fold in about an inch along each edge, we can staple them together like this."

They started stapling, placing each staple about six inches apart.

"Hope you've got more staples," said Nick.

"Don't worry, there's boxes of the stuff. I'll get them in a moment."

The parachute took shape. "Right, we'll add more staples later, but let's get the cords attached first—I guess we'll need to cut little holes for them all around the edges. Here, double the material over at the edge like this, then stick your finger into the doubled-over bit to bunch up the material, then cut it off—uh, just take your finger out first."

The result was a more or less circular hole about half an inch in diameter.

"Okay, let's do ten holes, evenly spaced around the edge. With two of them where the sheets overlap."

"How do we attach the phone cords? They've got all that crap on the ends, they won't fit through our holes."

"We've got a pair of wire cutters in our toolbox."

"Okay, just need to get more staples!"

She dashed off, coming back a minute later with more boxes of staples and the wire cutters. Without much effort, Nick nipped off the end of one of their phone cables.

"We're in business!" he said triumphantly, getting to work on the other cables.

"Do we use the stretchy ones and the straight ones?"

"Well, doesn't look like we've got enough of one kind for both parachutes, but I don't want to mix them. So let's do straight ones on the first chute and stretchy ones on the next."

He thought a bit more. "But we'll have a few left over, so let's use stretchy ones for joining them all to the harness. Hopefully it'll put less stress on the holes in the fabric."

"What kind of knots?"

"Figure-eights?"

"What, like this?"

"Perfect!"

They stood back and looked at the result.

"Okay, now we need to put figure-eight loops at the loose ends so we can thread through two stretchy cables, each one through five loops and through our jacket sleeves, from the shoulders to the wrists, so we can tie them together in the front."

"You start looping, I'll get the sports bags."

She rushed back in a minute later. "No idea whose they are. Hope nobody gets the urge to play racquetball."

"Perfect."

Five minutes later, the first completed parachute was folded in a complex zigzag style, two loose ends secured to the sports bag's loops and another two loops of cord attached below.

"Okay, we're done! Now the next parachute."

"Uh, are you sure? I'm actually not that keen on this, you know. Maybe I'll just take my chances . . ."

"Jesus, no, you can't back out now, Tash. Look out the window. See all that smoke? Nothing is going to stop it. And even if you don't die from smoke inhalation, the whole building is getting weaker and weaker all the time. It's going to collapse, Tash. There is no other way out."

"But . . . jumping out a window with that on my back? I . . . I . . . look, I'm beyond terrified."

A shape plummeted past the window. They both flinched. Tash screamed.

"Oh my God! That was a man! Did he . . . did he just . . . jump?"

"Shit. I figure he was up by the top floor. The smoke's much worse up there, it must have just become too much for him."

Tash stared wide-eyed out the window.

"There's going to be a lot more, Tash. The smoke's bad now, but you have no idea how bad it's going to get. Wouldn't you rather jump with a parachute?"

"Oh God . . . okay, let's get the other one done."

Fifteen minutes later, the smoke was chokingly dense and they were both wearing their shirts around their faces, but the second parachute was ready.

"God, I can hardly see," gasped Tash. "Let's hurry. Still not keen, just desperate."

"Wait, need to get . . . hammer." Nick coughed. "Need to break the window."

He rummaged in the toolbox for the hammer and used its sharp talons to smash out a window. Then he stepped into the makeshift harness's leg loops and put the main loops over his shoulders.

"Dammit! I haven't shown you how to land yet!"

"It's too late, just tell me!"

"Okay. So you land with both feet together. Got it?"

"Both feet together."

"With your body twisted to one side. Okay?"

"Body twisted to the left."

"Good. So you'll land and then crumple onto your right side: feet, knees, hips, shoulder, and roll, absorbing your fall."

"Feet together, body twisted to the left, crumple onto my right side, feet. knees, hips, shoulder, and roll. Got it!"

"Okay, I'll go first. Wish me luck!"

They gave each other a clumsy hug. Tash was crying. Nick perched on the window frame.

"Wait," gulped Tash. "How will I know you've landed safely?"

Nick looked down at the antlike people on the ground, barely visible through the swirling debris of office paper and smoke.

"Uh . . . if I can, I'll get those people to form a big cross, okay?"

"Hardly the right connotations, but okay! Go!"

As Nick jumped, he flung the crude parachute into the air above him. The air caught it with a *whack* and it billowed into something like the proper shape. Nick felt it slow his acceleration, and he dropped his arms stiffly downward to make sure the harness didn't slip up over his shoulders.

A second later, he heard a loud flapping noise from above and watched as one of the panels tore loose from its staples. Then the parachute ripped in two and gravity claimed him once again, the fabric battering the air loudly and uselessly above him as he fell.

Chapter 20

"Nearly done," he said, coughing. "We just need more staples now."

"How many?"

"Another two—*cough*—in between each one we've got now."

"You have done this before, haven't you?"

Nod. "Just enough to know—*cough*—we need a helluva lot more staples."

* * *

Nick leapt, flinging the crude parachute into the air above him, instantly dropping his arms to stop the jacket from tugging up over his shoulders. At first he plummeted with the now-familiar stomach-clenching panic, then the air caught the parachute with a whack. Nick felt it slow his acceleration and looked up, panic giving way to fear.

The fabric and staples held, but he was still accelerating. Ripples of air rushed across the fabric, vibrating faster and faster. Then a staple closest to the center of the parachute tore, allowing more air to rush through. The fabric flapped frantically, tearing more staples loose.

Then the parachute ripped in two.

Chapter 21

"One last thing. We need—*cough*—a hole in the center of each sheet."

"Won't it—*cough*—just make us fall quicker?"

"Maybe. But it'll guide air through the hole so the air isn't forced out between the staples."

He bunched the fabric and cut, forming a ragged circular opening.

"Won't it just tear the fabric around the hole?"

"I really hope not. You want to do yours?"

"Don't trust myself to do it right."

"Okay, I'll do it."

* * *

The fabric and staples held, but he was still accelerating. Ripples of air friction rushed across the fabric, causing it to vibrate faster and faster. But the parachute held.

Then the wind carried him into the building.

As the parachute slid down the side of the building, he swung against the glass. The parachute tipped and was smashed flat by the wind. Nick clutched at the side of the building in a desperate attempt to grab onto a smashed-out window, but he was dropping too fast. He fell faster and faster, the chute, unable to open, flapping uselessly above him.

Chapter 22

"Okay! We're done! But we need to launch from around the corner—*cough*—or the wind will just blow us back into the building."

"I'm shaking so much . . . I don't know if I can walk."

"It's not far, I'll see you there. I just need to fetch a fire extinguisher."

They met at the door of what they thought was an empty office. But as Nick drew back the fire extinguisher to smash the window, a wheezing voice piped up through the smoky haze.

"Hey . . . what's . . . going on?"

A man sat on the floor leaning against a wall partition, his shirt tied around his face. His opened his red, streaming eyes and looked at them accusingly.

"Gareth!" said Tash. "We're, uh, evacuating."

Nick smashed the window and cleared the remnants from the frame. Gareth tried to get to his feet. "You've got . . . you've got . . . parachutes?"

Tash nodded hesitantly and Gareth grabbed her by the arm. "Do you have a spare? You've got to give me one! Please!"

Nick seized Gareth's hand and hurled him away from Tash as Gareth started to panic. "Gareth, get back! Tash, this could get messy. I think you need to go first. And when you land, tell the people to form an X so I can tell you're okay."

Gareth came back in a crouch, waiting for an opportunity to pounce.

Terrified, Tash climbed onto the window frame, took a last look back, and leapt, flinging her chute above her.

Nick turned to look. She dropped. Her chute opened. It stayed open. The

137

gentle breeze kept her away from the building and the flames. Then she was swallowed up by the haze and swirling paper.

"Now give me your parachute!" Gareth's hands would have ripped it apart if Nick hadn't punched him in the face. Gareth slumped down to the floor again, sobbing, his face in his hands.

Nick turned back to the window, peering into the void, waiting. One way or another, Tash must have landed by now. He turned as he heard footsteps rushing toward him, then he was tumbling over backward with Gareth still clinging to him.

As they fell through the paper blizzard, the parachute trapped between them, he saw, on the ground, the shape of a cross made of people.

Chapter 23

"Your parachute! Give me your parachute!" Gareth would have ripped it apart if Nick hadn't punched him in the face. Gareth slumped down to the floor again, sobbing, his face in his hands.

Nick turned back to the window, clambered quickly over the frame, and leapt just as Gareth lunged desperately for him, clutching at Nick's elbow. As Nick threw his chute in the air, Gareth tumbled out the window, screaming.

The parachute popped open and held, braking Nick's fall. Gareth dropped from sight into the swirling blizzard of paper.

Nick looked up. The chute was vibrating but holding, but he was still falling a lot faster than he wanted. He was through the paper debris. On the ground, a few firemen and medics were forming into an X-shape and looking up at him openmouthed. Next to them, two medics were tending to a woman lying next to a limply flapping parachute. Then Nick smashed feetfirst into the concrete plaza, pain howling up through his legs.

A fireman loomed over him. "Don't move!" He turned away. "Medics! This man needs help!"

"Listen," gasped Nick as two medics ran up with a stretcher. "Important. You have to—"

"Broken legs, probably multiple fractures," said one of the medics.

"Tell them—tell them—" gasped Nick. "Have to get the firemen out!"

The other medic sank a syringe into his shoulder and pushed the plunger.

"Tell them . . . tell them . . ." whispered Nick, fast losing consciousness.

"Sure, we'll tell them," soothed the medic. "Right, let's get him out of here before someone else jumps out the window! Jesus, what a day!"

"He's not going to make it, is he?" said the first medic.

"Not a chance," Nick heard, faintly. "His femurs have gone straight through his hips. Massive internal hemorrhaging. But the woman will live. Incredible escape."

Chapter 24

"How's that freaky dude with the gas mask?" Nick overheard someone say. "That's what you call being prepared."

"Having a goddamned parachute is what I'd call being prepared," came the reply.

"A gas mask?" said Nick. He was on the ninety-fourth floor, scavenging for anything potentially useful.

"Yeah, dude looks totally freaky. He's down that way."

"Sounds like someone I might know," said Nick. "I'll go say hello."

"Down that way" was a row of small, miraculously intact offices, one or two people in each. They all had windows onto the corridor—cracked, yet still intact—and all had their doors closed. Locked too, Nick suspected. Clean air was a precious resource up here.

In the fourth office along, a lone man sat behind his desk, wearing, as his colleagues had reported, a gas mask. Nick didn't know anything about gas masks, but this one looked more like something out of a science fiction movie than a First World War trench.

The man had his phone to his ear as he dialed. Nick wondered what it would sound like talking on the phone to a man wearing a gas mask. Like being called up by Darth Vader. Or maybe his friends and family had gotten used to it. Despite the situation, Nick couldn't help laughing. Better not lose it completely, he thought.

The man pulled the mask away from his face and spoke into the phone for a few seconds, then put it down again, replaced his gas mask, and made a note on the pad in front of him. Nick knocked on his window. The man ignored him. Nick knocked again, waving with his other hand. The man finally looked up and stared at Nick for a few seconds through his visor. The gas mask turned vigorously from side to side, then pointed back down at the desk.

Nick shrugged and walked back up the corridor to where the two men were still standing by some broken-out windows.

"The guy with the gas mask—turns out I don't know him, but do you have any idea what he's working on?" he asked.

"All those guys down there, they're traders. Mostly they're on our open plan floor upstairs, but these guys are an overflow."

"What kind of markets?"

"Derivatives. You know, short selling and options and all that. I hear there's a bear run on the airlines right now."

His friend laughed sourly. "Those guys are probably making millions out of this. Probably dumping our own shares too."

"Thanks," said Nick. He didn't know much about options, but he understood greed. He looked around and found a notepad and marker on a nearby, unattended desk. He scrawled something on a sheet of paper and took it back to Gas Mask's window.

The man was back on the phone. He saw Nick stop at his window and waved him away. Nick waited until he put the receiver down again, held the sheet of paper up to the window, and pointed at it.

Gas Mask looked at it curiously. Nick pointed to himself, then to the interior of the office. Gas Mask gave an elaborate, full-body sigh. He stood up and walked to his side of the window, pulled the mask aside, and said loudly. "What have you got?"

Again, Nick pointed at himself and then to the office interior. Gas Mask rolled his eyes, elaborately removed his mask—revealing a narrow, belligerent face—and unlocked his door. Nick exhaled, getting ready for some fresher air. The door opened, Nick slipped inside, and the door closed and locked behind him. The man quickly bent down to ram a jacket into the gap at the base of the door and straightened up again. The air was delicious, despite the man's bad breath. Maybe that's why he needs the gas mask, thought Nick, and he almost burst out laughing again.

Gas Mask talked fast. "Okay, I'm like super busy here, so what have you got?"

Nick put his sheet of paper on the desk. The message read, "I have a red-hot tip for you."

Nick looked at Gas Mask. "Like that says, I've got some inside information. But I'll need something from you for it."

"What, you just walk in hoping to make a quick buck? Well, okay, why not? You want a percentage? If it works out, sure, we can do a deal. Ten percent of the profits. So what's the tip?"

Nick had a strong suspicion Gas Mask thought he was a complete sucker. Well, that was okay, as long as the trader stayed on the hook. "You can keep your money," he said.

"Yeah? So what's the deal? What do you want?"

"Ten minutes' use of your gas mask."

"You must be joking, pal. How do I know you'll bring it back? What do you need it for, anyway?" The man moved between Nick and the gas mask. But he also took another quick look at Nick's note. "Don't think you can just take it off me. I was in the marines in Desert Storm. Never thought the gas mask would come in useful, but I find it pays to be prepared."

"Desert Storm? In Iraq? Looks like the enemy's followed you onto home soil."

"No way is this Saddam. Hundred to nothing it's some other jihadi fruitcakes. Not my war anymore though."

"But you fought for America?"

"You questioning me? Damn right I fought for America. Sergeant First Class."

"All right, then how about you help me rescue the thousand people stuck up here."

"And how are you intending to do that?"

"There are three stairwells in the building. I'm betting at least one of them can be cleared enough to let us all get down it. But the smoke's too thick to even reach the damage. That's why I need that gas mask."

"You said ten minutes."

"Enough for a recon. But if I'd taken longer and cleared a staircase, would you have complained?"

"What about the fire department? Surely they're the staircase clearance experts around here?"

"We don't have time to wait for them."

The man pointed to his gas mask. "I've got time."

"You don't get it. I'm an engineer and know this building's structure. It'll collapse in half an hour, tops."

"Say what?"

"The plane buckled the internal columns and now they're melting too. See those cracks in your ceiling? They're growing. Hear that grinding noise? The tower's slowly collapsing. We're living on borrowed time."

"Is that right, Mr. Engineer? What's the comparative tensile strength of reinforced versus ordinary concrete?"

Nick took a deep breath of fresh air, held it, and exhaled. He might not get much more of it. "Okay, so I'm not really an engineer," he said, looking Gas Mask straight in the eye.

Gas Mask broke into a grin and clapped Nick on the shoulder. "You know what? I'm not a fucking marine."

He crouched down and rummaged in a cabinet, then pulled out a second gas mask. "Here you go. Used to work for a military contractor. These are samples. Hope they actually work. Normally I wouldn't bet my life on it, but it looks like today could be an exception. Name's Drake, by the way."

"Nick," said Nick. They shook hands.

"So here's the thing, Nick. Because it appears some crazy fucker in this very building decided to insure the World Trade Center, I've just made a killing. I'd like to make sure I get the chance to spend it."

"Me, I'm just keen to stay alive."

Drake grinned and helped Nick with the straps. Nick's vision closed in and his breathing hissed mechanically, like he was wearing scuba gear.

"So let's go check these stairwells of yours, Nick."

144

* * *

"Which one?" rasped Drake.

Nick had to smile. It *was* just like talking to Darth Vader. Not that he sounded any different himself.

Okay, which stairwell? Thinking about it, he'd only taken other people's words for it that they were impassable, he'd never actually seen the proof for himself.

Nick pointed to the closest one. Stairwell C, the one closest to the plane's impact. This was the one someone had said had collapsed. Maybe, but that didn't mean there wasn't a way down.

"This one," he said. They pushed the door open and smoke gushed out. Nick ducked, holding his breath. Drake gave him an odd look. Of course, stupid, he was wearing a gas mask. He straightened up, deliberately putting his head in the smoke, and breathed in deeply. The gas mask appeared to work.

They walked through the door and let it swing shut behind them. It felt awfully final, like walking into Chernobyl while it was in full meltdown. After all, thought Nick, they had little chance of getting all the way down to the impact zone, clearing the stairwell, and making it back up again with enough time left to herd everyone else down before the collapse.

And Nick felt guilty about involving this Drake guy in his almost certainly suicidal recon. He shook his head. Not going ahead was the suicidal thing.

"Ready?" Drake hissed. Nick gave him a thumbs-up and they charged down the stairs, Drake taking the lead. Nick got the impression that was just the way Drake rolled.

The only way to descend was at full tilt, they quickly realized, using the handrail to swing themselves around the landings.

Down, down, down. Fortunately the smoke didn't seem to get any thicker. What did get worse as they descended was the damage. The ceiling—the underside of the stairs they'd just run down—had big chunks missing, plaster that had shattered on the stairs and that they had to jump over. The walls had large cracks and gaps, the staircase's handrail was buckled and often loose in their grip, and it looked like their feet could go through the stairs at any moment.

How the hell were they going to clear any debris anyway? They didn't have a shovel between them. No heavy-duty gloves, no crowbar . . . well, maybe they'd find some bits of rebar or something along the way.

Just before they'd left Drake's office, Drake had grabbed a small backpack out of the same cabinet he'd been keeping the second gas mask in, and it was now bouncing up and down on his back. Heck, maybe it was stuffed with grappling hooks and rope ladders. Or just his sandwiches and a stash of banknotes. Nick made a mental note to ask.

They heard a crash from below and the smoke seemed to shiver. Then it went dark. They hadn't even noticed the lighting before, simply that it had been light. Now it was dark except for the fluorescent strips on the stairs and walls and the intermittent orange glow from beneath them somewhere.

Two floors farther down, the air got thicker, a mixture of smoke and dust. Now they could barely see ten yards. "Hang on," said Drake, and seconds later, a flashlight beam switched on. "Got one for you too." He passed Nick another flashlight. Chalk one up for the backpack. Flashlights in one hand, handrail in the other, they continued their fevered descent.

As Nick swung himself around a landing, eyes fixed on the stairs his flashlight illuminated right in front of him, he heard a squawk of shock from just below, followed seconds later by the echoing sound of Drake's flashlight hitting something far below and shattering. Just behind him, Nick looked up from the cracked tiles of the landing he'd just leapt down to—to see that the next flight of stairs had simply disappeared, and Drake was hanging one-handed from the handrail, dangling over empty space.

"Mind giving me a hand here, buddy?" he gasped.

Quickly dropping his flashlight and wrapping his right hand firmly around the handrail, Nick grasped a strap of Drake's backpack and pulled. Drake got a foot back on the landing and, with Nick's help, pulled himself back to firm ground.

"Fucking hell, that was close," said Drake as they peered into the murky abyss with the help of the remaining flashlight. Through the fog of dust and smoke, they couldn't see where the staircase began again, if it even did.

"We should try another stairwell," said Nick.

"Give me the flashlight," demanded Drake, and he shone the beam onto the handrail, showing its now-twisted and buckled shape as it disappeared into the haze.

He gave the flashlight back to Nick and delved into his backpack once again, pulling out two coils of what looked like nylon roof rack straps, buckles at one end. Goddamn, thought Nick, wish I'd found this character a lot earlier.

Working swiftly, Drake fed each strap around his belt, around the handrail, and through the strap's buckle. Then he mounted the handrail and slid down on his stomach, feetfirst, the handrail bending ominously but staying more or less in place.

"Didn't learn this in the marines either," he said.

This can't possibly work, thought Nick. And sure enough, the straps got caught on an obstruction just a few feet down. Nick shrugged at the pointlessness of the exercise. Should have just moved across to another stairwell. But Drake simply undid the end of one strap, refastened it on the lower side of the obstruction, then repeated the operation with the other strap.

Leaning over the handrail, Nick kept the flashlight trained on Drake until he disappeared beneath him. Then came a squawked scream and a crash, followed by a drawn-out groan of pain.

"You okay?" shouted Nick.

"Christ! Ran . . . out of . . . handrail," came the response. "Think . . . broke something."

"How far down are you?" called Nick.

"Not . . . so far. Landed on . . . piece of the staircase. But . . . nowhere to go now . . . Christ . . . painful."

Oh well, at least I know this stairwell's a bust, thought Nick. And rather than just leave the man in agony, may as well jump myself and save some time. Head first should do it. Just a second or two of weightlessness and I'm back in the meeting room. Somehow the idea of jumping in the dark didn't feel nearly as terrifying as it did in broad daylight.

"Don't worry," he shouted and tumbled forward over the handrail. A moment later, his shoulder caught on something sharp and solid and he spun around, swooped through empty space, and smashed legs first into something solid. He heard his left leg snap and he screamed with shock and pain.

"What the fuck?" said Drake, from right next to him.

Lying down on what felt like stairs, Nick reached out—and found Drake's arm.

"Fuck are you doing? Thought you . . . might rescue me . . . not . . . copy me," Drake groaned.

"Leg . . . broken," rasped Nick.

"Think . . . just . . . my arm," replied Drake. "Going to see . . . where these stairs go."

He started crawling up the stairs, swearing and gasping as he went. Seconds later, Nick heard him opening a door, letting some light shine through. Nick had a second to look around at his shattered, gaping hell of mangled concrete, hanging cables, and twisted metal before Drake disappeared through the door and let it close behind him, leaving Nick in darkness again.

A few seconds later, the door opened again. "Nick? Think I'll try another staircase. No hard feelings."

"No, wait!" The door closed.

Oh, great, thought Nick through waves of agony. He tried to drag himself up the stairs, but the pain was just too much. He lay back, groaning.

Then there was an enormous rending crash somewhere up above and debris came raining down the stairwell, a piece slashing into Nick's shoulder and making him cry out.

What the hell? It was too early for the main collapse, but it definitely wasn't worth waiting for. Nick dragged himself to the edge of the stairs and plunged downward, headfirst. He counted to six.

Chapter 25

They took Nick some time to find. Although he knew he'd seen them on one of his recon missions, he couldn't remember which floor they were on. Finally he found them in the southwest corner of the ninety-fourth floor: three large free-standing electric fans. Obviously, some of the people with desks on the sunny side of this floor had trouble staying cool in summer.

But—damn—the fans weren't where they'd been the last time he'd seen them. Now they were being used in an attempt to draw cleaner air into the building through some smashed-out windows. It wasn't working very effectively—the incoming air looked as poisonous as the air it was replacing—but Nick doubted he'd be able to convince the nearby office workers of that.

Nearby, a woman was on the phone. "I want you to know you've always made me proud," she said. "Always. You and your brother. You tell him that. Yes, of course I'll be fine. I need to run. Love you."

She put the phone down slowly. Then she looked up, blinking, and saw Nick. "You look a bit lost. Anything I can help you with?"

Nick smiled awkwardly, amazed at how deeply engrained the impulse was in some people to offer help to others.

"No. Um, look, I'm sorry to intrude, it's just that . . ."

"Please, I'd rather be doing something useful than just sit here feeling helpless."

"Thank you. I just came past and noticed your fans here . . . and was wondering if there were any more around."

"Those fans? Well now, I'm pretty sure there's another one or two stashed in a closet nearby. We often have more out in the middle of summer. Come with me."

She led Nick to a row of closets and, sure enough, found two more fans. "You're welcome to these," she said. "Which floor are you on?"

"Um, on the ninety-third floor?"

"Well, if we make it out of here in one piece, I guess I know where to come find you." She smiled.

"I can't thank you enough," said Nick.

"No problem. You know, you remind me so much of my own son. I was just on the phone to him and my grandchildren." She pointed at the beaming family in the photograph on her desk.

Nick picked up the two fans, feeling desperately uncomfortable. The woman looked up again and dabbed her eyes with a tissue. Nick gave her a quick hug and she held on tightly for a moment. "Well, you'd better get along before I go all to pieces," she said.

A minute later, Nick was lugging the fans down the stairs, blinking back tears from blurry eyes. Down on the eighty-sixth floor, he got the fans into an empty meeting room and opened his toolbox—he thought of it as his now, anyway. Using screwdrivers, wire cutters, and brute force, he soon had the fan blades and motors separated from the rest of the assembly. Holding one of the motors with his arm outstretched, he stood in place and whirled around. Excellent: the fan rotated in the breeze of the gentle air friction. Even better, he could feel the fan blades resisting his motion.

Now, how on Earth could he hold two fans while free-falling from the building? One, he didn't think he'd be able to hold on to them if they did actually create the air resistance he needed. And two, the blades of one fan would probably mash into the blades of the other.

He put the fan down and searched for a cleaning closet. Sure enough, he found a mop with a wooden handle, which he quickly broke in two by leaning it against a desk and slamming a foot down on it.

After hammering out a nearby window, he gripped one of the fans by the motor and taped his fist tightly to it with duct tape. Ripping it all off again would be pretty painful, but Nick figured if he got to that point, it would be the least of his pains. Then he surprised a woman gasping for breath at a window by asking her to tape his other hand to the motor of the other fan.

Under Nick's direction, she taped the broken mop pole between Nick's fists, creating a spacer that would keep the blades apart. "I don't know—*cough*—whether you're insanely brave or just insane," she said.

"Well, I've already tried homemade bungee cords and parachutes, but you never know, this could be the one that works."

The woman looked at him in pure bewilderment.

"Well, wish me luck," said Nick. "If I could just use your window?"

The woman shuffled uncertainly to one side, still trying to process what was happening. Nick maneuvered his fan blades and arms carefully out through the window frame and held them as high as he could.

"Break a leg," he muttered to himself and leapt.

For a stomach-churning moment, nothing happened. As he dropped like a stone, Nick felt this would be the most embarrassing death he'd suffered yet. Then the fan blades started rotating, whizzing faster and faster, louder and louder, higher and higher pitched. But while it felt like he was slowing down as the blades accelerated, he was starting to spin around and around himself, as if he was stuck on the end of a power drill. He shut his eyes to blot out the whirling view. Damn, he hadn't thought of this.

From the other tower, he could hear a few people shouting encouragement. If he could maintain this speed all the way down, he had a real chance of surviving. If only the fans didn't fail. If only the spinning didn't make him feel so hideously ill.

Nick opened his eyes and looked up. The fans were a screaming blur. There was no way they were designed for anything like this. He gulped. And sure enough, the right-hand fan popped right off the motor shaft and spun away, followed a moment later by the other.

The shouts changed to screams of horror as gravity hurled him to the unforgiving ground.

Oh well, thought Nick. At least the spinning had stopped.

Chapter 26

"Well, I'm certainly glad you're getting so much enjoyment from my single malt," said Quentin.

"It's truly bottomless," agreed Nick, holding up his refilled glass. "Your client spent his money well."

"Seriously though, each time you . . . reappear . . . you don't even suffer any physical effects? Not from the alcohol, but—"

"Except for the disorientation, none at all. No fatigue, no drunkenness, no hangover . . . and no pain, thank Christ. On the other hand, I don't get any more in shape. And those stairs don't get any easier."

"And emotionally—and mentally?"

"Well, mentally, I keep learning, obviously. Emotionally? I veer from debilitating panic to total detachment. The last time I fell to the ground, I started counting firemen."

"You know," said Quentin thoughtfully, putting his glass aside, "have you considered that you might be rerunning some kind of self-inflicted mental experiment?"

"You'll have to explain that," said Nick, puzzled.

"Well, okay. Imagine that you were here, the plane hit the building, you tried to escape, the tower collapsed—but somehow, you survived. You're in bad shape physically, in some kind of coma."

"Okay . . ."

"And in your mind, you're rerunning events, trying to figure out some way in which you could have escaped intact."

"So I'm simply hallucinating your existence? The main problem with that is you presumably don't feel like you're just a figment of my imagination. Do you?"

"Young man, I'm in no position to judge my own state of mind right now. Between shock and rather severe inebriation, nothing feels real, I can assure you."

"But if I pinch you—like that?"

"Hurts. Thank you. So I'm still real. I don't know whether to be relieved or disappointed."

"I'm convinced this is real. It's my assumption that everything will replay itself until I, at least, survive. And hopefully, if I find a way to survive, other people will be able to escape too."

"Hmm. There are different kinds of reality though. Spent much time playing computer games?"

"I was briefly addicted to *Doom II*. Battling psychotically violent aliens on some hellish world. Why?"

"Well, to have become, as you say, addicted, the experience must have been subjectively convincing, yes?"

"Uh, it never felt like reality, but the fear, the visceral tension, that was certainly real."

"And this was when—some years ago?"

"Five or so years ago."

"And since then, computer games have become far more lifelike, yes?"

"Absolutely, although I haven't played for years. You're saying we're just characters in a game? And . . . I'm being played by somebody for the thrill of it?"

"What do you think?"

"There's just way too much detail. My entire lifetime of memories, and presumably yours too. And . . ." Nick opened one of the books on Quentin's desk to a random page and slowly flipped the pages. He pointed to the text. "Look at this and think about the conversation we're having. Would a game be able to maintain this level of detail?"

"Are you familiar with Moore's law? A conjecture by Moore, the Intel executive?"

"Yeah, that sounds familiar. It's about computer chips, isn't it? How they keep getting more and more powerful, doubling in processing power every couple of years?"

"That's the one. Following Moore's logic, in just ten years' time, computers will be about thirty times more powerful than they are today. In twenty years' time, well, I thought I'd given up arithmetic, but, oh, I think we're talking about a thousand times more powerful."

"I think I see where you're headed."

"Exactly. How much longer will it be before game reality becomes just as rich and complex as 'real' reality? And if you, as a player, were somehow wired directly to the computer . . . what if you could experience the virtual character's reality directly, a direct feed straight into the brain?"

"And you . . ."

"My character is also programmed to experience a lifelike reality. Maybe another real-world game player is wired into my virtual character. Or maybe the game designer programmed my character to experience—or at least exhibit—self-awareness."

"So you're saying that, twenty or thirty years into the future, the Twin Towers has become a computer game."

"And your character is played over and over again, with the players learning the best moves, until they escape to safety and win the game."

"And then?"

"Maybe your real-world player plays a different game. Maybe he starts again from the beginning. Maybe he sells the game to someone else."

"Okay, give me that pad of yours. And a pen."

Quentin pushed a pad and pen across the desk. "Look, I'm not saying I believe my theory, but it does seem to cover the bases."

"Well, let's see if it covers this base," said Nick, writing grimly in big letters across the pad. "There."

He showed Quentin the message, then held it up in front of his own eyes and stared straight at it.

"FUCK YOU, I'M NOT PLAYING ANYMORE. STOP THE GAME. I QUIT."

"How much longer have we got?" asked Quentin.

"Building collapses at one minute to ten."

"Eighteen minutes."

"Fine. I'm sitting here just like this for eighteen minutes, then. Going to bore the shit out of my game player."

"Me too then. Best keep absolutely quiet."

"Sure." Nick rested his elbows on the desk, got comfortable in his chair, and stared hard at his message.

Eighteen minutes later, the building collapsed right on schedule.

Chapter 27

Nick found a spare, out-of-the-way desk in an abandoned office, wrote his message out on a pad again, and stared at it until the building collapsed.

Chapter 28

"So it's obviously not a game."

"No, no game player would spend fifty-six minutes staring at a piece of paper."

"Thank God for that. I definitely prefer living in the real world, even if only temporarily. However—"

"Oh, no. Oh, no."

"What?"

"You've got another theory. You're determined to convince me this isn't real."

"Well, in the end I'm hoping to convince you it is. I'd like to get home to my wife, you know." Quentin smiled. "No pressure, of course, but it looks like you could use some motivation too."

Nick shrugged. "Okay, let's hear the next theory."

"This also depends on Moore's law—and the development of vastly powerful computers in, let's say, twenty or thirty years' time."

"Okay."

"It also depends on the insurance industry remaining just as painfully ungenerous as it is now."

"That's a certainty."

"Right. So imagine today's tragedy sparks a torrent of litigation. The victims' families' lawyers argue that the fireproofing wasn't adequate, the elevators should have functioned better, the roof doors shouldn't have been locked, the evacuation procedure wasn't fit for purpose, and who knows what else. Now imagine the litigation drags on and on and on, as litigation tends to do. Until, twenty or more years from now, one side or the other creates a computer model of the South Tower, packs it with simulated versions of everyone who was here on the day, and sets your simulated persona loose to see if there's a way out: to show, one way or the other, who or what—besides the evil terrorists themselves—can be blamed for our outcome."

"Well, Mr. Straw Man, that shouldn't take long to tear apart."

"Be my guest."

"If they're able to model the tower so exactly, why do they need me to show them the faults? They have to program in the malfunctioning elevators and locked doors. If they really want to see if there's a way to escape, why program just one person to learn from one rerun to the next? If everyone could learn progressively what doesn't work, we'd soon find a way that does. Do you know how difficult it is to get people to accept what I've learned along the way? Besides yourself?"

"Well, while your argument does rely on the insurance industry—or the legal industry—doing something rational, I do tend to agree with you. Which leaves me with one conclusion."

"Which is?"

"We've found an honest-to-God glitch in the workings of the universe. And Nick, it's your destiny to use it to do something incredible. Not because it'll square things with your brother, although I'm sure it will. But because you have a streak of pure stubborn and neither this building nor the people in it are going to stop you."

"Well, shucks. But I'm afraid you haven't exactly left me much time. We get flattened again in, oh, two minutes or so."

"Well, dammit, we've barely touched this absurdly expensive whisky. Bottoms up!"

"Tops down!"

For some reason, they found this very funny.

Chapter 29

Nick stood looking out a smashed-out window. Feeling the late summer breeze, looking at the blue sky, trying to ignore the smoke, the helicopters, the screams, the sirens, the fear, the unutterably unfair responsibility that some inexplicable fate had loaded onto his shoulders.

He looked at the aluminum-clad pillars on either side of the window. He felt a kind of paternal affection for them—they'd so nearly let him defy gravity—but he just couldn't face another attempt yet. Maybe later.

He rapped on the cool aluminum. Not a hint of the blistering heat that had hit him just a few floors down.

A tiny dust mote of a thought hovered quietly and politely in his mind. After intentionally ignoring it for a minute or so, Nick sighed and gave it the attention it itched for. He shrugged, reached out his right hand to the pillar to his left—and felt around its outer corner.

Before, he'd actively avoided exploring the outer faces of the columns. He'd been terrified that shifting his weight or even his attention would unbalance him enough to send him hurtling into the abyss. But now, with his feet on the still-solid floor, he stretched out his arm, curled his hand around the corner, and, stretching further, felt a recessed vertical groove, a half-inch-wide crevice running up the column's outer face.

The crevice stretched as high and as low as he could reach. He turned and felt the pillar on his right with his left hand. It had exactly the same recessed crevice, also extending both up and down.

He thought for a minute or so as the world carried on going to hell.

Somehow he found all the panic and confusion strangely relaxing. If only all those other people and all their effort could relieve him of his endlessly recurring fate.

He turned back inside. At a nearby desk, a young man finished a phone call to some loved one. "Be brave, be strong, I love you," he said and put the receiver down reverently on its cradle. "Goddamn answering machine," he said to nobody in particular.

Nick gave him a few seconds. "Sorry to cut in on your thoughts," he said, "but—uh—how do they clean the windows here?"

"Huh? Oh yeah. There's an automated rig with brushes that goes up and down the columns. It's controlled from the roof. You could probably escape on it—if only the doors to the goddamn roof were open."

Chapter 30

"What the fuck are you doing?" said Gareth.

"Oh, hello, Gareth, nice to see you," Nick replied. "Want to help me take this computer apart?"

"Are you fucking mental? The building's burning down with us in it and you want me to help you do computer maintenance? Whose computer is this, anyway?"

"Guy called Chris. He headed up to the roof, said I was welcome to his PC. You can head up and ask him if you like. Or you can help me with this, like I said."

"You're such a smartass, aren't you? Unless you're building a teleportation device, you really are wasting your time."

"Maybe I am."

"Fuck you." Gareth gave Nick a final sneering glare and swaggered off.

Nick sighed and carried on dismembering the PC. One more screw and the back came off, exposing its internal workings. He quickly undid more screws, a litter of dismembered computer parts growing on the desk.

"Hey, looked like you and Gareth really hit it off."

Nick looked up. A young man—Japanese or Korean, Nick guessed—sat down on the desk opposite Nick and surveyed the computer parts.

"Took me a couple of weeks to reach outright animosity," the man continued. "What's your secret?"

Nick smiled. "Just a gift I have. I'm Nick," he said, extending his right hand.

The young man shook. "Gwang. Looks like you have a plan."

"I'm looking for a strip of metal like an inch and a half long, hopefully with a hole for a bolt drilled through it."

"Um, like a clasp of some sort?"

"Wouldn't be strong enough. The bolt would need to support my weight."

"I'm intrigued. Mind sharing?"

"Sure. Although you might think it's crazy."

"If there's a chance it could save my ass, I don't care about crazy."

"Okay. So here's what I'm thinking. You know all these vertical columns running up and down the sides of the building? Each one has a track recessed into it for the window cleaning gondola."

"Huh? You're trying to escape on the gondola . . . or fix the gondola? But they say we can't get onto the roof."

"No, but if I can find the right shaped strips and put handles on them, I should be able to insert the strips into the tracks and, uh, climb down."

"Holy cow. You mean like ice picks? That sort of slide down the gondola tracks? Won't you just freefall?"

"Difficult to explain without seeing for yourself. Come over to the window and I'll show you. Here, take this screwdriver."

Nick hung on to Gwang's left arm while he used the other to poke the screwdriver into one of the grooves. "Okay, I think I see what you mean," said Gwang. "The tracks are basically C-shaped grooves running all the way up and down, with just a very narrow gap between the horns of the C. So if the ice pick broadens out at the tip, you can pull back on it and control your rate of descent."

"Exactly. The tip of the ice pick would have to be a short metal strip at right angles to the rest of the ice pick. You'd need to rotate it ninety degrees to insert it into the groove and then twist it back again to make it secure."

Gwang nodded. "You'd need two devices though, like with proper ice picks. And you'll need a harness, or your arms will just give up. No way could you just hang on long enough to get all the way down."

"Well, I only need to get below the impact zone, but yeah, I take your point."

"Okay. So if you had a strip of metal just the right size to fit into the

162

groove, and you attach it to some kind of handle you can grab on to, then you need to run a rope or cord, I don't know, like electric cord, through the handle, attached to some kind of hip harness . . ." Gwang looked around.

"Sports bags should work."

"You got it, wait here."

"Not going anywhere," said Nick as Gwang rushed off.

A minute later, Gwang came back with a couple of empty sports bags. "I hope their owners will forgive us. I'm sure I can turn these into functional harnesses in no time. Any luck with those metal strips? And the handles?"

"Not yet. What I really need is a workshop. Or even just a hacksaw and a vice grip."

Gwang smiled. "You're in luck. Maybe you should come over to my cubicle. It's just down here."

One look at Gwang's cubicle and Nick burst out laughing. On a shelf above his desk was a menagerie of half-built creatures made from nuts, bolts, springs, and other bits of metal. Gwang opened his desk drawers to reveal racks of metal fittings and equipment that included a hacksaw, vice grip, battery-operated drill, screwdrivers, and a soldering iron. Nick shook his head, grinning. "God, I wish I'd found you earlier."

"My lunchtime hobby." Gwang smiled. "I make these for my daughter."

"Well, let's make sure you finish them. You think you can help me make a rig for each of us?"

"Well, I'd say some of the stuff in your PC looks promising."

* * *

"Random as pi, but they should work," said Gwang, looking at the collections of pirated hardware, cables, and sports bags that comprised their escape gear. Nick inspected the "ice picks" and nodded. Sawn-off plastic dustpan and brush handles, bolted to short strips of steel set at right angles to the handles. Holes drilled into the handles, electric cable running through the holes, and the cable secured to the straps of sports bags, which they'd wear like diapers.

"Okay," said Nick. "Time to test them out."

He fastened one of the sports bags around his butt and leaned backward out of a window, Gwang holding on to him by the straps. With his right hand, he inserted an ice pick tip into the gondola track on his right and twisted the handle down to secure it, then did the same with his left hand, plugging into the gondola track on his left. He leaned back further. Everything held. Pulling on his right hand, he unweighted his left hand and slid the ice pick up and down with ease. Then he pulled on his left hand and slid the right-hand ice pick up and down. He pulled back on both hands and bent his knees, crouching down to transfer his weight onto the sports bag. Feeling confident, he stepped backward so that both feet were pressed against the tower's vertical glass cliff face, and he "walked" up and down for a few small steps.

He pulled himself back into the window. "Works like a charm. You try yours."

Gwang's trial was equally successful. "Okay, let's head down to eighty-five," said Nick.

"Give me a minute. I need to make a quick phone call."

Nick checked the knots while Gwang made his call from a few desks away, his back to Nick. Nick only caught the end of it.

". . . trying very hard to be there for your birthday like I said, Princess, but if I don't make it, Mommy's got my present for you. I hope you like it. No, it's not a pony. You'll see. Well, it's something for your dolls. They'll like it too. Maybe, Princess. Daddy's got to go now. Love you." He turned back to Nick with a sigh. "Okay, let's go."

"One last thing," said Nick. He picked a hammer out of the toolbox and stuffed it into his belt.

"Thought you were planning to finish your argument with Gareth for a moment," said Gwang. "What's that for?"

"It's my patent window-opening device. For getting back into the building lower down."

Gwang nodded. "Good thinking."

They headed down stairwell A. Conditions hadn't changed: smoky but breathable. "Been thinking," said Gwang, "it's probably better to slot both your ice picks into the same groove. That way the column gives you some shielding from any flames coming through the window."

"Got it."

They were about to turn into floor eighty-five's fire door when Nick stopped Gwang with a hand on his shoulder. "Listen."

Footsteps up above stopped abruptly. They waited for more but heard nothing.

Gwang looked puzzled. "Gareth," Nick said quietly. "Let's go."

They steered their way through, across and over the rubble of the eighty-fifth floor, and found a broken-out window on the north side. Silently, they put on their sports bag diapers.

"Ah, just one thing," said Gwang. "Do you mind if I go first? Someone has to be the guinea pig and I'm volunteering."

"You sure?" asked Nick. "Because I'm kind of used to this."

"It's my engineering, so it's my job to go first," said Gwang. "Besides, with my glasses on I can't see much more than fifty yards. Helps with the vertigo."

"Better take the hammer," said Nick, passing it over.

Gwang put the hammer through his belt and, with Nick hanging on to him from inside, stepped onto the window ledge and reached out with his right hand.

"The clip's gone in the track," he said. He pulled this way and that. "Feels like it's going to work."

Gwang took his right foot off the window ledge, swung himself out, and planted his foot on the column below his right hand. He wiggled the makeshift harness into a more or less comfortable position. Then he breathed out heavily, swung himself out into space, and clipped in with his left hand.

He put his left foot on the column. Leaned back. Everything held.

"Whew. Here goes."

Unweighting one hand after another and shuffling his feet down the pillar a few inches at a time, he quickly got his technique under control and picked up speed. He looked up at Nick. "Easy as cake," he said, grinning nervously.

He descended a few yards, then looked at his right-hand ice pick, a look of horror on his face. "Plastic's tearing," he shouted.

"Come back up," shouted Nick. "Quick!"

"It's gone!" Gwang swung to his left, out of control, throwing the left-hand ice pick away and grabbing frantically at the other one. With both hands on it, he repositioned himself, leaning back, getting his breath back under control. But now his harness was only supported on one side. He had to carry almost all his weight on his arms and the one remaining ice pick. He pulled himself forward and tried to shift it up the groove.

"Keep going, you can do it!" shouted Nick.

Gwang repeated the movement. "It's jammed," he screamed. "The tip of the other pick's still in the groove!" Nick could see the sweat pouring from his face.

"I . . . can't . . . hold on . . . any longer." Gwang's hands slipped off the handle. He dropped, tumbled out of his harness, and was gone.

Nick stood back from the window and sank to his knees, trembling.

"You . . . fucker!" shouted Gareth. He'd been watching from another window. He strode up to Nick and threw him backward so hard his head bounced off the wall. "You fucking killed him!"

Nick shook his throbbing head, furious with himself. "You're right. We should have used wider washers. Sorry, Gwang." He looked at his watch and sighed. "Next time."

Chapter 31

They were on the eighty-fifth floor, heading for the window. A loud thump came from the other side of the door to stairwell A. "That'll be Gareth, I expect," said Nick.

Gwang smiled. "Good thing you wedged the door shut."

"Yeah, better hurry though. Won't take him long to get around to one of the other doors."

At the window, they quickly stepped into their sports bag diapers. "I'll go first," said Nick.

Gwang looked like he wanted to argue, then simply shrugged.

This time, they'd braced the connections with oversized washers and secured their hands to the ice pick handles with prodigious amounts of duct tape. "You know what they say," Gwang had observed cheerfully, "if it breaks, you simply weren't using enough duct tape." Nick had just nodded grimly.

Nick swung himself out the window and twisted his second clip into the gondola track. He straddled the pillar, a foot on either side of it. His harness felt surprisingly secure. "Look out below," he said and began his descent.

Weight on top clip, weight off bottom clip. Lower bottom clip by a foot. Weight on both clips. Shuffle both feet down. Weight off top clip, lower top clip a foot, weight on both clips. Shuffle both feet down. Nick quickly got into the rhythm. Quickly, he passed the next level of windows and kept going.

"You're doing great," called Gwang from above. "I'm going to start following you."

Nick looked up. "Okay! But take the pillar to my left, all right?"

"Sure thing," Gwang replied, and Nick breathed a sigh of relief. The last thing he wanted was 150 pounds crashing down on him from above if anything went wrong with Gwang's rig.

The next time he looked up, Gwang was climbing down confidently. "Whoo-hoo!" Gwang yelled. "If this wasn't so terrifying, I could do it for fun!"

"Remember to wash some windows on your way," shouted Nick in response.

"You can talk, you're a disgrace," replied Gwang. "You've left your filthy footprints all the way down."

"The real vandalism starts in a couple of minutes," shouted Nick.

"Jesus, look at that."

Nick glanced at Gwang. He was looking inside the window between them. Nick followed his eyes and saw devastation, smoke, and burning . . . oh God, he didn't want to know. He hurried on. Then he remembered.

"Slow down, slow down!" he shouted, looking at his watch. He settled on his harness and leaned back.

"What do you mean?" asked Gwang, almost level with Nick, twisting to look down. "Ahh! Shouldn't have done that—even with my eyesight, it still looks a long way down." He faced the column again. "What do you mean, slow down?"

"If I remember right, we're about to have a bit of fire action in a moment or so," yelled Nick.

"If you remember right? What do you mean?"

"Tell you later. Here it comes . . . now!"

A giant tongue of fire roared out of a window below and to the left of them. Fortunately, the breeze blew the worst of the heat away.

"Shit, that's hot!" screamed Gwang. "I see what you mean."

"Wait . . . wait . . . okay, let's go!"

The flames subsided and they hurried on down. A minute later, they were below the fire. "Just one more floor!" shouted Nick.

Another endless minute. Then: "Okay! Here we are!"

They stopped, side by side, Gwang on Nick's left. Nick unclipped his left-hand ice pick to reach for the hammer in his belt. "Shit! Shit! Shit! Fucking duct tape—I can't use my fingers!"

"What about the other window? The one on your right?"

"No luck, it's still solid."

"You'll have to rip through the duct tape with your teeth!"

"Okay!" Nick unclipped his left hand again, found a loose end of duct tape, and started to peel it off his hand with his teeth. "It's working!" Finally, he extracted the hammer from his belt. "Should have attached this somehow," he shouted, "but too late to worry now. Okay, look away!"

Gwang looked to his left. Nick swung the hammer back and hit the glass. Not hard enough. Nick took another swing and the hammer bounced back, almost leaping out of his grip. Damn. His left arm wasn't strong enough for a good blow, and neither was his left hand strong enough to keep a good grip on the hammer.

"You're not left-handed, are you?" shouted Gwang. "Give me the hammer so I can use my right arm!" He unclipped his right hand and used his teeth to tear at the duct tape. A half minute passed like torture. "Ready!"

Nick held out the hammer for Gwang to grab. "Sure you got it?"

"Got it! All right, watch out!"

His second swing burst through the glass, and he quickly cleared the rough granules from as much of the window frame as he could reach. He threw the hammer in through the window, then hooked his right leg inside and reached his hand around the column. He unclipped himself from the gondola track and swung himself inside.

"Your turn!"

"Just a sec." Nick looked up. Gareth was right above, leaning out of a window, watching them with a look of pure hatred. Nick lifted his left fist above his head and showed him his middle finger. At least it was capable of that.

Moments later, he was inside the building. "Put it there," shouted Gwang, holding up his right hand.

"Way to go!" Nick shouted, smacking it with his left. Abruptly, they both started to shake, leaning against the window frame as nervous tension got the better of them. "Oh man, oh man, that was terrifying."

"Next time, let's find a nice long rope," Gwang said.

The floor shook and there was a deafening roar from above.

"What the fuck's that?"

"Sounds like a whole floor collapsed. We've got to get the fuck out of here. We don't have much time."

"What do you mean? Where are you getting this stuff?"

"I'll tell you when we're out—just take it from me that this building's going down in just a few minutes."

"Let's go! Stairs or elevator?"

"We've got fifteen minutes. I don't trust the elevators—can we do seventy-six floors in ten minutes?"

"Eight floors a minute? Let's give it a try."

"Yeah. Just pick up that hammer first, will you?"

A moment later they were whirling down the closest staircase three steps at a time. One-two-three-four swing left, one-two-three-four swing left. On and on, down and down, two flights of stairs per floor, like a living clock.

"Floor sixty-eight! How's our timing?

"About a minute! Keep going!"

On they went.

"Forty-two!"

Nick had a stair to go before the next landing. He lifted his wrist to look at his watch and tumbled to the floor, cursing.

"Hope that wasn't your ankle!"

"That was my ankle! Ow! Jesus!"

"Get up, let's get to the elevators!"

Gwang held the door open and grabbed Nick around the waist and they staggered to the elevator bank. Gwang punched the down arrow. Something started humming.

"One of them's moving!"

The lights told their story. The elevator was climbing from the thirtieth floor. Seconds later, the doors pinged open. They charged in, and Gwang hit 1 and the Door Close button.

Nothing happened for a few fateful seconds. Then the doors whooshed shut and they were on their way. The numbers fell away rapidly. They were past floor thirty-five. Thirty. Twenty-five.

A grating noise and a lurch. They both exclaimed at once. "Shit!" Then a crunch that knocked the elevator, and them, sideways. The elevator jolted to a halt, throwing them both to the floor. "Fuck!"

Gwang hit the Door Open button. Nothing. He pushed other buttons at random. Nothing. They leapt at the doors and tried to wrench them apart, but it was hopeless.

"We'll have to smash through the side," said Nick grimly, swinging his hammer.

Gwang pointed at the cavity Nick was making in the sheetrock panel. "You've obviously done this before too," he said.

The sheetrock gave a token resistance before crumbling. "Hope there's nothing too solid on the other side!" Nick took a few more swings, then gave the hammer to Gwang, who attacked the wall in a frenzy, smashing an outline of a two-foot-square hole. He wrenched the square of sheetrock away, leaving them facing another wall. Gwang took another swing. "More sheetrock."

"We can do this!"

Nick took the hammer back and carried on pounding as Gwang wiped sweat off his forehead, then his hands.

Another swing and they heard tiles clattering onto a floor. Light came through the hole. "Nearly there!"

More swings, more clattering tiles and sheetrock debris, more light. "Stand back," said Gwang. He took a running start and lashed out with a foot. The sheetrock gave way. "Go!"

Nick launched himself through the knee-high hole, scraping himself painfully as he dragged himself through, twisting his ankle again as his foot caught on the edge of the hole. They'd broken through into another bathroom at waist height. He tumbled painfully to the floor and rolled out of the way. Seconds later, Gwang landed next to him.

"Stairway!" And they were off, Nick crying out with pain at every step.

"How much time?"

"Don't know. You go ahead."

"No! I'm not leaving you!"

"Go—just go! I'm going as fast as I can!"

Gwang looked desperate. Then he fled, moving twice as fast as Nick.

Nick looked at his watch, then stopped. He sat down. The staircase shook.

Chapter 32

"You know what I think, man? You're a quantum."

"Right over my head, Gwang. Want to come down to my level? Particle physics wasn't my thing."

Nick gripped a metal strip in a pair of pliers while Gwang dripped solder in place. "It's simple. Imagine a wall with a great big gap in it."

"I don't really have to imagine that, Gwang. Got quite a few around here."

"Not these walls. A hypothetical wall."

"Okay."

"Now, imagine you shoot a bullet through the gap. What happens to the bullet?"

"It carries on straight until it smacks into something?"

"Okay. Now imagine there's a flood and a wave of water comes through that big old gap in the wall. What does the wave do?"

"It spreads out, in every direction."

"Exactly. Now imagine you're in a pitch-dark room with a wall dividing it in half. And there's just one tiny hole in the wall."

"But I can't see the hole because it's pitch-dark."

"Blow on the solder for a moment. Thanks. Correct. But now imagine someone in the other half of the room is shining a flashlight through the hole, straight at you. What do you see?"

"I see a bright light where the hole is."

"So is the light behaving like the bullet or like the wave?"

"Like the bullet."

"Yes. Pass that . . . yes, thanks. Now imagine there are two tiny holes in

173

the wall, a yard apart. One hole is slightly to your left, the other slightly to your right. What do you see now?"

"Uh . . . I see two bright points of light."

"Is the light still behaving like a bullet?"

"I guess not. If it was, I'd just see one hole, or neither."

"So what's the light behaving like now?"

"Like a wave. Comes through the holes and spreads out."

"Exactly. So sometimes light behaves like a particle—a bullet—and sometimes it behaves like a wave."

"Okay, but what does that have to do with me?"

"Wait. Here's the fun part. Do you know what makes the light behave either like a particle or like a wave?"

"Not a fucking clue, Gwang. But I'm worried we'll be dead long before you get to the point."

"Okay, I'll leave out some of the detail. It turns out what makes the light behave like a particle some of the time and a wave some of the time . . . is whether or not the wave is being observed."

"That doesn't make sense."

"No, it doesn't. Hold that steady. And that's why nobody can make sense of quantum physics."

"And that's why I'm a quantum? Because I make no sense?"

"No, no, no. Here's why. Under certain conditions, when nobody's looking, light will behave as both a particle *and* a wave."

"But only when nobody's looking. So how do we know it's behaving like a particle and a wave?"

"Because we've set up some fancy apparatus to tell us what it's done after it's done it."

"And it shows us the light's behaved in both ways?"

"No. Depending on how we look at the results, it shows us only one way or the other."

"So the light's actually acted in both possible ways, but we can only see one? That's insane."

"Yes. But it gets crazier. Because the universe's timeline actually had to split in two to let that happen. And that's why you're a quantum. Okay, let's strap on the duct tape. Ah, remember to leave the ends loose."

"Right, Gwang, you're making perfect sense now. So every time some theoretical entity observes me dying, time splits?"

"Exactly. And I'm guessing it will keep splitting in two until you behave in whatever way lets you survive."

"Uh, Gwang? Has this got anything to do with that cat—you know, the one that's both alive and dead at the same time?"

"Schrödinger's cat. Yes, it's the same sort of thing."

"Except in this case, there are any number of potential kinds of deaths and nondeaths?"

"Sure. Quantum physics doesn't limit that number, I don't think."

"Okay, great, I'm glad you've cleared that up."

"No problem, man."

"Uh, Gwang? You don't really believe this quantum horseshit theory of yours, do you?"

"What, are you crazy? But this solder's finally dry. Time to head for the windows."

"Like a wave or like a particle?"

"Your choice, man. Just as long as we come out of this box alive. Right, all done. Let's go!"

* * *

"Let's get an elevator! Not enough time for the stairs!"

"Okay." Gwang hit the Down button, his hands still shaking. "Can't believe it's working."

They watched the numbers until the elevator doors binged open in front of them. They leapt in, and while Gwang pushed the first floor button, Nick was already swinging the hammer at the elevator's side wall.

"What the fuck are you doing?"

"Elevator shaft's buckled. We're about to get stuck!"

"Where?"

"Floor twenty-three!"

Gwang jabbed 23.

"No, hit twenty-five! Safer!"

Gwang jabbed again.

"God, I'm such an idiot," sighed Nick, shaking his head. "Hadn't even thought of that."

"This happened the last time?"

"Yes, but now we're in fresh territory."

Gwang looked at him dubiously. The elevator slowed, grated, and stopped. "Doors open, doors open, doors open," prayed Nick. They did. "Staircase this way!" Nick threw down the hammer and they were off. Through the door. Down the stairs.

In the stairwell, a team of firemen were heading up, laden with gear. "The building's collapsing!" shouted Nick. "You've got to get the fuck out! You've got five minutes!" They dashed past the firemen, who paused in indecision, looking at each other. "Follow us!" Then Nick and Gwang were gone, flying down the stairs, floor after floor.

More firemen. "Building's about to collapse! Go down! Go down!"

"But what about—"

"No time! Follow us!"

The firemen turned, still laden.

"Drop your gear! Come on! No time!"

They rushed down.

"Gonna make it!" They burst through the door marked 1 and out onto the mezzanine level and kept running.

"This way!" shouted Gwang and they ran down an escalator. Everything was a blur: people shouting, pointing, waving, Nick and Gwang shouting back, "Get out! Get out! Building's collapsing! Get out!"

Then they were out, running across the plaza in the sunshine filtering through the smoke, running and shouting, careful not to slip in the slush of blood and jet fuel, trying not to look at the no-longer-human lumps of flesh and bone as they ran past, beyond the plaza and across a street.

"We've done it!" screamed Gwang. "We've done it!" He hugged Nick.

176

Nick looked back at the South Tower. His eyes traveled up, past the flames and smoke still erupting from the upper floors. Something caught his eye. Falling from high, high in the North Tower was what looked like a woman, skirt and shirt flapping. People screamed. He turned away. Seconds later, there was a thud. He looked back. Black hair fanned around her lifeless head. Her white shirt brutally discolored. White. Not turquoise. Still, he felt like he'd been kneed in the stomach.

He looked back up at the South Tower, body slumped, breath coming in short gasps.

Gwang grabbed him. "We've gotta get farther away. Come on, man!"

Nick shook himself loose. "You go on. Got something I need to do."

He walked back across the plaza, firemen and police and Gwang all shouting at him.

He looked at his watch. He sighed. Now.

II

Part Two

Chapter 33

"Tash!"

Where on Earth was she? He'd needed a few minutes on his own to put his thoughts in order, but now he couldn't find Tash anywhere. He'd been to the 107th floor, he'd been all over this one, he'd asked about her on other floors. Quite a few people knew her or recognized Nick's description of a "chic, thirtyish female Indian executive," but no one knew where she was.

Strangely, Nick hadn't bumped into Gareth or Uday either. Not that he particularly wanted to meet them again—for all he cared, Gareth could have jumped out a window. Oh my God, could Tash have been one of the jumpers?

Nick felt a dagger of ice deep inside. While he hadn't dared admit it to himself before, it was now all too clear what he felt for her. But surely she would never have jumped. She'd been absolutely horrified to witness the other jumpers.

"Tash!"

Could she be in a closed meeting room, huddled with her company lawyers, trying to find a loophole out of Gareth's disastrous contract?

"Tash!"

Some of the people Nick saw were talking on phones or leaning out of cleared windows; most just hunkered down on the floor, conserving oxygen and waiting.

Nick banged on a meeting room door. An unknown voice told him to go away. This wasn't Tash's floor, anyway. But where was she? Where were

181

Uday and Gareth?

"Tash!" Nick banged on another meeting room door. Was that a noise inside? A gasp? Nick knocked again. "Tash!" Nothing. Nick turned away. A thump, like a chair being kicked over. Nick threw the door open.

The room was dark, the blinds closed and the lights off. But at the far end, he could make out two or three people huddled together. It looked like two of them were holding the other down over the table.

"Just fuck off now," said an Irish-accented voice. "This is a private party and you're not invited."

One of the figures—a woman—seemed to be writhing on her back, grunting. Oh God, what have I interrupted, thought Nick, taking a step back. Except that accent had sounded a bit unnatural. In fact—

He walked farther into the darkened room, letting in more light from the door behind him, exposing a familiar face.

"Fuck off, Boy Scout," Gareth snarled in his normal accent. "I said you're not invited."

For a moment, he was transfixed. No, it couldn't be. It just couldn't. Please God no. Gareth had one hand pressed down on the woman's throat. Uday, head turned away from Nick, was trying to control her violently struggling legs.

The woman bucked, trying to turn her face to Nick. Tash.

Without thinking, Nick charged past Uday and launched himself at Gareth, knocking him backward. Tash made a gurgling, rasping, coughing sound. Uday let go of her and hurled Nick after Gareth so that he tumbled headfirst into the wall with a horrible crunch.

"Grab her!" shouted Gareth, and Uday let go of Nick.

"Shit!" grunted Uday. It sounded like he'd fallen over. Then he screamed in shock and pain.

Nick backed away from the dented panel of sheetrock and blood shot from his nose. More blood from his forehead seeped into his eyes. He twisted around, wiping his eyes clear. He could just make out Uday on the floor, screaming, and Nick realized there was a pencil sticking out of Uday's right eye. Tash was trying to lash at Gareth with another pencil but tripped over Uday, who was trying to get up. As she pulled herself up again, Gareth ran for the door.

"Tash! Oh my God!"

Tash hugged him desperately. "You got here just in time! Are you all right?"

Nick wiped at his eyes again. It carried on gushing from his broken nose, saturating his shirt and Tash's turquoise blouse.

"I'm fine. Better than him," he said, nodding his head at Uday, whimpering on the floor. "Wait here, I'm going after Gareth."

Nick raced for the door, and found Gareth just yards away, trying to dodge past Ms. Morallis, who'd come to investigate the noise. With Nick right on his heels, Gareth shoved Morallis aside and raced off. She went down, making a gulping noise, staring horrified at Nick's bleeding face. Nick stepped over her and chased after Gareth, both of them gasping for breath in the smoke-laden air. Too late, Gareth noticed the smashed-open window in front of him and tried to veer to one side just as Nick hurled him through it.

Nick fell to his knees and watched Gareth twisting through the air. Behind him, Tash screamed something incomprehensible. Then Nick was ejected into space, Uday's animal scream following him.

Nick turned in the air, a sprawling half somersault. Looking up, he saw Uday falling toward him, arms and legs flailing. Above Uday, framed in the open window, Tash howled in rage and horror.

Chapter 34

As the airliner tore through five floors of the South Tower, Nick put out his right hand to stop his fall and regretted it a moment later. He sat up, groaning in agony, holding his wrist gingerly. Gareth sneered at him with cold malice. Nick glared back in revulsion.

"Well, well, it looks like our new risk analyst just broke his wrist," Gareth gloated.

Nick stood up and offered Tash his shaking left hand, desperately trying to get his emotions under control. Guilt. Rage. Powerlessness. Guilt. Tash looked at his face and recoiled visibly. Gareth smirked.

"Well, well, things have taken a turn for the worse, haven't they?" Gareth said, pointing at the window. "I'm wondering how long your new job's going to last. Not to mention your new employer's new job."

"Fuck off, Gareth," said Tash. "Nick? Are you okay? What happened to your wrist?"

Nick shook his head. "It'll be all right, just sprained."

"Good, let's get out of here. Gareth, you can stay for all I care."

Gareth watched them leave the room. "Catch you later," he called after them.

Nick followed Tash, joining the herd heading for the stairs. His thoughts seethed. What was that knowing look Gareth had given him? Triumph? Gloating? Could Gareth also be part of this time loop nightmare? Did he also remember everything? And if so, how many times had he . . . how many times had he overpowered Tash in that meeting room? And then?

Was it possible? Had Gareth just waited for Nick to head off on his own selfish missions, then got together with Uday to lure Tash to the ninety-fourth floor meeting room, where they could . . .

Nick felt ill with guilt. Obviously, he wasn't going to let it happen again. Just as obviously, he couldn't let Tash ever know what had happened. But what about Gareth? Logic and counterlogic clashed backward and forward. Hadn't he already settled the score with him by hurling him out the window? And hadn't Tash settled the score with Uday? But what kind of punishment was that when Gareth, seconds later, was sitting just feet away, smirking at him? And what was one quick fall from a window when, right now, he could be gloating over every time he'd . . .

He bent over, shaking. "I just need a minute. I'll catch up," he said to Tash and turned back.

Gareth was still in the room, sitting on the floor with his back to the wall. "Oh, it's the Boy Scout. Come back for some relationship counseling?"

"Shut up," said Nick, standing in front of him, glaring down in indecision, fists clenched.

"Because you and me, we both know she needs a firm hand."

Nick reached down with his good hand. He was about to grab Gareth by the collar, but instead, Gareth threw himself sideways and collapsed to the floor, holding his face as if he'd been hit.

"Nick! What in God's name are you doing?" Tash burst through the doorway and glared at him. "I thought you were an adult, but you're no more grown up than him!"

"What? No! I didn't . . . it's not what you—"

"For God's sake! I don't want to hear it. I'm really disappointed in you. Where the hell are your priorities?" She whirled around and stormed off.

Nick stood, speechless, hands limp at his sides. Gareth grinned up at him. "Well, well, I may know a thing or two about fucking up, but you just made me look like an amateur, so you did."

Nick headed for the door. He gave no indication that he'd noticed Gareth's imitation of an Irish accent. Still, Gareth's laugh followed him out of the room.

* * *

"Tash."

"What?"

"Look, I need to apologize for what happened earlier. I shouldn't have approached Gareth."

"Approached him? You hit him! Just because he taunted you? He was just reacting, it hasn't exactly been a great day for him."

"Did you see me hit him?"

"I saw you bending over him and him flying backward."

"I'd bent down to help him up, but he heard you walking in and improvised. I've got a sprained wrist, I'm not about to start hitting anyone."

Tash glared at him, thinking. She shook her head and sighed. "What a piece of work. He's been poison since day one. But why did you turn back—why did you need to talk to him?"

"I'm tempted to say I wanted to get him moving, for his safety."

"I should have done that. It was probably my responsibility."

"Except you're not his boss and he would have taken it out on you."

"Anyway, why did you confront him?"

Nick was silent for a moment, biting his lip.

"Well? Did you want his restaurant tips? Misogyny advice? Come on, what was it?"

"Okay. Remember your bully on the slide—the one whose collarbone you broke?"

"No! How did you know about that?"

"I wish there was a quicker way to get past this bit. You told me, like you told me about your family disowning you—"

"Whoa! Did you drug my drink in Boston?"

"You know I didn't. We're in a time loop—I keep waking up just as the plane hits our building, exactly the same scenario time after time after time. I can tell you about your schools—all four of them—the first album you bought—Cyndi Lauper—"

"Oh my God. Okay. I'm not saying I believe you, because it's just too

186

insane and I'm probably just having a delusion of my own, but how long do these time loops last?"

"Fifty-six minutes."

"That's awfully exact. Fifty-six minutes from impact. So we have just, what, half an hour left? Until what?"

"Until the building collapses. Too much structural damage downstairs."

"Shit, the building collapses? Well, I guess that's better than asphyxiating. Okay, so following this extraordinary line of reasoning, how does Gareth fit in?"

"Okay, this gets weirder and weirder. So sometimes my time loops don't last all fifty-six minutes."

"Because you get killed sooner?"

"Correct. You've seen those people jumping out the windows, right? Well, sometimes there's someone pushing them."

"No way! What are you saying, that Gareth—"

"When everyone's given up hope of rescue, he decides to settle the odd score."

"Hang on. So every fifty-six minutes—or less—you're either crushed by the building or get pushed out of it?"

"Or other outcomes I'd rather not go into."

"And you remember them all? How do you cope?"

Nick pulled a Xanax out of his pocket. Tash's face fell.

"Oh, brilliant, you're on psychoactives. And you almost had me believing your story. Please . . . just leave me alone."

"Dammit, Tash, you've got this all wrong. If I was just hallucinating, how would I know about your Dr. Pepper phase or your orthodontist with bad breath?"

"I said leave me alone. If I've only got half an hour left, at least leave me in peace. You stay here, I'm going somewhere else. Don't even think of following me. And to think I actually hired you."

Wrist in agony, stomach convulsing, Nick cursed himself impotently until he couldn't bear doing nothing a moment longer. He headed up to the ninety-fourth floor. No Gareth, Uday, or Tash on the staircase, or on the ninety-fourth floor itself. The door to the meeting room was open. No one inside. Nick slipped in, leaving the door open. Without knowing exactly why, he walked to the far end of the unlit room. The scene of the crime. He heard voices from just outside the door, and without thinking, dropped to his knees and crawled under the table.

Just in time. Footsteps and voices came inside. Faintly, Nick heard the meeting room door snicking shut. "So the two of us have been putting our heads together," he heard Gareth say, "and we believe—strongly believe—that there's a way out of this contract mess. And we think it's right for you to take it to Grendan."

"Say again?" Tash. "You have a solution, but you want me to take the credit? Or do you just want to set me up to look stupid?"

"Well, all right, it was really Uday's idea to involve you as his line manager. I didn't want to, but so it goes."

"Seriously, this could be good for all three of us." Uday.

Gareth again: "If you don't want to consider it, we'll have to take it to Grendan ourselves. But we'll have to explain that you weren't interested."

"All right, we'll see." Tash. "So what is it? What have you got?"

"Uday? Show her."

A thump, followed by sounds of a struggle.

"What are you doing? No! Let me go! Take your hands off me!"

Nick crawled out from under the table. In the half dark, no one noticed him until Tash, now flat on her back on the table, saw him raise his arm. Too late, Gareth and Uday turned. A brief moment later, both of them were lying on the carpet with damaged skulls.

Nick put down the hammer and hugged Tash with his good arm. She dissolved into his shoulder.

"I'm worried I hit them too hard," he said after a minute.

Tash drew back and looked at her still inactive attackers. "Not hard enough," she said grimly. Then she appeared to remember something and narrowed her eyes slightly.

Uh-oh, thought Nick.

Tash lifted her hand to slow things down while she got her thoughts straight. "So, according to your time loop theory, are you saying this has happened before? Me . . . and them?"

Nick looked stricken. He shook his head slowly. "Jesus no, it runs differently every time, depending on—on what I do. Normally I end up being Gareth's target, one way or another."

"So where did you come from just now?"

"I came looking for you. Someone said you'd gone off with Gareth and Uday, so I started searching for you. I heard you cry out and rushed in."

"The door's closed."

"I know, I closed it behind me as I came through. I didn't want anyone to see or hear what I'd do to these guys."

"Yes, I see you came prepared—like you knew something might happen."

"I've told you how dangerous Gareth is. I've been walking around with a hammer in my pants for some time now."

Tash was forced to smile.

Nick carried on. "But I didn't expect him to drag Uday into his plans, that was a surprise."

"All right. And the Xanax?"

"A few . . . time loops . . . ago, I was starting to feel completely traumatized. I found these in someone's desk drawer. When it feels like I'm about to go catatonic, I take one. Otherwise I'd have completely lost it a long time ago."

"All right, so what now?"

"So now I'd like to have a little chitchat with our friend Gareth, because I have a suspicion he might know something about this time loop business."

"Do you think he's up to it?"

They looked at Gareth, who was leaking blood into the carpet from a wound above his right ear. Nick gave him a shove with his foot and an eye opened slightly. "Looks like he's waking up."

"Okay, I'll leave you to it. Thanks." She slipped off the table, straightened her dress, and walked, slightly shakily, to the door, closing it behind her as she went out.

"Wakey, wakey, Gareth."

"Fuck . . . you . . . Boy . . . Scout."

Careful not to get too much blood on himself, Nick dragged Gareth into a chair with one hand, where Gareth immediately slumped over and almost fell out. There were a few used water glasses on the table, presumably from an earlier meeting, and Nick grabbed one that was still half full. He held Gareth upright and tilted the glass to his lips. Gareth took a small sip, the rest trickling down his chin.

Nick put the glass back on the table. Picking up the hammer again, he stood in front of Gareth, who was staying more or less upright now, although his eyes were a long way from focused.

"So what would you like to tell me, Gareth?"

"Oh, aren't you just the saint," Gareth slurred. "As if you don't want the same thing."

"Tell me the truth or you go straight out of a window. Was this the first time this happened?"

"You'd like to know . . . wouldn't . . . you?"

Nick looked into Gareth's eyes, but they weren't focused on anything. Was Gareth hinting at what Nick feared or was he simply being malicious?

Nick banged Gareth hard on one knee with the hammer. Gareth's leg leapt reflexively and he almost fell over. Using the hammer, Nick kept him upright. "You know, I've never believed in violent interrogation, but I think I've just become a big fan. Have you assaulted Tash before?"

"More . . . water."

Nick pushed the glass along the tabletop until Gareth could reach it. He took a sip, seeming not to notice how much drooled down his chin onto his shirt. "What do you care?" he said. "We'll all soon be dead anyway."

Nick did an involuntary double blink that Gareth didn't seem to notice.

May as well just get to the point, thought Nick. "Because of the time loops?"

Gareth finally managed to focus on him, staring at him as if he was insane. "The fuck you talking about? We'll be dead because my life is unmitigated shit, that's why. I work with the most gorgeous woman in the building and she treats me like a cockroach. I pull off the deal of the decade and we burst into flame. And"—gesturing dismissively at Uday—"the only person

190

in the building that respects me is a spineless suck-up that's afraid of his own pathetic shadow. That's why."

Nick went slack with surprise and relief. Which is when Uday leapt up off the carpet, grabbed the hammer out of his hand, slammed the meaty end into Gareth's head, and burst into tears.

As Nick watched, horrified, Uday spat into Gareth's unconscious, slumped face and sobbed, "That's for every time you humiliated me. That's . . . that's for Martina Becker, who had time for me . . . until you assaulted her too. And . . . that's for me."

Uday turned to Nick in horrified realization. "I'm sorry, but you're a witness now," he said, and before Nick could react, swung the hammer into his forehead.

Chapter 35

Nick hit the floor, carefully keeping his wrists out of harm's way. He turned to look at Gareth, who was sneering as maliciously as ever. "Well, well, Mr. Boy Scout fell down. Happy landing?"

Nick got to his feet and helped Tash up. Then he ruffled Gareth's hair, causing him to recoil with a snarl. "Better repack your box, Gareth." Then, to Tash: "We'd better get the hell out of here. But first, let's have a quick word with Grendan. I think I may have a simple plan for a financial rescue."

Seconds later, as the rest of the staff trudged toward the stairwell, Grendan came into the room. "Well, this had better be good. Now that we're liable for two fucking towers, our shitstorm has gone nuclear."

He glared at Gareth, then turned to Nick. "So what have you got, kid?"

Nick pointed at a piece of paper he'd been frantically writing on. "This is a list of publicly owned security-focused companies that I've been watching. CCTV, bomb detection, airport scanners, etcetera. Their stock prices will be going through the roof in the next hour or so."

Grendan took the list and gave it a quick scan. "You've checked these stocks out?"

"Medium caps, all of them. They'll take off like rockets once some money starts to move into them."

"Well, for fuck's sake, what are we waiting for?" He whirled around and screamed down the corridor. "Don! Stefan! Alistair! Get your asses back here pronto, you've got some trading to do! Lazy fuckers. Nick, good call. Proof there's a silver panty liner in every shitstorm. Just hope the internet hasn't shut down. Let's go! Let's go!"

"What was that all about?" said Tash once they were out of the room.

Nick smiled. "Some tips from an extraordinary person upstairs."

"Huh? When did you—"

"All will be revealed. But first, we need to source some tools—I'm going to need your help."

* * *

They were still on the ninety-third floor when a frightened young woman came up to Tash. "Miss Singh? You've got a phone call."

Tash took the cell phone from her. "Who is it?" she said.

"Miss Natasha Singh?" The phone was on speaker and a tinny male voice boomed out. "I'm calling from the *Wall Street Journal*. Can you confirm your company insured the World Trade Center?"

"Jesus! Do you not realize what's going on up here?"

"That's exactly the issue, Miss Singh. Can you confirm your company's exposure?"

"No, I'm not going to confirm or deny that, thank you!" Tash ended the call with an angry stab and handed back the phone. "Can you believe it? Can you fucking believe it? While we're trying to stay alive and hundreds of firefighters put their lives on the line, the investment community sticks in the knife. Shit, we'd better go talk to Grendan again."

Grendan was still in his office. He greeted them with a plastic grin. "My two favorite employees! What can I do for you?"

"I just got a call from some vulture at the WSJ," said Tash.

"Excellent! Excellent! And what did you tell them?"

"'I can neither confirm nor deny our exposure, blah blah,'" said Tash, using air quotes.

"Perfect! Our stock's tanking as we speak, like a lead submarine that's lost an argument with an iceberg."

"And that's good?"

"Good? It's like Christmas got moved to the Fourth of July. You see, it appears as if some unidentified people got wind of Gareth's little contract half an hour ago and short-shat our stock into a downward vertical pattern. And now you and the *Journal* have made the rumor official. Which means, in a few minutes' time, you'd have to scrape our shares off the sea bottom with a shovel. Which is exactly what we'll be doing. By the truckload."

"I don't—"

"Because tomorrow, when the market hears we're only in for twelve percent of the loss, we'll rebound like a Bangkok bar girl's ping-pong ball."

Tash shook her head. "Twelve percent?"

"Turns out our liability wasn't such a big liability after all."

"And those unidentified sellers you mentioned?"

"Hmm, I wonder," Grendan said, tapping his nose.

"And . . . and Gareth?"

"I do believe he's been quietly rehired. Perhaps even with a bonus. Your new hire can stay, of course. His tips are working out quite niftily too."

"You do realize we're not actually going to be rescued before we asphyxiate or get crushed by twenty stories of collapsing building, don't you?"

"Well, I'm still hoping to get out of here before it turns tits up, but if not, well, my family will inherit a fuckload of money, my dear Miss Singh. Partly due to your guileless performance on the phone just now, of course."

Tash took a deep breath. She closed her eyes for a moment. Nick suspected she was trying to count silently to ten, but in the end she didn't appear to get past one.

"Grendan? I'll tell you what. Why don't you take my job and shove it up your ugly fat ass? And then crawl away and die?"

"Miss Singh, Miss Singh—"

"Shut up, you malodorous sweaty prick! You have the manners and cultural attributes of a sewage trench. You put on this self-inflated air of some kind of folklore legend but you're just another grasping, bullying, lecherous creep! Fuck off!"

With that, she punched him in the nose, then kneed him in the crotch for good measure. He went down, curled into a ball. "Find the silver panty liner on that, you toxic sack of shit," Tash told him.

* * *

"So what are we looking for again?" asked Tash.

They were up on the 103rd floor, the floor with the safe. They'd checked up on the woman in the wheelchair to see if she was okay—Nick still felt guilty about the way they'd treated her—and were now ransacking the floor's utility rooms and cabinets.

"Anything that could get us out of the building alive. We won't know what it is until we see it."

"What about this? Looks like enough bubble wrap to float a battleship. Any use?"

"Hmm. Maybe if there was literally a roomful of the stuff, we could wrap ourselves up in it and throw ourselves out of a window. But a few boxes ain't gonna cut it, sorry."

"Spoilsport."

Tash carried on looking. After a while, she looked over at Nick in concern. "Uh, Nick, you okay?"

Nick shook his head slowly. "Lost in thought."

"You've barely moved in the last minute. What's up?"

"Sure you want to know?"

"Come on, out with it."

Nick sighed. "Okay. Tash, I've told you all about my family—"

"You have?"

"Ah. I keep forgetting what's happened when. Must have been in other loops, I guess."

"I don't know how I feel about all those other versions of me, you know."

"When we finally get out of here, I'll tell you about some of the heroic things you've done along the way."

"It's a deal. In the meantime, you were saying about your family?"

"Sure. What I told you was that my parents and older brother were killed by a truck that carried on straight when it was signaling a turn."

Nick leant back against a desk. Tash came and sat next to him. "Oh Jesus, that's awful. I'm sorry."

"And I was driving at the time."

"That's horrific. Were you badly hurt?"

"Barely a scratch. And now . . . when I remember that truck, sometimes it's signaling, and then other times it isn't."

Tash took his hand and squeezed it. "The human mind has an incredible talent for generating guilt, you know."

Nick looked off into the distance. "I've been telling people about that truck for ten years. In my head, I can see it, hear it, feel it. Thing is? It's not even true."

"What—what do you mean? Is your family still—"

"No, they died all right. But there was only one person responsible. Me."

Tash looked at him. "Tell me," she coaxed, gently.

"Yeah. It's been long enough. So here's what really happened. We used to have a small fishing boat, my Dad's pride and joy, tiny cabin and outboard engine. Used to tow it off to wherever we went on vacations and fish, mostly for bass. We'd have it on a trailer and to get the boat into the water could get quite tricky, you'd reverse the van slowly until the trailer sat deep enough in the water to float the boat off the trailer.

"It's not at all easy to reverse with a trailer behind you, but I'd gotten fairly good at it. My brother tried it once and jackknifed the trailer and slammed the boat into a wall, so I was the trailer guy.

"Mostly, we'd take the boat to inland lakes. But then we decided to take it down to the coast, to Savannah."

"Down in Georgia?"

"Yeah. My mother's sister had moved there with her husband and they invited us down there to stay a couple of weeks one summer. So there we are, and on this particular day, it's just our family, going fishing. So I launch the boat into this tidal river, reversing the trailer down a concrete slipway, and off we go, leaving my mother in the van on the shore, reading some Patricia Cornwell novel. My Dad tried to persuade her to come with us, but she said she'd get seasick on the ocean.

"We spend a few hours out on the boat and then head back in. My Dad's caught a red snapper about this big, a monster, and I know he's totally thrilled. My brother's driving and he nudges the boat up to the slipway and I hop out, like knee deep, and wade up the concrete. I notice there's a bit of a current. Anyway, I fetch the van, with my mother still glued to her Patricia Cornwell, and back it down the slipway with the trailer behind me.

"And I'm thinking I'll reverse until the van's back wheels are just in the water, which is what I always do, but I haven't noticed how fast the tide's been going out. So suddenly the trailer runs out of slipway and just tips down into the water, bam.

"And that's when I ram my foot on the gas, trying to pull it straight out again. It was like when you rub a bit of spit on a scratch you've made on the car because if you do it quickly enough, maybe it didn't actually happen in the first place, if that makes any sense to you. But I've put the car in neutral, not drive, so we just keep rolling back. Then I panic and move the gearshift, but now I've put it in reverse again, so we shoot straight backward. This is when my mother starts to panic. Me too. I ram on the brakes, but we've hit this patch of seaweed growing on the slipway, so we just carry on sliding backward and bam, we go over the edge of the slipway and right into the water, slewing around so the van goes in sort of sideways with the passenger side down.

"So I climb out the open window as we go over and leap back onto the slipway—it's all happening like a slow-motion nightmare—and slip on the seaweed and fall flat on my face. But my mother is still in the passenger seat and now the whole van's sinking underwater. Not to mention there's a strong current dragging the van away from the slipway. I don't even know if it's hit bottom, either. So then my dad leaps in off the boat and swims through the current, grabs the driver's side doorpost and dives into the side window as it's going under. And disappears. The water's just liquid mud, you can't see an inch into it. He doesn't come up again.

"My brother's screaming at me, I don't know what, but he's maneuvered the boat in the current to try and keep it level with where he thinks the car is now, and I realize he's shouting at me to swim to the boat so he can rescue our parents. So I dive in the water and swim like crazy for the boat and he dives into the water and disappears. I get on board and steer it back to where the car should be, but there's nothing. So now I jump in the water and dive down and get knocked into God knows what by the current, a dead tree or something, and the current feels like it's going to ram me under this thing and not let go—I can't see a thing—and I panic and thrash around and finally get to the surface again and the boat's gone and I'm just trying to get to the shore so I can kind of mark where the car might be, but of course I have no idea anymore, the way that current's moving.

"And then I get to the shore and just kind of collapse, and there's people helping me up and shouting and pointing. Then I'm just . . . I don't know. Waiting. Praying. They find my brother washed up somewhere a few minutes later, do CPR on him for ages, but no luck. They find the car and trailer once the tide's completely out. They're both inside it. I guess my mother couldn't get out of her seatbelt—she had it on because the car used to make a warning noise at you if you don't—and my dad couldn't undo it either, or she panicked or something.

"But basically, if I hadn't been so goddamn cocky, if I'd just been a bit more cautious, or if I hadn't just panicked when the trailer went over the edge of that slipway, or if I'd stayed in the fucking car when it fell in instead of scurrying out like a frightened rat and helped my mother out before—before—" Nick's chest heaved. Tash held him tight while he made incoherent noises into her neck.

* * *

"Jesus, Nick, I can see why you'd rather not remember that. I wouldn't. But I guess you've realized it's time to stop blaming yourself."

Nick shook his head. "What do you mean? I am to blame."

"Come off it, Nick, anyone who's ever worked in insurance knows tragedies happen when people get into unfamiliar situations. Regardless of what the tide was doing, that slipway was a deathtrap, and it shouldn't have had seaweed growing on it. If you'd gotten a lawyer on the case, they'd have sued the pants off whoever was in charge of it."

Nick wiped his eyes with his sleeve.

"And why were you left to deal with it? What about your mother's sister? The one who lived in Savannah?"

"Oh yeah, her. All she could think about was how she now lived just a couple of miles from the place where I killed her sister. I never saw her again when she wasn't hysterical."

"Well, that's helpful. So how did you deal with it all? Surely not by just telling everyone a story about a truck and half convincing yourself it's true?"

"That became my official story, something I could tell new friends and colleagues, while I suppressed the reality with alcohol, cheap drugs, and self-deception."

"You don't strike me as an alcohol abuser. Forgive me for saying so, but you're a bit of a control freak. In a good way, of course."

"Not back then I wasn't. Things really spiraled, until I ended up in a school with inmates rather than classmates. But I finally found a way to give my life some purpose—as you say, by imposing control on hazardous situations. Or trying to, anyway."

"Of course: assessing insurance risk. While—I'm just making assumptions here—presumably having some strange relationships that probably didn't work out for the best."

"Bull's-eye."

"Nick . . . am I the first person you've told the real story to? Out of choice, I mean?"

"As opposed to people who were paid by the state to listen to it? Correct."

"Because that's a bit of a breakthrough, isn't it? Finally facing the demon?"

"Or is it just because, well, here we are?"

"Me and you? Oh, you mean here we are in another out-of-control situation. And you figure maybe you finally have a shot at redemption."

"If I can fix this, I think I can put a lot of demons behind me."

"Or maybe you'll end up making every catastrophe on the planet your personal responsibility."

Nick ran his fingers through his hair, digging into his scalp.

"You've got to stop torturing yourself, Nick. You didn't fly these planes into the towers. You weren't responsible for airport security."

"But I've been talking about air safety for ages. I bet those terrorists just walked right into the pilots' cabins. If only I'd been more convincing."

"You think the terrorists wouldn't have found other ways to commit their atrocities? Like you said earlier, they're the ones with the motivation and the time. Nick. Look at me. You were not to blame. Not back then. And not today."

"On some level, I know you're right. I just wish I could believe it. On the other hand . . . if I take some responsibility for today, I don't have to become a victim."

"You know that makes no sense, right?"

"Welcome to my world. Uh, talking about victims, this is not exactly related, but . . . do you know Martina Becker?"

"Martina? She worked here until a few months ago. Then one day she just handed in her notice and left. Went back to Germany, I think. Why? How do you know her?"

"Ah, someone mentioned her earlier. Doesn't matter."

"Was this in one of your 'resets'?"

"Yeah, it's a bit fuzzy. I was wondering if she was important somehow."

Tash looked at him seriously. "So let me get this straight. Every time you die, everybody—everything—gets reset to the moment of impact? But you're the only person who remembers the previous times?"

"That's certainly what it looks like, yeah."

"But are you sure you actually die each time? I mean, maybe you get reset just an instant before you actually die."

"Well, there's usually plenty of pain at the time, but I don't recall experiencing any slow fade-out, no tunnels of light or angels or anything like that."

"So maybe you're not dying? Maybe you're just a time traveler?"

"Just a time traveler, she says. Just the first one ever, in the history of, well, history."

"Okay, but what do you think?"

"Well . . . if I am a time traveler, and I keep going back to the same point in time, shouldn't I keep bumping into my earlier self? Every time I wake up in that meeting room again, I should already be there. In fact, there would be, like, fifty of me crammed into that room by now. I'd also be exhibiting some fairly nasty injuries that I've picked up along the way."

"Damn damn damn! This is just such a complete headfuck! I guess you're right—it can't be time travel—but the alternative seems so awful, with everyone except you dying every fifty-six minutes. And perhaps you're not returning to the *same* tower and the *same* people, but to a parallel-universe tower . . . and by now you've used up fifty parallel universes' worth of towers and people and firemen."

"Wait, wait. I see what you're saying, but could that mean every time I get reset, I have the chance to save all the other people in all the towers in parallel universes that I haven't 'used up' yet? And if I'm not reset, there's simply no hope for any of them?"

"But what about *me*, Nick? If I don't get out of here alive, now, in these fifty-six minutes . . . do I survive? Me, this me? Not the next me who's there the next time you're reset, but this version of me, the one who's here with you now?" Tears ran down Tash's cheeks, leaving stripes through the grime, then smears as she angrily wiped them away. Nick reached out to hug her and was pushed away.

"So what I'm trying to say, Nick, is that if you're playing some long game, if you think it doesn't matter how many times you get reset because you think you'll figure this all out and get everyone out of the towers eventually . . . every single time until then, all of the rest of us up here are all dying for real. We do not. Get. To come. Back."

This time she let Nick hold her and sobbed against his chest while he stroked her back. Then she gently pushed him away again, looking him in the eye and blinking back more tears. "So if you know a way to get some people out before the building collapses, maybe you should tell us. Because maybe we want to go on living in this universe, because it's the only one we have."

Nick blinked, openmouthed. Tash stared at him in disbelief. "You do know, don't you! You do know!"

"No! I don't! I . . . oh God, I can't take this!"

201

"Because you're so wrapped up in being the man who saves everybody that you're not even trying to save the few you could! Am I right?"

"I don't know! It's not like that. I saved your life once, but it was a complete fluke—you might not survive an escape like that again. And if I concentrate on saving just you, nobody else gets to survive. Do you want to live at everyone else's expense?"

"Do you swear you're telling the truth?"

"Yes. I've saved you once, but I died in the attempt. And another time, two of us escaped. Me and Gwang."

"Gwang! The gadget guy?"

"Yes. But then I walked back into the building."

"Jesus. Why?"

"Because Gwang wasn't you."

"Come here." Tash wrapped her arms around Nick. "You really saved me?"

"I threw you out of an eighty-fifth-floor window with a homemade parachute."

"You bastard." Tash sniffed, squeezing as hard as she could. "I love you."

Chapter 36

Nick and Tash were ransacking the kitchens on 107.

"What are we looking for again?"

"Rope, cables, tablecloths, whatever."

"Hmm, you'll probably want to take a look at these parachutes here. Sorry, sorry, that's not funny. Just a bit stressed out."

"Rope ladders and grappling hooks would be good too."

"Haven't seen any of them . . . got a whole lot of bunting though. Must be for when they have parties up here."

"Let's see?" Nick had a quick look at the multicolored bunting. "String's too thin, unfortunately."

"What if we plait a few strands together?"

"Do we have that much? We'd need loads of it—and it would take forever to plait enough."

"How much would we need?"

"A hundred yards? At least?"

"Not going to happen. What else is here . . . some ribbon . . . balloons . . . cake candles . . . party hats . . ."

"Did you say balloons?"

"Yeah, there's loads. White balloons, red balloons, and blue balloons."

"Let's see. Whoa, that's a lot of balloons. Maybe they do that party thing where they put them all in a big net hanging from the ceiling."

"Yeah, I guess. All we need is some helium now. And loads of string."

"We've got the bunting string—but we'd need to get the bunting flags off it somehow. Pass a balloon, let's see how big it inflates."

Nick stretched the balloon, put the end to his lips, coughed painfully, and puffed into it. Half a minute later, the balloon was double the size of Nick's head, while Nick had his hands on his knees, coughing spasmodically. He let the balloon go and it whizzed around his head before landing on the floor.

"The size—*cough*—is fine—*cough*—but we need a gas canister—*cough*—or a—*cough*—balloon pump."

"I don't see a gas canister anywhere. But I doubt they'd have wanted the balloons to stay up in the ceiling. There's normally the big moment when they pull the net apart and the balloons all fall down on everyone."

"So there—*cough*—must be a balloon pump then."

"Or . . . voilà! Two balloon pumps!" Tash held them up proudly.

"Beautiful! What about the net?"

"Here it is. No, here they are—two of them! But . . . what's the point if we don't have helium?"

"Well, we're not trying to fly to New Jersey, we just want to fall less fast—we'd be using them as a kind of parachute, really."

"Seriously? You think it could work?"

"It all depends on how many balloons we can inflate. Come on, let's take all this stuff downstairs before someone else gets ideas."

They bundled everything into a couple of shopping bags they found in the cabinet and headed for the stairs. They'd just gotten through the door when they heard a loud voice behind them.

"Hang on a moment. Have you just taken these items from the kitchen?"

They turned around. It was a large bald man. Nick thought he remembered him from earlier but struggled to place him.

"And you are?" said Nick.

"Kitchen manager. And we still have laws against looting, you know. Serious laws. So come on, hand it all over."

He reached for the bags and Nick and Tash took a step back.

"You're not the kitchen manager," said Tash. "You're just trying to take these for yourself."

The man grabbed Tash's wrist with one hand and tried to wrench her bag away with the other. "Don't fuck with me, bitch!" he snarled.

Before Nick could react, Tash rammed her knee into the man's groin and he let go, doubling up with a little whimper.

"Way to go!" said Nick admiringly. "Come on, we'd better get out of here."

They hurried down the stairs, pausing a few flights later. There was no noise of pursuit.

"Hell, I didn't know I was going to do that until I'd done it," said Tash, elated. "Maybe I should have started years ago."

"Got news for you. You did exactly that to your boss Grendan, just an hour or so ago."

Tash laughed until she choked. "Just the once?"

"Afraid so."

They carried on down, coughing with laughter.

The eighty-fifth floor was deserted, the thick smoke making it impossible to even see from one end to the other. Nick tore off his shirtsleeves and tied them around their faces, covering their noses and mouths.

"Let's find a room on the north side, it should have the cleanest air once I knock out a window."

They dashed into a small meeting room, toppled the table on its side, and pushed it out of the way, then laid the first net down on the floor.

A minute later they were frantically pumping up balloons, taking turns to breathe from the window that Nick smashed out with a meat tenderizer.

"What made you bring that along?" asked Tash.

"Just in case I got the opportunity to knock together a quick filet mignon," deadpanned Nick.

"I'd advise you to start with higher quality steak."

"Or maybe just a cooking lesson. So I knew we'd have a window to bash out, but I was also nervous about that guy—I'd noticed him paying a lot of attention to the balloon I blew up."

"Would you have used that on him?"

"I'm glad I didn't have to find out. But you handled things perfectly. You're kind of amazing, really. Proud to be working for you."

"Aw, shucks. So how many of these balloons do we need?"

"As many as we can blow up. How many do we have?"

"Four bags of fifty."

"Okay, well, as many as we can stuff into the nets, anyway."

"And how do we attach ourselves to the nets?"

"I've been wondering. What I'm thinking is we use some electric cords or phone cords to harness ourselves to the nets—and also to seal up the nets, of course."

"Right. I thought we might just tie ourselves into the nets with the balloons."

"Ah, right. Could do. Depends on how full the nets get, the more balloons the better. I guess . . . if you're inside the net, there's more chance you'd end up hitting the ground face-first. Even if we had real parachutes, a face-first landing would do a lot of damage. But if you're dangling below the net, you're more likely to land feetfirst, which is more survivable."

"How survivable?"

"Pretty good, I'd say. It's not just the area the balloons take up that'll slow us down, it's the turbulence of the air going through the balloons—and their vibration."

"As long as they don't just burst."

"Sure, which is why we're slightly underinflating them. Must say, tying these stupid knots is a pain on the fingers."

"You're not kidding. One more thing: are we going to be jumping individually or together?"

"Uh . . . I was assuming individually, but—"

"Nick, I am utterly terrified, okay?"

"Yeah, me too, actually. Um, to answer your question, I guess jumping out together shouldn't make us fall any faster, with the two nets of balloons above us and us harnessed together. And it'll definitely be less terrifying."

At that moment, a massive explosion somewhere above shook the floor. The balloon Nick was busy tying shot from his grip straight into Tash's face and she screamed.

"Oh Christ, no! Not another plane!"

"No, one of the floors above us collapsing," said Nick grimly, looking at his watch. "We'd better hurry."

"Wish these balloon pumps were a bit bigger."

* * *

"We're doing okay, we've almost filled the first net. You carry on, I'm going to get some harness cords."

Nick dashed out. Phone cords? He grabbed one but couldn't get it loose from the actual phone receiver. And damn, he didn't have the wire cutters with him. What about . . . aha—ethernet cables. He detached one from a desktop computer. Thin, flexible, and easy enough to tie together. Two minutes later, he rushed back into the "balloon room" with twenty of them stuffed into a couple of sports bags.

The first net was now overflowing with balloons. Moving around the net, he and Tash tied an ethernet cable through each corner. Damn, they weren't long enough to meet in the center. "Okay, let's tie loops on the ends, okay? Then I'll thread another cable through the four loops . . . and pull . . . and close the net . . . and thread another cable around the mouth of the net to keep in the balloons . . . and . . . success!"

"How will we get the balloons out the window?"

"Well, there's still plenty of give in the net, we should be able to wiggle the whole thing out."

"Aren't they going to burst on the glass fragments in the window frame?"

"Yeah, we need to do some tidying up first. Also need to make a couple of harnesses from these other cables."

"Okay, I'll tenderize the windows, you tie the harnesses."

Less than a minute later, Nick held up one of the repurposed sports bags. "Okay, try this on for size."

He helped Tash climbed into the makeshift harness's leg loops and she pulled them up to her groin. "Chose a bad day to wear a skirt—stop laughing!" She put the sports bag's straps over her shoulders like.a backpack. More cables connected the leg loops and sports bag straps behind Tash's back. Doubled-up cables connected her to the cables in the mouth of the bulging balloon net.

"Great, now we just have to push the balloons through the window."

Together, they wiggled the squirming net through the window, squeezing and shaking individual, stubborn balloons. As more of the net emerged on the outside of the window, a merry riot of red, white, and blue, the breeze buffeted it and Tash grimaced with apprehension.

Then the net was completely out, tugging gently at Tash's harness. She stood with feet wide apart, bracing herself in the open window.

"What do we do when we land?"

"Keep your knees together before impact. Then bend your knees and fall sideways so your hips and shoulders take some of the impact, okay?"

"Got it. Knees together, bend knees, fall sideways, hip, shoulder. Right, better get going on your parachute."

Nick turned away and surreptitiously checked his watch. 9:56. Less than three minutes left. He spread the second net out on the floor and they carried on inflating balloons and dropping them onto the net.

Nick glanced out the window. "Haven't heard any of them pop yet."

Tash said nothing. Sweat was beading on her forehead. The balloon in her hands burst off the pump nozzle, whizzed around her head, and shot out the window. She exhaled and picked up another balloon.

Then Armageddon broke out above and Nick hurled Tash screaming out the window. As the first crash turned into a second and a third, Nick kept his eyes on Tash, her arms and legs flailing, falling below the balloons and out of view. Then the balloons jerked and the net tightened and Tash's triumphant scream was just audible through the howling roar of the building's accelerating collapse.

"It works!"

Chapter 37

"Tash. I have a way to get the two of us out. I need to get some stuff from the kitchen first. But we'll need a bunch of ethernet cables—twenty or more. Can you get those and I'll see you on the eighty-fifth floor—north side—in ten minutes?"

"But—but—hey! Hey!" But Nick was already gone.

Ten minutes later, Nick charged out of the stairwell door on the eighty-fifth floor with two full shopping bags. Tash stood nearby, looking this way and that, fidgeting with her watch. The smoke was already uncomfortably thick. A few other people milled around, still deciding what to do, glancing at Tash and Nick suspiciously.

"The smoke's less bad in some of the conference rooms," Nick told them. "There's a bunch of people in the one just around the corner."

Glad to be told what to do, the people headed off. "What about you two?" one of them asked.

"Got some PC security to take care of quickly," Nick replied, holding up the bags. "We'll join you as soon as we can. Tash, let's start in the far corner there."

"Good thinking," said Tash decisively, and they turned and strode off. Nick expected to hear a challenge from behind them, but they heard nothing. When they reached the corner, Tash looked back. "All gone."

"Thank God. It would have been hard to explain why I've got two bags full of balloons, nets, and a meat tenderizer. Let's go into the meeting room over there. Damn, forgot to tell you before—we need a couple of sports bags too."

209

Tash looked at him openmouthed as he attacked a window. "All will be revealed." Nick smiled. "But we need to move fast."

Twenty minutes later, Tash's bulging, bobbing, red, white, and blue net was surging in the breeze, and they were frantically filling Nick's net with more balloons.

"Nearly there," said Nick, sweating.

"I know the building's on fire and everything," said Tash, hoarse from coughing, "but still, you look like a man with a serious deadline. Do you know something I don't?"

"We've got at least ten minutes," said Nick, checking his watch again. "I'll explain later."

"You obviously know a lot more about this building than you made out."

"Let's say I've learned a hell of a lot since I got here this morning. But hopefully it'll all be over soon."

"One way or another."

"I'm actually pretty confident this'll work. Seriously."

"Well, we're not going to survive this smoke much longer anyway."

"You're right. Okay, let's tie up this net."

A deafening explosion came from above them. They reflexively cowered as more ceiling board crashed down just outside the door.

"On schedule," said Nick, teeth gritted.

"Sounded like the building's collapsing," said Tash, eyes wide.

"You're right, but we still have a few minutes."

"You really do have some explaining to do, you know."

Two minutes later, they were wrestling Nick's balloons out the window, where they joined Tash's, tugging gently in the breeze.

"Okay, now we fasten our harnesses together. Ready?"

Deep breath. "Ready."

They stood face-to-face and Nick tied the necessary knots. "Okay, done. We're going to leap straight out, on three, okay?"

Tash's "okay" came out as a whimper. Nick grabbed her around the waist and kissed her for a second.

"Okay," she said, trying to smile. "On three."

"One. Two. Three."

They leapt sideways, holding on to each other, cables trailing, balloons dragging. For a second they plummeted together, gasping, then they felt the braking effect of over a hundred violently agitated balloons straining against air friction.

They slowed down.

"Oh my God, it's working!" cried Tash. "It's working!"

They were clear of the blizzard of swirling paper and smoke. Nick kept looking up. The balloons were vibrating too fast.

There was a series of pops. Then they were falling faster. More popping. Tash screamed. They held on to each other as tightly as they could as their fall became a gut-swooping plummet.

Chapter 38

U p on the ninety-seventh floor, Nick frantically scoured the closets for anything useful. Tash and Gwang were doing the same, on the other side of the floor. A creaking, crunching, grinding noise froze them in place as the floor jolted beneath them.

"Oh my God!" screamed a nearby woman. "The floor's collapsing!"

A moment later, the noise and the motion subsided.

"If that happens again, I think we're headed straight for street level," said a man.

"Then let's get as much weight off the floor as we can," said Nick.

"What do you mean?"

Nick gestured at the rows and rows of heavy metal cabinets, stretching in all directions around them.

"These things, we have to get rid of them. And fast."

"But we can't throw them out the window!"

"No, but maybe we can push them down an elevator shaft."

"That's crazy," said the man.

"What's crazy is just waiting to die," retorted the woman. "I'm with that man. Just tell us what to do."

"Okay, so the elevator doors are all jammed shut, but the side walls of the elevator shafts are just sheetrock. We just need to smash through that, line up the cabinets, and push them through the hole. Make sense? Who's going to help me?"

He looked around. There was a ragged chorus of agreement.

"Which elevator shaft?" someone asked. "The nearby ones only go down as far as the seventy-eighth floor. We'll probably just set ourselves on fire if we break into those."

"Good point," Nick thought aloud. "Are there any elevators that go all the way down?"

"Sure, there's two. They don't have doors on this floor, though—they go straight up to the observation deck."

"Great. If there's no doors, we can smash through from any direction, the shafts will just be sheetrock all the way around. Can you lead us to one?"

"Sure, just down this way."

It took just a couple of minutes to bash a desk-sized hole through the sheetrock, revealing a dark cavity and dimly visible vertical cables. Some smoke wafted out, but not much.

"One more swing," said a panting man, slamming his empty fire extinguisher at a ragged flap of sheetrock. He hit it too hard and his swing almost carried him into the gap. He stumbled and let go of the extinguisher with a curse and it tumbled into the void. They all held their breaths. Silence. "I can't believe—" Then they heard a dull, echoing clatter.

"Long way down," someone said.

"If that hit the elevator roof, they must have gotten one heck of a fright," said the man who'd been wielding the extinguisher, looking embarrassed.

"They're going to get an even bigger fright when we drop our furniture on their heads," said another.

"Sounded like it hit concrete," said Nick. "The elevator must still be above us somewhere."

"Whoa—if it's up there, why hasn't someone used it to get down?"

"It's not at the top floor," said a woman. "I just phoned someone who said they were up there."

"Well, if the shaft's buckled, it would probably have just stopped wherever it was at the time of the impact."

"I guess we could take a look."

"I'm not sticking my head through that hole. If the elevator comes down—"

"I'll take a quick look," said Nick. "I think we'd hear something if it started moving. The rest of you, start dragging those cabinets along here."

He got down on his knees and poked his head through the hole, peering down, then up. "Too dark to see anything. Hello! Hello!" he shouted. "Hello-o!"

His voice echoed back at him, gradually dying away. He wasn't sure, but he thought he heard a faint response—a faint cry, maybe.

"Anyone hear something?" asked Nick, turning back to a couple of people who'd just dragged up the first cabinet.

They shrugged and shook their heads. Nick tried again. "Hey! Hey! Heyyy!"

A definite response. More than one voice. Followed by thumping.

Nick crawled backward and stood up. "It's up there somewhere, with people in it. You guys start chucking the cabinets down the shaft, I'm going to go up a few floors and see if I can find them."

"Take this fire extinguisher," someone offered.

"Thanks."

"Timber!" shouted a man as he and a couple of others slid a desk into the hole. It lurched over and disappeared.

Nick jogged toward the stairs, looking for Tash, and had almost reached them before he heard the muffled crunch of the desk's impact. Spotting Tash, he quickly explained his intention, then headed up the stairs.

He guessed the elevator had been at least six floors higher, so he'd get out at 103. Make a quick hole. Take a look. Repeat as necessary.

The hammer went through the sheetrock like a blunt knife through butter. As soon as he had a hole, Nick screamed into it. "Hey! Anyone there!"

Tash's voice came up from below. "We can hear you, Nick!"

The elevator had to be still higher. "Okay! You guys stay quiet a moment, I need to listen for anyone in the elevator. Hey! Hey! Anyone there!"

A muffled shout and the stomping of feet.

"Okay! I hear you! Hold tight, I'm coming!"

Nick hit the stairs again. Another two floors. There was nobody around. He smashed through more sheetrock. Ripped it aside and saw another layer beyond it. He heard banging from the other side.

Seconds later, he'd smashed a hole right through into the elevator. He heard a small girl's voice. "Mommy! Are we going to be all right now?"

"I hope so honey," came her mother's voice, shaky with stress.

"Are we ever glad you're here," said a man, presumably the father.

Nick had broken through just above the floor of the elevator, a few feet higher than the floor Nick stood on. To make the hole big enough for the family to escape, he'd have to swing the fire extinguisher quite a bit higher.

"Just a moment," he said. He cleared a nearby desk with a single, violent swipe and dragged it over.

Standing on top of it, he enlarged the hole, then paused for an uncontrollable coughing fit.

"Pass me that thing, I'll do the rest," said the father. Nick passed the fire extinguisher through the hole and seconds later, more sheetrock exploded outward. Half a minute later, the job was done.

"Great, lie on your stomachs and push yourselves out backward!"

The little girl came out first, wrapping her arms fiercely around Nick's neck. "You're going to have to let go now," he soothed. Finally she did and he lowered her to the floor.

"Mommy! Come on! Mommy!" she called, gulping tears.

Her mother came next, followed by her brother and, finally, her father, who shook Nick's hand in profound thanks.

"What happened?" he murmured to Nick. "We get hit too?"

"Passenger jet," said Nick. "Hit about twenty floors down. We're completely cut off up here. Staircases are blocked or just shattered."

"Jesus. Don't tell them." His eyes darted toward his family. "They came to visit me at work, we were planning on going up to the viewing deck. Then the other tower got hit, and we could see how those guys over there were suffering. Not something you want young kids to see."

"Yeah, I've certainly seen a lot of things I'd put in that category," said Nick with a sigh, attracting a curious look from the father.

"So, any ideas?" asked the father.

"You can come back down the stairs, help us out a bit down there," said Nick. "We're trying to drop most of the heavy furniture down the elevator shaft to get the weight off the floor—that's how we heard you guys, actually."

"Take the weight off the floor? You mean . . . you think the floors might collapse?" He kept his voice as low as possible. Fortunately, his wife had her hands full distracting the children.

"Uh, yeah. Some of the floors have started to buckle already—the impact plus the burning fuel isn't doing the support pillars any good."

"Well, no good trying to push the furniture into the elevator shaft on this floor—the elevator's in the way." The father looked speculative. "You haven't found any elevator technicians anywhere, have you? You seem to have gotten around a bit."

His wife interrupted them. "Sorry to butt in, but do you have any kind of plan? Things are getting kind of tense here."

"Sure, honey. We were discussing getting the elevator working, but—"

Her expression stopped him cold. "No way are we getting back in any elevator."

"I was just about to say I haven't found any elevator people anywhere," said Nick. "I think we may as well head down to my colleagues a few floors down."

"Well, okay. We need to do something, I can't hold these two in check much longer. Come on, children, we're heading down the stairs."

As they opened the door to the stairs, acrid smoke drifted out. The young girl started to cry. "Are we going to die, Mommy?" she asked, gripping her mother's hand.

"Charlie, listen to me," said her father, crouching down with his hands on her shoulders. "I promise you we'll be fine. But we do need to go down these stairs a few floors. Now, I'm going to carry you on my back, okay? You'll be perfectly safe, I promise."

His daughter climbed onto his back and they went down the dimly lit, smoke-filled staircase as fast as they could, the parents coughing, the children whimpering with fear.

"Okay, we're getting out onto this floor here," said Nick. With relief, they followed him out of the staircase. The others had a line of cabinets positioned in front of the elevator shaft and as Nick walked up, another cabinet was pitched into space, sending up a dully echoing smash a few

216

seconds later.

"Want to help?" asked Nick, but the father shook his head.

"How far above the impact are we?" he asked.

"Nearly fifteen floors."

"Right. Now I know you said the stairs are all blocked up," he said quietly, "but I need to see that with my own eyes. So I'm going exploring."

To his wife and children, he said, "All right kids, you need to stay here with these people for a few minutes while Daddy finds the best way down. Okay?"

The children nodded fearfully while his wife tried to keep her emotions under control. "You'll be okay, won't you?" she said. "No heroics, all right? And come back as fast as you can."

They hugged briefly and the father headed to stairwell C. He was back in less than a minute. "Not a chance, it's pure hell down that one. I'll carry on down the one we were on."

"Stairwell A?" said Nick. "I've been told that's—"

"I hear you, but I need to see for myself. And who knows, maybe someone's cleared the debris by now. Maybe there's even a working elevator down there." And off he went.

"What can we do?"

"Actually, you know what, you can all help," said Nick. "You can drag along all the chairs you can find and we can pitch them down the elevator shaft in between the cabinets."

"Thanks," said the mother. "Doing nothing wouldn't be good for them right now."

Almost cheerfully, the children rounded up the nearby chairs and soon had a mob of them ready to go down the elevator shaft.

"I want to throw one down," begged the boy.

"Mommy, can we throw them down the hole? Please?" implored his sister.

Another desk had just gone sailing into the abyss.

"It's not safe," said their mother firmly.

"But I want to," wailed the little girl. "Please let me? Please?"

"I can hold on to them while they do it," said Tash. "It'll keep their minds off things."

Their mother shrugged and nodded.

"Yay!" cried the girl.

"Me first!" cried the boy.

One by one, they took it in turns to jettison the chairs—genuine Aerons, Nick noted.

"This is the best," said the boy gleefully.

"The bestest," agreed his sister, pitching another thousand-dollar chair into the gaping mouth of oblivion.

Their mother nodded, smiling bravely, between anxious glances at her watch.

"I'd like to organize a desk party on the floor above us," said one of the office workers. "What do you say?"

"Good idea, go for it," agreed Nick, and the man hurried off. As he opened the door to stairwell A, the children's father lurched out, gasping. About to speak, he was seized by a sudden coughing fit. He held up a hand, waiting for it to pass.

Then the roaring started and the floor tilted. Nick fell through the stairwell door as the man went over backward. The staircase shook like a maddened snake and threw them tumbling into space.

The last thing Nick saw was the face of his watch. Their floor-lightening work hadn't bought them one extra second.

Chapter 39

"Nice work, Gwang."

Together, they'd rescued the family from their elevator and brought them down to the ninety-third floor. The father, counter to advice, had gone off in search of a way down, while his wife and children got settled in the closest meeting room.

Gwang was looking thoughtful. "I couldn't help noticing the aluminum panels in the elevator," he mused.

"Mm-hmm. These wall columns have got aluminum paneling too."

"You're right. I don't know why it's taken me so long to figure it out. Tell me if you know this already, but molten aluminum is actually massively explosive."

"Aluminum? Seriously? Like Coke cans? But surely aluminum gets heated to melting point all the time when it's smelted."

"Yes, very, very carefully. Because if it comes into contact with water when it's in liquid form? Ker-bam."

"I suggest we get ourselves some liquid aluminum then. Any idea how?"

"No, but I know who we can ask."

"Funny, I think I do too."

* * *

Rosalyn nodded thoughtfully. "Actually, it's even more powerful than TNT—two or three times more explosive."

"Wow. Where do we get us some melted aluminum?"

"Well . . . there's probably something like a hundred tons of the stuff downstairs."

"What? You mean the support columns?"

"Fortunately not, they'll be made of steel. I mean the plane. The TV's saying it was a Boeing 767. That thing's fuselage and wings are pure aluminum, now being roasted in a roaring fire."

"Oh, Jesus."

"And come to think of it, since the plane would have sheared through at least one water pipe—"

"There's loads of water swilling about downstairs. I've seen it."

"Then in that case . . ."

"Oh my God."

"No hang on, hang on. There's just one more thing you need to get the full kerblooey. A catalyst."

"And that would be . . . ?"

"Iron oxide."

"What, you mean rust? Shouldn't be much of that downstairs."

"Or gypsum."

"Gypsum. Where do you find gypsum?"

"Pass me that hammer for just a moment."

"Ah, sure, here. Why?"

"Thanks."

Rosalyn swung the hammer into one of the partition walls next to her desk, leaving a deep dent. Then she flipped the hammer over and used its claws to rip out a chunk of fibrous gray-white material. She handed it to Nick.

"Gypsum."

"So you're saying—"

"I'm saying the burning jet fuel is not the thing we need to fear. What it's heating up is."

"Oh Jesus. You've just explained why this building keeps falling down every fifty-six minutes."

"Yes, it would explain exactly . . . hang on. What did you just say? Every fifty-six minutes?"

"Sorry, don't mind me, just . . . babbling."

"Okay, it's just that . . . it must be close to fifty-six minutes from the time of impact, um, right now, if that matters."

Nick looked at his watch and sighed. "Give me a minute, I'll be right back," he said as the building started to shake.

Chapter 40

"Guys, we need to build a bomb, and Rosalyn here has the recipe. You know the doors to the rooftop? They're locked. And if we want to be rescued, there's only one way through them."

"Whoa, you said I had the recipe?"

"Exactly. A mixture of molten aluminum"—Nick held up a Coke can he'd scavenged from a bin—"gypsum"—he rapped a knuckle against one of the office partitions—"and water."

"Well, that would certainly blow the bloody doors off," said Rosalyn.

Tash looked skeptical. "An aluminum bomb?"

"Three times more bang than TNT," said Nick.

"Molten aluminum?" said Gwang. "So that would have to be a two-stage process. First the melting, then the mixing."

"Exactly," said Nick. "So . . . what's the melting point of aluminum? Rosalyn?"

"Not too high, actually, about twelve hundred Fahrenheit."

"So it shouldn't be too hard to melt some? I mean, could we just hold some aluminum over a gas flame, for example?"

"Ah, not really. People put aluminum cookware on gas burners all the time. As fast as you heat up your saucepan, it transfers the heat to something else: water, soup, noodles, or just the surrounding air."

"Damn. You're saying we need some kind of kiln."

"Basically. You have to heat up the entire surface at once."

"There's a pizza oven upstairs," said Tash.

Rosalyn shook her head. "Not quite hot enough."

Nick frowned. "Uh, assuming we did have a kiln that could get to twelve hundred degrees, what would we collect the molten aluminum in?"

"That's simple. Any other kind of steel container. Steel and copper melt at a far higher temperature than aluminum."

"So another cooking pot, basically," said Gwang.

"As long as it's not aluminum. There must be something in one of the kitchens upstairs."

"Let's hope so," said Nick. "And there's definitely a gas burner up there. So forget about a kiln—what if we just put a cooking pot over a gas flame and then insulate the hell out of it?"

"Okay, that could work . . . something like cement or ceramic would do it."

"What about this sheetrock? From what you say, it would only cause an explosion if we were to add water."

"Yeah, the gypsum won't burn, although the outer layer will. It's just paper."

"How would you shape it around the pot though?" asked Tash.

Gwang looked around. "Hey, what about a ceramic planter? Wedge a stainless steel or copper cooking pot in it, knock out the bottom of the planter to give the gas flame maximum contact with the pot, stuff the gaps around the pot with ripped-up sheetrock, shred soda cans into it, put on the lid . . . then more sheetrock on top of that."

Rosalyn nodded. "Forget the pot lid, it's just more stuff to heat up. Just sheetrock on top is fine. Okay, so . . . say we get a pot of molten aluminum. How do you combine it with water and gypsum without blowing yourself up in the explosion?"

"Umm . . . how long will the aluminum stay liquid?" asked Gwang.

"A few minutes—ten, fifteen maybe?" said Rosalyn.

"Okay, so we'd premix the gypsum fiber and water in a separate pot, then set up a tilting and pouring mechanism." He looked around, then picked up a desk lamp, examined its conical lampshade, and opened and closed its extendable arm. "In fact, with a bit of surgery, this will be perfect for the job. Tell you what, if you two sort out the aluminum side of things, Tash can help me with the pouring mechanism, okay?"

"How much time would you need?" asked Nick.

"Five, ten minutes maybe?" said Gwang.

"It'll take longer than that to get our gas melter going," said Rosalyn.

"That's what worries me. And we'll still need to attract a helicopter once we get onto the roof. Um. Gwang, could you pass me your safety gloves and visor? If you guys get on with the pourer, I'll see you up at the roof door in fifteen minutes."

Tash and Gwang looked puzzled. With a gasp, Rosalyn caught on. "Nick, that's crazy! You'll be incinerated!"

Nick had already scavenged two coffee mugs and put them into his briefcase. "Tash! See that metal trophy on that desk? Yes, thanks! And these computer cables . . . see you upstairs!"

* * *

Nick burst through the door to stairwell A, the staircase with the least smoke. Twelve, maybe thirteen floors to go, ten seconds per floor: two minutes. But how far could he get down before the stairs became impassable?

The stairwell's echoing growl made Nick feel like he was descending the throat of an angry demon. He ran down flight after flight, his way lit only by fluorescent paint and flickers of fire visible through holes in the stairwell walls. The demon's eyes, Nick thought. No mystery what or who was the prey.

Floor eighty-one. The door was too hot to touch. Shit. Carry on down. Eighty. He touched the door. Hot but not unbearable. He quickly tied one of his computer cables through the handles of the trophy. Deal of the Month, it said in beautifully engraved lettering. He tied another computer cable to the first. Copper, not fiber, he hoped.

Ripped-sleeve bandanna over his nose and mouth. Safety visor over that. Safety gloves on. Deep breath. He pushed the door open and stepped inside. Straight into hell. His brain refused to confront the blast of heat, the carnage, the noise, or the gut-punching smell. But that was okay; he was only looking for one thing. It was either here or it wasn't.

Holding his breath against the heat, he took another step into the nightmare. The demon roared, as if it was trying to kill him with fear alone. There! A jet of steaming white liquid falling from ceiling to floor. Gone. Then again. Nick stepped two paces closer, stumbled on something, almost went down. He put a hand on the floor and was scorched right through his glove as he pushed himself back upright. He swung the trophy from its computer-cord rope, right into the steaming white-hot gush, and instantly pulled it back. It dribbled liquid metal. He grabbed a handle and poured a tiny trickle into one of the mugs. The other was broken. Sweat trickled into his eyes. Half blind, he put the mug down, swung the trophy. Nothing. Again.

There was a gush like a wide-open bath faucet. He jumped back and pulled the cord simultaneously, grabbed the mug and trophy, and ran for the door. He had no free hand. Shit. Then the door opened in his face and he charged through and the door closed behind him.

Tash smacked his head over and over with her bare hands. "Your hair's on fire, you fucking lunatic!"

He added the mug's contents to what was in the trophy and ran. Two stairs at a time. Three. Tash was somewhere behind him. His leg muscles screamed in pain. He gasped for more air, chest heaving. Coughing violently, he climbed on. Down below, the defied beast roared its rage.

* * *

Up at Floor 105, Malcolm was waiting to pull the fire door open. Through his pain, Nick couldn't help smiling. Malcolm's expensive jacket and tie were gone, and one torn-off arm of his silk shirt was tied round his lower face. Nick rushed through the door, heading for Stairwell B, and Malcolm dashed ahead of him to throw that door open too. Upstairs, the ragged opening next to 107's fire door was large enough that Nick barely had to duck. He sped up and people stood back to let him pass. "They're up the first escalator!" shouted Malcolm. The escalator was still stationary and

Nick took the stairs three at a time. Someone else was standing inside the revolving door and started turning it the moment Nick got in.

In the corner to the left of the roller door, Gwang slid a large cooking pot, one-third full with a fibrous mush, against the wall. Together, Jerome and Obie heaved a metal filing cabinet into position up against it, holding it in place. Then they pushed a slightly smaller cabinet into position, blocking the pot into the corner.

"Perfect," shouted Gwang. He maneuvered a sheetrock-and-duct-tape funnel into position above the saucepan, similarly trapped between filing cabinets and wall. "Okay, everyone back down the stairs—except you, Nick!" Gwang pulled at a cord dangling from the roller door housing under the ceiling. The cord was connected to others that stretched all the way down the stairs.

Nick placed the trophy carefully on top of the larger filing cabinet. Gwang tied the cord to one of the handles, taking a quick look in the bowl of the trophy. "How long?" he asked.

"It's been seven minutes."

Gwang grinned. "I'm crazy impressed. Mad hair, by the way." He pulled the knot tight.

"How do we make sure the trophy doesn't slide around when it's tipped over?"

"Good question. Um." Gwang extracted a wad of gum from his mouth. "Knew this wasn't just a nervous habit." Carefully, he tilted the trophy back, squashed the gum under its base—the edge nearest the wall—and squashed the edge down again. "Tension!" he shouted down the stairs. The cord went tight, lifting the unstuck edge, tilting the trophy toward the wall . "Stop!"

"Now let's get the hell out of here!"

They raced down the stairs. On the upper side of the revolving door, Jerome held the cord. Nick took it from him and Jerome followed Gwang through the revolving door and further down the stairs.

"What's in the filing cabinets?" shouted Nick.

"Just documents!" yelled Gwang. "Didn't want any extra shrapnel."

Nick nodded and backed into the revolving door so that one of its thick glass panels almost entirely sealed him into it. He left just enough of a gap for the cord to move freely. He looked up the stairs. From here, he couldn't see the bomb at all.

"Here goes!" Head down, eyes closed, he let out the cord slowly, more and more, until it went slack. Then his eardrums imploded and the glass doors burst into a million bits that lashed against his body and visor. He sagged to the floor, eyes closed, expecting to open them again back in the meeting room.

Oh God, what now? He was being shaken by the shoulder. He opened his eyes to see Tash looking at him worriedly. She beamed to see him alive and shouted in his face. He pointed at his ears and shook his head. She shouted again and pointed up the stairs. He tried to stand and found that he could. He brushed off a thousand crumbs of glass, then shook more out of his clothes, wincing from the still-developing blisters all over his body. Slowly, he climbed the stairs, holding onto the banister for balance. He could dimly hear the noise of helicopters and sirens coming from above.

Now he was high enough to see a pall of acrid gray smoke, scorched walls and ceiling, shredded paper everywhere, two mutilated filing cabinets lying on their backs, and a gaping hole to the left of the door. "We've fucking done it!" he tried to shout, producing only a croaking cough that he could barely hear.

He ducked through the hole onto a raised rooftop walkway—and stopped in dismay. The people climbing out behind him bumped eagerly past, then turned to look at each other in horror.

"Come and get us, you goddamn helicopters!" shouted Jerome, rushing through the door behind them. Then he stopped, sagged to his knees, and cried. More people came out onto the rooftop, wild exultation changing instantly to shocked despair.

Up here, the smoke was a solid black mass. They could see each other but almost nothing else. Not even the sun was visible. Far away, a helicopter could be heard thudding in the sky, but there was no way the pilot could possibly see them, let alone rescue them.

The would-be escapees stood, sat, and knelt on the walkway, coughing uncontrollably in utter defeat. "Going back inside," said Obie, and slowly they all ducked back through the maimed wall. Nick limped behind, dripping blood and despair.

Chapter 41

"Nick," asked Rico. "Have you tried the window cleaning gondola yet?"

"Fuck."

Rico, Gwang, Tash, and Rosalyn turned to look at Nick. "Any reason you're smacking yourself in the head?" asked Tash.

"Because it seems I completely forgot about it." He looked at his hands, still surprised not to see blisters all over them. "Yes, of course, the gondola! How do you operate it?"

Rosalyn shrugged. "Gwang? Any idea?"

"There are two different window cleaning systems," said Gwang. "There's an unmanned window cleaner that does most of the tower's windows and a manually operated gondola that just does the wider windows near the top. The automatic one must be operated from the rooftop, and the manual one must be operated from the gondola itself."

"Wait! They weren't cleaning the windows this morning, were they?"

"They're always cleaning the windows. It takes like months to do the whole building."

"Mr. Sandini?"

"Ms. Morallis, so nice to see you. Is that my contract?"

"Indeed, sorry to intrude, if you could just—"

"Tear it in two, of course. There you go, Ms. Morallis, so kind of you."

"Well. I wish you the best of luck in your chosen career, Sandini. I hear McDonald's is hiring."

"Lucky for you then, Ms. Morallis. Although I'm not sure the customers will appreciate you spitting in their food. Goodbye, Ms. Morallis. Sorry, Tash, you were saying?"

"Nice to see you making friends with our HR director. Uh, if someone was using the gondola this morning, shouldn't he be trying to rescue people with it?"

"Maybe the mechanism jammed," said Gwang. "It's happened before."

"Maybe it lost power."

"Maybe he was on the gondola when we got hit."

"That could have been nasty."

"He would have been wearing a harness though, surely."

"He might have been standing up there looking across at the North Tower. Might not have had his harness on."

"And the way we were sent flying . . ."

"He wouldn't have stood a chance."

"And what would have happened to the gondola?"

"Judging by the way the walls came down in our offices, it could have been ripped right out of its rails and thrown off."

"I haven't seen it down on the ground though."

"It'd be in pieces, scattered among all the other wreckage."

"But if someone was using it, why would the roof doors be locked?"

"Well, if it's up there, we need to get on the roof."

"Which is problematic." Nick shuddered.

"But what if we could?"

"Then there's still a security fence you'd have to get through."

"What about remote control? Could the port authority operate the window cleaner from their control center? Anyone know?"

"No idea. But if it's the same control center that unlocks the doors to the roof, they're not picking up the phone."

"And how many of these things are there? One per tower or one for each face of the building?"

"One of each per tower. The rails for them go right around the rooftop."

"And how many people could you fit on the gondola—and the other thing?"

"The automatic cleaner is just a metal frame with brushes. You could maybe hang on it, but I don't think you could stand on it. But the manual one, the gondola, is about ten or twelve feet across. I think it's only designed for two people, there's like a well at each end, but I'd guess it can take a lot more weight than that."

"You could probably put two or three people in each well, so maybe six in total, but that might strain the guide rails. But once we get it down here, we can do two trips past the impact zone."

"If it could even get this low. I've never seen it doing our windows here. And then what? Go all the way to the bottom? That would take some time."

"We just need to get below the seventy-eighth floor, maybe the seventy-sixth for safety. Then we can smash open a window or two and get back inside, then walk down the stairs from there."

"But won't we get roasted on the way?"

"We'd need some kind of panel to shield us from the heat."

"Okay. This wall board should be good insulation. There's plenty of it."

"Should we split up and look for the gondola? Each of us look out a different side of the tower?"

"Let's do it. Careful you don't fall out."

"Been there, done that, thanks."

Gwang's yell brought them back to a smashed-out, north-facing window, where he was seething with impatience. "The gondola's almost directly above us. Looks like it's by the observation deck windows. Take a look."

"I haven't seen it from the observation deck though?" said Nick.

"Maybe it's just above it?"

Nick poked his head out the window and looked up. "I see it. It's almost hidden by the smoke from the North Tower, damn."

"Yeah, you'd literally need a gas mask up there."

"Why is it there at all? Why isn't it all the way up?"

"Maybe the window cleaner guy was using it and got engulfed by the smoke? Or maybe the mechanism jammed on him?"

Nick swung himself back inside. "Okay, I've got a plan. Gwang, I'll need your craft hammer, the one with the narrow tip."

"Sure. But what would you use for a gas mask?"

"Give me a few minutes. Tash and Rosalyn, why don't you get a couple of panels to shield us from the flames, then wait here by the windows? If this works, we'll pick you up on the way down."

"Is this the best window to wait at?"

"This one next to it would be better, but I need to open it. You got that hammer, Gwang?"

Gwang handed over the hammer. Nick aimed its narrower point at the glass and smashed it out with one violent strike. "Gwang, you and Rico can break through into the observation deck. I'll fetch a gas mask and see you up there. Tash and Rosalyn, we'll pick you and those panels up in a few minutes!" He ran off with Gwang and Rico on his heels.

* * *

"That's it up there," said Rico, pointing.

"Out of our reach though," sighed Nick.

Up on the 107th floor, they looked despondently up at the bottom of the gondola, half-hidden in choking smoke. No wonder Nick hadn't noticed it before; they could only see the very bottom through the top of the window.

"So near and so far," said Gwang. "We need a ladder. There must be one somewhere to help them clean the insides of the windows or change the lightbulbs."

"There's a service corridor down there," Nick said, pointing. "Let's go."

They checked two storage rooms with no success. Another had been locked. "What about these tables?" said Nick. "We can stack them and climb on top."

Coughing with the effort, they dragged three tables to the window under the gondola.

A minute later, they had a two-story ziggurat, two tables supporting one. Rico climbed up while Nick and Gwang held the tables steady. Nick passed him the hammer and he attacked the window, coughing spasmodically in the thicker layer of smoke just below the ceiling.

"Better put this on," shouted Gwang, handing up the gas mask.

232

Rico put it over his head and gave a thumbs-up. On his next hammer strike, the entire window disintegrated into the abyss, Rico frantically grabbing onto one of the vertical columns to stop himself from toppling after it.

"Watch out below!" yelled Rico.

As smoke from the North Tower drifted in through the window, people responded with fear and anger. "You trying to kill us, dude?" shouted the large bald man.

Nick's heart sank. Oh God, not him again, he thought. This was all they needed. He ignored him and looked back up. From below, the gondola looked like a simple rectangular platform with diagonal tubular metal struts for strength. On either side, steel struts pointed diagonally downward to plug into the vertical tracks in the columns—the rails he'd used for his one successful escape.

Rico was looking down, hypnotized by the quarter-mile drop. His knees started to wobble. Slowly, he sat down and took off the gas mask. He shook his head. "I can't do this," he said.

"No sweat, come on down," said Nick. They swapped places, Nick donning the gas mask.

"Hey, you might need this," said Gwang, handing him the sports bag with his tools in it. Nick pulled it on over his shoulders to keep his hands free.

"I think I can get a good grip on the strut at the end," Nick said, looking up, "and then wedge a foot into that diagonal strut below it."

He looked down for a final word with Gwang and Rico and couldn't help looking all the way down to the plaza below. Standing on an unstable table made it that much worse. He swayed and grabbed the nearest column to steady himself.

"Okay, wish me luck," he said, wiping his sweating palms on his trousers. He braced himself against the ceiling with his left hand. With his right, he reached out and pushed against the bottom of the gondola. It was completely steady, still locked into its vertical tracks on either side.

He wiped his hands again. "Okay, hold these tables steady." He reached for the horizontal strut at the base of the gondola and grabbed it with both hands. Then he swung himself out the window, lunging upward with his right foot for the angle created by the right-hand down-strut. It took him two attempts to land his foot. He twisted to his right, moving his right hand up and out of sight, feeling for more support. Thank fuck, he found something: a vertical flat panel he could get his fingers around. But if he released his left hand at this point, his right hand would just slide straight downward. He paused a moment. There had to be something better above his right hand. He pulled up with his left arm, lunged as high as he could with his right, and grasped a round diagonal strut. Now it was a race between how fast he could find a higher handhold and how soon his hands got too sweaty to cling on. He swung both legs back, then forward and up, got his left foot around the other side of the down-strut and into the angle it created with the vertical column, then jerked himself up with his left hand to get his right all the way up onto the rail running around the top of the gondola. Planting his right foot against the base of the gondola, he pulled himself up and fell into it, breathing in shuddering gasps, then slowly got to his feet.

He was in a square three-feet-by-three-feet mesh basket with horizontal struts between him and the basket at the other end of the gondola. The basket came up to his waist, and Nick bent his uncontrollably wobbling legs to get even lower until he'd gotten his breathing—and sweating—under control.

"I'm in!" he shouted, squeakily.

"Great! Bring it down!" came the faint reply.

"Sure!" Nick looked for the controls. Just his luck. They were on a panel at the front of the other basket.

"Oh, for fuck's sake," he muttered, almost crying with frustration. He grabbed the rail and dragged himself across. It reminded him of a playground jungle gym. Easy enough in theory, except now there was no way he could keep from seeing the quarter-mile gulf below him. Bile rose in his throat. He finally sank into the next basket and sat down, hugging himself, eyes closed.

"You all right, man?"

"All over it," Nick replied, but it came out as a croak.

"Nick?"

"Coming!" Nick stood up again, looked at the control panel, and sighed. They needed a key. "Give me a minute," he called, taking the sports bag off his shoulders.

Two minutes later, Nick punched the Down button and almost cried with relief as the gondola shuddered into action, whining down its two tracks. In moments, it descended to the level of the lookout deck's floor, and Nick brought it to a stop. Gwang and Rico climbed into the empty basket, holding their breath.

"Ready?"

"Oh . . . God . . . yeah . . . ready," muttered Gwang. Rico was too terrified to speak.

Nick punched the down button again and they descended slowly. "What on Earth did you do to the controls?" said Gwang, pointing at the wires dangling from the control box.

"Damn thing needed a key."

"So, what—you hotwired it?"

"Damn right. Good thing you gave me those tools."

"You have an interesting youth?"

"Had some unconventional classmates, yeah."

"Unconventional school too, I'm thinking."

"Well . . . now you know, I guess."

"Secret's safe with me. Oh, fuck—Nick!"

Just above them, the bald man swung himself out of the cleared window, froze for a moment, then dropped, landing sprawled on the gondola's crossbars and yelling with pain. Gwang grabbed his leg to keep him from falling off.

The gondola lurched to a halt. Nick pushed buttons in vain.

"Dude, this thing can't take all our wait," shouted Nick. "It can only evacuate two or three people at a time."

"Well, fuck you," the bald man shouted back, dragging himself upright. "You think you own this thing? Someone else can get out."

Nick tried the Down button again and the gondola juddered downward a

235

few inches before stopping again.

"Hey, mister!" shouted Nick. "We're not going anywhere! You need to get out. I'll send it back up in a minute!"

Leaning over, the bald man steadied himself against a vertical column, then got to his feet, standing on the gondola's rail. "You want fewer people in here? Fine." Without warning, he stamped viciously on Rico's head. As Rico sagged dazedly, his attacker picked him up by the armpits and held him over the side.

The bald man turned back to Nick. "Now drive this fucking thing before I drop him," he snarled. "Let's go!"

Then Nick saw movement through the window in front of them. A moment later, he was showered in glass granules as someone smashed their way through.

"Morons!" Nick shouted. "This thing's gonna collapse!"

Another man launched himself through the cleared window. As he landed on the overladen gondola, it pulled loose from its right-hand track, spilling himself, the bald man, Rico, Gwang, Nick, and finally the gondola itself, into the abyss.

As Nick tumbled through the air, he thought he heard Tash screaming his name.

Chapter 42

"**S**hit!" Nick banged his head backward against a wall, making it shake. "Shit, shit, shit!"

Everyone looked at him.

"I've just thought of something I should have figured out a few lifetimes ago. Could have saved us all a hell of a lot of trouble."

"Well, at least you got there in the end. What is it?" asked Tash.

"Who owns this building again? We need to give them a phone call."

* * *

Rosalyn took the phone from Nick. "Hi, I'm calling for Mr. Silverstein from up in the World Trade Center. I have some extremely urgent information from his insurance company.

"Yes, I'm sure he's very busy right now, but I have to tell him how he can stop the towers from collapsing.

"Look, if you want to save him ten billion dollars, I advise you to put me through now.

"Thank you.

"Hello? Hello? Is that Mr. Silverstein?

"Good morning, my name's Rosalyn Croft. I'm a senior building insurance assessor at Wolff Coburg, up in the South Tower. That's right, *your* South Tower. I understand our firm is partly liable for the World Trade Center.

"Yes, I'm up on the ninety-third floor, that's right. Mr. Silverstein, please listen carefully, this is incredibly urgent if you want a chance to save the towers. At the moment, there's tons of water flowing from severed pipes up here. At the same time, the aluminum from the airplane fuselages is being melted by the jet fuel blaze. When the water meets the molten aluminum, it will set off explosions that will collapse both buildings. You have to get the water turned off *now*.

"No, you have to do it right now or you'll lose both your buildings. Are you following me, Mr. Silverstein?

"Damn." She put the phone down.

"What did he say?"

"Either we lost reception or he thought I was just some crank."

"Shit. Never mind. Time for another brainstorm, I think."

* * *

They'd moved the tables and chairs against the wall and were sitting on the floor in the empty half of the meeting room.

"Okay!" shouted Tash. "Thanks for taking some time out of your busy schedules." (Sour laughs and coughing.) "I figured you'd all like to work out a way to get the hell out of this building. First, a sitrep from disaster simulation expert Nick Sandini, who's spent God knows how long researching this building—and who also appears to be a time traveler." (Puzzled looks.) "Nick, over to you."

"Thanks, Tash. Thanks for your attention, everyone. I'm not sure Tash believes the time travel part, but here's the situation. The building's on fire from the seventy-eighth floor up to the eighty-third. Each of the three stairwells is either collapsed, blocked, or on fire. The elevator shafts are mostly full of smoke, and there's no working elevator up here. The doors to the roof are locked, plus the smoke's too dense up there for a helicopter to even get close.

"There don't appear to be any parachutes in the building, and nothing we can use to make some. I've looked. There's no rappelling gear or bungee cords. No fire hoses. I can't find anything that would let us build a glider or helicopter.

"Time is not on our side. You may have noticed the floor's tilting ever so slightly? Basically, the building's buckling and won't stay upright much longer, so we need to come up with some new ideas and fast. Tash, you're the chair."

"Thank you, Nick. Okay, who's first? Yes, Rico?"

"Uh, how about toilet plungers? Use their suction power to climb down the building." He mimed the action.

Nick grimaced. "I've actually tried that one. I'll spare you the details, but it didn't work as well as in the movies."

"Nice try, Rico. Who's next? Sandi?"

"What about a tightrope cable? Remember that French guy—what was his name, Petit? The guy who walked between the towers years ago? Who knows, maybe he left his tightrope cable upstairs somewhere."

"You want us to do tightrope walking?"

"No, no—we rig up some kind of gondola, or just a pulley-and-harness system, to ferry us over."

"Nick, what do you think?"

"Far as I remember, that Petit guy used a crossbow to shoot over some fishing line, then used that to pull over a thicker line, and finally the cable. We'd need all that, plus all the pulleys and whatever to get us across. But I don't believe the cable's still in the building."

Rico. "Plenty of cable in the elevator shafts."

"Especially if they're not being used for elevators," agreed Sandi.

"Nick, any comments?"

"It's a really interesting idea, but realistically, how would we cut the elevator cable? Plus, it would take hours to get everything ready. We don't have that long. It would also take too long to get people across to the other tower. Sorry."

"Okay. Next?"

"What about a rope ladder made from electric cable?"

"Nice idea, Eric, but we don't have enough time to construct it and get more than one or two of us past the impact zone."

Rico. "Hey, Eric! How about your rubber band collection? Got enough for a bungee cord?"

"Sure, you can be the test pilot."

"Okay, seriously, next?"

Gwang. "We were talking about the elevator cables . . . what if we contacted the fire department and got them to cut through one of the cables near the ground floor, then we haul it up here, attach some kind of harness to it, and lower people past the fire? Ah, it's crazy, forget it."

"Whoa, Gwang! It's not crazy at all. Problem is, it would still take too much time—we'd only be able to rescue a handful of people like that. And there's still the fire coming out of the windows to get past."

"So the fire department attaches multiple harnesses at the bottom of the cable, plus a bunch of asbestos suits."

"What do you think, Nick?"

"Could we drag up that much cable? It wouldn't be too heavy?"

Gwang. "We'd need to use a cable from the express elevators or the freight elevators, one that goes all the way down to where someone can cut them. We don't have to access the cable from this floor. We can go down to, I don't know . . ."

"The eighty-sixth floor might be okay, we'd just have to bash through the men's room wall to get to the shaft. Don't worry, I've done it before."

Rosalyn. "Dying to hear that story, but I guess I can wait."

"Okay, floor eighty-six. That still gives us well over three hundred yards of cable we need to haul out of the elevator shaft. The beginning would be the hardest part; every yard we pull out of the shaft will lighten the load."

"Time's ticking, guys. We don't have to work out all the details right now. Why not get the fire department on the case in the meantime?"

"Good thinking, Tash. Who's got a signal? If we use the landline, we just get the port authority."

Sandi waved them all to silence. "I'm ringing . . . and I'm through! Who wants the phone?"

"Gwang? You understand the concept best."

"Hello? Fire department, please, I'm up in the South Tower. Yes, I know, but I need to discuss an escape plan with someone . . . no, we can't afford

to wait, we need to escape. Please put me through to someone. We have a
viable escape plan, but we need help—I need to talk to a fire department
officer now." Gwang looked around. "I'm on hold."

Rosalyn. "I'm just thinking . . . if you cut the elevator cable . . . won't it
be attached to a counterweight? Kind of like a seesaw, with elevator and
counterweight balancing each other?"

"Shit, you're right," said Nick.

"What do you mean?" said Tash.

"When you cut the cable, both elevator and counterweight will crash to
the basement and the cable will go straight down after them."

Rico shook his head. "Shit."

Rosalyn. "Maybe there's some kind of braking system that can keep the
counterweight up there. Let's not give up just yet."

They looked at Gwang, who shrugged. "Still on hold."

Tash. "Say we get the cable out and we get in these harnesses. How do we
get lowered down again? We'd need either a whole lot of people lowering
us from up here or some kind of braking system."

Eric sighed. "Er, yeah . . . and who decides who gets to survive and who
stays up here?"

Gwang raised a hand. "Hello! Yes! We're up in the South Tower. We'd like
your reaction to a possible escape plan. Here's what we're thinking: you cut
one of the express elevator cables and attach some harnesses and asbestos
suits to it, then we pull it back up here, get in the harnesses, and are lowered
down the elevator shaft. What do you think?"

The room went quiet.

"Officer? Right. Okay. I'll hold." He looked up. "He says sit tight. He's
going to discuss it quickly at his end."

"Great."

"Well, we're probably in the safest place right now," said Tash. "With all
the smoke coming through the vents, anywhere out in the open or near a
window is getting smoked out."

"Look at those guys," said Sandi, pointing at the TV at the far end of the
room, which was currently showing a team of firefighters rushing into the

building. "Come and get me! I'm all yours!"

"Hell, Sandi, if you're desperate for a man, I've got a brother who'll help you out."

"Well, I tell you what, Roxanne, if your brother got me out of this building, I'd let him fireman-carry me anywhere he liked."

"I'll let him know. He's a construction worker though, I'm not sure about his fireman-carry technique."

"You get him here, I'll teach him. Hey, maybe you can tell him to construct us a ladder."

Rico. "Or drive a crane up to the window."

"Wish I could, he's not answering his cell. Damn, he wanted me to watch the football game with him last night. Should have taken him up on that." Roxanne pulled out a tissue. "Doesn't look like I'll be getting another chance."

The room sank into silence. For a few seconds, everyone was lost in their own thoughts.

Nick took a breath. "So guys, what would you do if you managed to escape this place?"

"Well, I know what I'd do if we get out of here," said Roxanne. "I'd chuck in my job, sell my crummy loft apartment, and move to Italy. Teach English, marry an Italian, and live in an olive grove."

"Know what I'm gonna be doing?" said Eric. "Take a year off with my wife to explore South America, starting with a trip up the Amazon. Eat some piranhas. Photograph a jaguar."

"Your wife's on board with that?" joked Sandi.

"You know, I just called her. She said, you get out of there and don't even think of going back to work. She said, since we got married you've been talking about the Amazon, well, we're buying tickets tomorrow. I hope we are. I sure hope we are."

Sandi. "What about you, Rico?"

"You know what? I'm going to take some time to record my music. Move somewhere I can have my own studio. Play in a salsa band. Sing my own songs."

"Olé!" said Sandi. "Me, I'm going to write a novel. *How I Got Rescued from the World Trade Center by the Hunkiest Firefighter in Manhattan."*

"Sounds steamy," said Roxanne.

"Steamy? You'll barely be able to see the pages! But seriously, that's what I'd like to do: kick back and write. Come tomorrow, they can take their underwriting and shove it."

"Tash? You've gone a bit quiet."

"You know what? I'm tired of trying to be the token Asian female hoping to change shit from within. I think it's time to launch my own insurance dot-com business and do some ass-kicking from the outside."

"Atta girl!"

"Whoo-hoo!"

"Well, Tash," said Rico, deadpan, "you need some brains and expertise in that there little enterprise of yours, you be sure to talk to this here Big Swinging Dick."

"Fascist pig! Swivel on this!" Tash held up a finger.

"Well now, I don't mind if I do, young lady."

"Eurgh—get away!"

"One way or another," said Eric, "it doesn't sound like the company's going to have too many employees come tomorrow. What about you, Nick? Going to hand in your notice on your second day?"

Sandi, with a salacious smile. "Yeah, Nick, how's your fireman's carry?"

"Ah, well, uh—"

Rosalyn. "Nick, seems like you might know more than us about all of this. We are going to get out of here, aren't we?"

"I wasn't sure, but you've made me more and more confident, yeah."

Roxanne. "Huh? Why am I feeling some kind of undercurrent here? Tash?"

Tash took her eyes off Sandi, midglare. "Sorry, what was that?"

Gwang waved a hand at them and they all looked at him intently. "Yes, I'm still here. Oh. I see. Oh. Okay. All right. Goodbye then."

Gwang handed back the phone. He looked around and sighed. "So. One, the counterweights would drag the cut cables to the bottom. But two, they think the express elevator cables were all severed anyway, because they all crashed right to the basement when the plane hit."

"So that's it?" said Tash.

"He says to sit tight."

"Shit."

"Just what I was thinking."

Then screams of excitement came from outside. The children from the elevator. "Nick!" yelled their father. Nick rushed out of the meeting room to find the father stumbling toward him, coughing. "It's clear!" he croaked. "Stairwell A! It's clear!"

To Nick, it felt like the floor was shaking again. He put a hand against a wall to keep himself upright. No, it was just him.

"Daddy!" The children tugged at their father from behind as their mother tried to shush them.

"How far down did you get?" asked Nick.

"Floor seventy-seven. Past the blaze." He showed his bleeding, blistered hands. "Took some work, but we can get through now. Let's go, kids, hurry, hurry!" He scooped his daughter onto his shoulders. "You coming?" he asked Nick.

Nick leaned against the wall to support himself. He felt faint, disconnected from reality. His knees were limp. He took a deep breath and straightened. He looked at his watch, blew out a breath. "Sure," he said. "Let's have a look at these stairs."

The mother was looking at him in horror. "What's happening? You look like you're in shock. What do you know?" She put a hand on his shoulder. "You do know something, don't you?"

"Come on, hon," said the father, "don't want Ollie to get too far ahead."

Nick turned to call the others, then crouched over as the urge to vomit became uncontrollable. He sagged over, retching, as everyone else came hurrying toward the stairwell door. He waved away their gestures of aid and they carried on past him, confused.

The mother turned away, torn, then followed her husband, grasping his hand and squeezing it. He stopped to hug and kiss her, gave Nick a quick look, and hurried her on. Nick wiped at his mouth, shrugged, and followed, sneaking another quick look at his watch. It read 9:59.

III

Part Three

Chapter 43

The shattering, rending impact sent Nick and Tash flying to the floor. Nick rolled, leapt to his feet, and helped Tash up. "That was a second plane," he shouted. "The bad news is this building is going to collapse in less than an hour. The good news? There's a way out."

"Whoa, whoa—what? How do you know any of that?"

"It's complicated. Same way I know about your slide and the bully's broken collarbone. But I've also got the whole next hour mapped out in my head. First, I need to talk to Grendan, then get Gwang to rescue a family from a stuck elevator. I'll be back in a minute. In the meantime, can you round up Roxanne, Sandy, Rico and Eric and get them to come to meeting room F? The one over there with the TV? Everyone else, tell them to head down stairwell A."

"Look who you're taking orders from now," sneered Gareth. "Didn't you just hire him?"

"Gareth. Two words: Martina Becker."

Gareth's face went white.

Tash looked like she was about to fall over again, but she followed Nick out of the meeting room toward Grendan's office.

He was just putting his phone down. Then he picked it up and threw it at the wall, leaving an ugly dent. "Where's that Gareth asshole? He's really fucked it up now, the fucking cocksucking piece of fuck."

"Grendan," said Nick, improvising.

"The fuck do you want already? Can't you fucking see I'm in mid-fucking-tantrum here?"

"One second, Grendan. Tash, tell everyone else to head down stairwell A. It's the only way out. Tell them no matter what they're told, it's safe all the way down, they'll just need to move some debris out of the way."

Tash nodded, dazed.

Nick turned back to Grendan. "Grendan. You want to cut our liability to nothing? You need to phone Silverstein and tell him how to keep these buildings from collapsing. Let's go to your office, I'll explain what you need to tell him. In fact, I can even tell you how to make a little money on the side."

"Well, that certainly sounds interesting. Hang on a sec, there's the fucker now. Gareth, you fuckwipe coward, you running away?"

"Let him go, we don't need him. You just need to get Silverstein on the phone. Rosalyn! Can you come over here a second? I need you to explain to Grendan what happens when you mix molten aluminum and water."

"Stairwell A, guys!" yelled Tash behind him. "You've got to head down stairwell A! Roxanne, Sandi, over here, I need you quickly. Stairwell A, everyone! It's safe all the way down, just a little heavy lifting to do. Rico, over here a minute, please!"

* * *

"You gonna tell us how you know so much about us?"

"Yeah, are you like a TV magician or something?"

"I'll explain once we're safely out of here. But right now, all I've got time to say is that the way I know those details about you is the same way I know how to get us out of this building alive."

"Well, you already said stairwell A, so what are we waiting for?"

Nick shook his head. "There's hundreds of people up here, it's not just the people on this floor. One, someone's got to tell them about stairwell A—most of them are heading up to the roof, which is locked. Two, some of the doors onto stairwell A are jammed shut. And three, a lot of people are stuck in elevators or trapped behind debris. Now, on my own, there's very little I can do. Together? We can save a lot of lives."

"Man, I don't know. I'm, like, just so terrified."

"Sandi? Me too. So let me explain quickly, and then it's up to you whether you want to stay or head straight down the stairs. But grab one of these writing pads and a pen each, you'll need them."

* * *

The wide-eyed newswoman faced the camera, a live image of the burning South Tower behind her. "We've just heard from a man in the South Tower that there is a way down from above the impact. It appears one of the staircases, stairwell A, is still intact. And I believe we have . . . ah, Mr. Nick Sandini on the line now."

Nick's voice came out of the TV. "If you're watching this and you're in the South Tower, I want to tell you stairwell A is your only way out of here. If you're anywhere else and know someone who's up in the South Tower, call them now and tell them: stairwell A."

At the bottom of the screen, a ticker appeared: "SOUTH TOWER STAIRWELL A UNDAMAGED. IMMEDIATE EVACUATION ADVISED."

The newswoman continued. "What are conditions like up there, Mr. Sandini?"

"Getting worse fast. The floors and walls are buckling and there's an explosive mixture of molten aluminum and water brewing downstairs. So if anyone out there is able to switch off the water supply to the towers, do it now. Otherwise we probably have less than an hour to evacuate the towers before they collapse. No need for panic, but if you're in the South Tower, get moving now: stairwell A."

A few people who'd stopped to look at the TV looked around in horror and ran for the stairs. Another shouted into his phone, "Yeah, I'm on my way out. Yeah, I've heard. I'll see you soon, I love you all."

"Hey! Nick! Let's get moving—those stairs are going to be crowded."

Nick shouted down the corridor. "Sandi! Rico! Rosalyn! Eric! How're you doing with the other TV stations?" A chorus of positive shouts came back and Nick punched the air. "Okay, everyone, let's get moving—those

251

stairs are going to be crowded!"

His team headed for the stairs. Nick looked around. The floor was deserted except for Tash, Rosalyn, and himself. He checked his watch. Half an hour to go. He held the phone to one side. "Okay, what have I forgotten?"

"Nothing I can think of. All the TV networks are pushing your advice. Stairwell A's got people streaming down it."

"What about the injured people in the impact zone?"

"Not a lot we can do for them, Nick."

"What about the elevators? If they can get them running, we could load them up with injured people—probably not on the seventy-eighth floor, but maybe they could get as far as, I don't know, maybe floor seventy-six or something, just high enough to make a difference."

"Sure, but there'll be qualified emergency services people coming up in those elevators, they'll do a far better job than we can. They'll have stretchers and morphine and splints—that's their job, we've done ours."

"Yeah, but if the emergency people come up in the elevators and don't get to the floors where the injured people are? How much time will they waste climbing up another one or two or three floors? And then still have to get the injured people back down to the elevators?"

"Christ, Nick. If we don't know where the elevators are going to be, where would we take an injured person? And without a stretcher? Without anything? We'd do more damage than good. And frankly, I'm terrified. Let's go."

"Sure. You're right. Okay. Head for the stairs, I'm right behind you." Nick spoke into the phone again. "That's all I can think of. I'm heading down now."

He held the phone away from his mouth. "Okay, if anyone's still up here, it's time to go!" he shouted. Then he paused, held by the image on the TV screen. "Wait! Tash! See that helicopter view of the tower rooftops?"

"Covered in smoke, yeah. Let's go, for God's sake."

"Yeah, but look at that one corner of the North Tower. That must be the northwest corner. I bet they could land a chopper there."

"Except there's a security fence and radio antennas all over the place. And look at the wind blowing over the roof—you'd have to be crazy to even try."

"What about one of those monster Chinook helicopters? They're heavy as fuck, they can probably land in a hurricane. In fact, they don't even have to land, they can just hover in front of the tower and drop their tail on the edge of the rooftop to get people off the roof."

"Sure. And the fence? And the locked rooftop door?"

"Okay, what if they bring some sappers to clear the way and blow the door?"

"Seriously?"

"Sure. Shit." He shouted into the phone again. "Hey, are you still there?"

* * *

On CNN, the newswoman carried on. "We've just heard more from Nick Sandini in the South Tower, where apparently stairwell A is open all the way down. However, in the North Tower, there is still no way out from the upper floors. And we've had reports that the doors to the roof are locked.

"But apparently there's hope. Mr. Sandini, you have an idea how the people trapped in the North Tower can evacuate?"

"Yes, all the North Tower staircases are blocked. The only way out is through a rooftop evacuation with military Chinook helicopters. They won't be able to land on the North Tower because of the smoke and cables up there, but they should be able to touch down on the northwest corner of the tower, the windward corner, and evacuate people to nearby rooftops. But because the doors to the roof are locked, they'll need to first bring people with breathing equipment to cut through the security fences, blast through the roof door, and help people get to the roof. They'll need guide ropes and more breathing equipment."

"Thank you, Mr. Sandini. Let's take a closer look at that rooftop now. In the meantime, we are trying to contact senior officials from the air force and navy."

Seconds later, a new ticker appeared: NORTH TOWER: HEAD FOR 107TH FLOOR TO AWAIT EVACUATION.

On the TV, the camera cut between the view of the roof and a view of a man sitting next to the helicopter pilot, hovering close to the North Tower's roof. "Yes, the roof is almost completely obscured by smoke and landing would be extremely dangerous, but there does appear to be one corner, the northwest corner, where a Chinook helicopter might be able to touch down. As long as the locked door can be blown open—ah, we've just been told to vacate this airspace."

"Thank you. We're now going back to Mr. Nick Sandini on the ninety-third floor of the South Tower. Mr. Sandini?"

"As I said earlier, if anyone can turn off the water supply, turn it off now or it'll cause a massive explosion. Everyone in the South Tower, help everyone on your floor to stairwell A. In the North Tower, help them get to the roof."

He put the phone down and stood up. Only Tash was left in the room. "Okay! Let's get out of here!"

* * *

The staircase was a slow torrent of people of all sizes, ages, shapes, and nationalities. Many had tied pieces of fabric from their clothing around their faces to filter the smoke. Mostly they were silent, except for intermittent coughing and wheezing, saving their breath in the poisonous air and saving their energy for the ninety floors of stairs.

Some were being supported by others. Older people, overweight people, and, as they got lower, people with injuries: a woman with bleeding head wounds, someone limping on a bad ankle, a couple of people who were obviously suffering from smoke inhalation and had to stop sporadically for spasms of coughing.

The healthier overtook the injured and hurried on, barely sparing a glance for their slower comrades. Nick himself felt physically fit but emotionally drained. He still couldn't believe that this time he might actually escape his torture.

As Nick had learned on his previous descent to collect the molten aluminum, the debris on the stairs grew worse as they descended, along with the hellish howl of the wounded building. As the passed the eighty-first floor, the stairwell became an obstacle course and the ceilings looked as if they could fully disintegrate at any moment. In some places, flames were actually visible through gaps in the walls. Luckily, the lights were still on.

They noticed the stairs getting wetter and wetter with liquid pooling between the clumps of debris. Nick looked around and saw how the liquid was seeping from cracks in the walls—as they passed the next door, he saw it running out in a slow trickle, then a floor lower, flowing more strongly, dripping, gurgling, and gushing around them.

He lowered his bandanna and sniffed. He wasn't sure, but the chemical component of the toxic stew in the stairwell seemed a lot stronger. The liquid didn't have a particular color, or at least not one he could see in the murk.

Tash noticed him looking. "The plane must have cut all the water pipes," she suggested.

"Yeah, but I don't think it's just water." Nick touched a finger to the wet wall, tasted it, and spat. "Kerosene," he said. "Jet fuel. It obviously didn't all ignite when the plane hit."

"Holy shit," breathed Tash. "It could catch alight at any second if the fire spreads from one of the floors."

"Better keep it quiet," said Nick, gesturing at the people around them. The last thing they needed was to start a panic. He looked around for Rosalyn and found her a few steps in front of him and Tash. "Rosalyn, could you wait up a second?"

She stood aside until he caught up with her. "Rosalyn, how volatile is this jet fuel?" he said quietly.

"I've been thinking about that myself," she said. "Fortunately, it's a lot less flammable than gasoline. I mean, sure, once you get it burning, it goes up, like . . . well, jet fuel, but you need a fairly high air temperature to set it alight. It's the evaporated gas that burns, not the liquid."

"So that's why it doesn't have as much odor as gasoline?"

"Correct. It evaporates at about one hundred degrees Fahrenheit."

"So the stuff can't ignite while it's cooler than one hundred degrees?"

"I don't think so. Let's just hope it doesn't actually get that hot in here."

"Christ, it's pretty hot already and we haven't gotten past the worst of the impact zone yet."

They were all sweating and panting from the heat coming from the doorways and walls, while the jet fuel kept pouring down around and between their feet.

"The smell's getting worse," said Tash.

"Just hope nothing starts sparking," said Nick, looking apprehensively at a dangling lighting cable. Below them, someone casually dragged a big chunk of debris into the corner of the landing to clear more space. Nick thought he could see a bit of buckled metal sticking out of it. He grimaced.

A protracted scream of agony came from behind a doorway. Floor seventy-eight. The Sky Lobby, the floor where everyone who worked on the upper floors had to switch elevators. And the lowest floor of the impact zone.

When Nick had been in the Sky Lobby earlier that morning—eons and eons ago—there'd been over a hundred people there. Sure, they'd all been trying to evacuate, but even earlier, there'd been about fifty people there. How many had been there when the plane sliced through it? And could anyone have actually survived?

Nick took a deep breath. If he opened the door, what waited for him on the other side? And what use could he be? Surely anyone who'd survived the impact—and the fire—would have escaped already if they'd been able to. He was now just minutes away from safety. With someone who might be close to caring as much for him as he did for her.

He turned away. Tash had climbed back up the last flight of stairs and was standing in his way.

"We can't—" he said.

"We must," she said.

"Two minutes," he sighed.

"Two minutes," she agreed.

Nick turned back to the door and put his hand against it. Warm but not too hot. He opened it toward him. Smoke wafted out.

"Expected more smoke than this," said Nick.

They peered in. Hazy, but not impenetrable, not the choking smoke they'd experienced on the upper floors. The light was flickering orange. So something *was* on fire, but maybe most of the smoke was going out the windows.

Another gut-wrenching scream. Nick gripped Tash's hand. "Whatever we do, it needs to be fast."

They stepped inside and were immediately stripped of their bearings. It was like being inside a frozen explosion. Everything that had normally been solid, level, or upright now wasn't. Even the riot of dangling cables wasn't hanging straight down. Barely able to process what he was seeing, even Nick's sense of balance struggled to tell him which way was up.

A woman looked up at them from what might have been the floor or maybe a fallen-over wall. But she didn't have a waist, or legs. And those dangling cables . . . weren't cables. Tash turned away and vomited explosively, followed by Nick a moment later. Wiping his mouth, he said, "I think it's going to get worse."

It did. They shakily made their way beyond the woman. There were more bodies, bodies without heads, heads without much in the way of bodies.

"Anyone here?" shouted Nick. "Anyone . . . alive? If any of you can walk, you need to go down stairwell A now!"

Incredibly, a few people here and there stood up and picked their way toward Nick.

"Through that door, as fast as you can," he said to them. "Anyone else need help?"

"Over . . . here," came a faint reply.

Nick clambered over debris and body parts. Tash was retching behind him. His shoes slipped. He didn't look down.

"Where are you?"

"Here . . . over here."

Further away, from near the blazing fire in the distance, came another shuddering scream. Nick ignored it. He saw a man and a woman, each in one piece but drenched in blood. Trembling with shock, they looked at him with hope in their eyes.

Not exactly in one piece. The woman had lost most of an arm. The man held the end of a belt wrapped tightly around her upper arm. He had a gaping wound to the side of his head, bone showing through the blood.

"It's all right," the man said to the woman. "We're going to be rescued now." He smiled at her in a bloody grimace, then his eyes lost their focus and he relaxed his grip on the belt.

The woman screamed. "Lennox! Oh my God, oh my God . . ."

Nick grabbed the belt, which had started to unravel, and retightened it, tying it off. He sized her up. She was taller than Tash, and more solidly built. No way could they carry her out of here.

"They said . . . to stay up here," the woman gasped. "But then . . . but then . . ."

"Don't talk," said Nick, "you'll just inhale more smoke." He looked around. He couldn't see Tash.

"I . . . should have stayed . . . upstairs . . . like they said," the woman continued. "But I . . . I just . . . I . . ." She coughed violently.

"It's all right, it's all right," said Nick, holding back emotion, gasping for breath. "Tash!" he shouted. "Tash!"

"Over here! It's Kendra!"

"Oh Jesus. Can she move?"

"I think so. I think it's just a broken leg."

Just a broken leg? Nick screamed in frustration, a wordless howl. The woman flinched.

"What was that?" Tash called.

"Nothing. I'm coming!" Gently, he put a hand on the woman's good shoulder. "I'll be back. Just need to see if anyone can help."

The woman closed her eyes. Nick didn't know if she'd passed out or not, but at least she was still breathing. Although in a few minutes it wouldn't make any difference.

Nick clambered over more building and human debris. Tash knelt next to a young woman barely recognizable as Kendra, crumpled, leg at a crooked angle.

"I got to the bottom . . . but they said . . . was safe . . . to go up again," she whispered. "Then . . . waiting here for the elevator . . . looked like an airplane wing . . . straight through the wall . . . straight through everyone."

"Were you hit by the plane wing?" asked Nick.

"No, someone was hurled into me . . . that person . . . over there."

Nick and Tash turned. Kendra was pointing at a headless lump a few yards away.

"Had to get away . . . was on top of me. I . . . crawled over here. So hard . . . crawling over . . . everything."

"Could you walk if you held on to us?" Nick asked. "We need to get you down the stairs."

"I . . . I don't know. Hurts . . . so bad. Lift me up . . . and I'll see."

They got on either side of her and held her under her arms. "One, two, three, lift!" said Nick and they pulled her up between them. She shouted with pain, then controlled herself with a huge effort.

"Well done, you hang in there," said Tash.

"Let's try a few steps," said Nick. "Okay?"

Kendra nodded.

There was nowhere level to walk. On their second step, Kendra's broken leg caught on a chunk of ceiling board and she writhed with pain, almost toppling the three of them over.

"This is never going to work," said Tash. "We're just going to fall."

"We need a stretcher," said Nick. "Settle her here quickly, I'll sort something out."

"I've got her, don't worry," said Tash, holding Kendra upright.

Nick clambered off, returning seconds later with a battered piece of paneling. He put it down as level as he could. "Let's lay her on this."

They got her lying flat. "Now I need some straps or rope," said Nick. He looked around. A tangled piece of rope lay just feet away. He strode over and grabbed it. It squished in his grip. He dropped it, bile in his mouth, gasping with revulsion. He looked farther into the haze, strode another few yards, and removed a belt from a pair of trousers lying loose except for one leg.

He got back to the makeshift stretcher with four stained belts. Tash grimaced. Nick strapped Kendra firmly to the stretcher, one belt under her shoulders, one around her hips. He looked around again.

"Come on," said Tash. "Come on."

"Just a second." He reached out and grabbed a three-foot length of metal. "Splint. Help me."

Tash held the broken leg steady while Nick wrapped a belt around it and the splint and buckled it tight, and Kendra bit her teeth together and tears flew from her eyes. Then he used the final belt to strap both legs to the stretcher.

"Let's go."

Tash looked at his watch and raised her eyebrows. Nick shrugged. "We do what we can. If we don't get out, we do it better next time."

"Jesus. Let's make it this time."

They stood up. "I'll go in front," said Nick. "I'll be able to take more of her weight going down the stairs."

They lifted the stretcher. "Lucky you weigh so little," said Nick over his shoulder.

"He's a charmer," said Tash.

In a slurred voice, Kendra replied, "It's just . . . my dress. Makes . . . me look thinner."

Nick took a quick look behind him. She was sweating profusely, eyes losing focus. He faced forward again, carefully picking out the easiest route to the stairwell.

"Don't worry, we'll get you out in it again soon."

"I . . . do hope I can keep . . . my job," she replied faintly.

"Tash, what do you know about shock?" asked Nick.

"Keep warm? That's all I know."

"Well, it's sure hot enough around here."

As they carried Kendra past the woman with the missing arm, Nick hoped desperately that she would still be unconscious. But she had her eyes open and was trying to smile at them through her obvious pain.

"I'm so glad you rescue people have arrived now," she said.

"Yes, help is on its way," Nick replied, too ashamed to look her in the eye.

"I'll be right here," she said and closed her eyes again.

Seconds later, they were back at the stairs. Nick kicked the door open and they shuffled through.

The smell of jet fuel was even stronger. Then the lights went out. The only illumination was from glow-strips—fluorescent tape on the stairs and walls.

"How do you feel about this?" asked Nick.

"Not sure, to be honest, but let's go."

Nick started the descent, Tash following cautiously, Kendra gasping with every lurch.

"Better step up the pace," called Nick over his shoulder.

"I'm going to trip and throw her down the damn stairs."

"Well, we're also jarring her with every step we go down."

"I know, but it looks like she's passed out."

"That's definitely for the best, considering how painful this must be for her, but really, we both know this isn't going to work."

"Okay. You want to just abandon her? Yeah? Just leave her here?"

"Dammit, you know I don't. But we've got less than fifteen minutes to clear the building and seventy-eight stories to go. And God it's hot."

As they rounded the next landing, Nick tripped right over an exhausted middle-aged man sitting with his back against the wall. As he fell, Nick had a moment to see that the man had a lit match in one hand, a cigarette in the other.

The man looked up in horror, watching the stretcher descending on him, and dropped the lit match. Before it even reached the puddle of jet fuel below it, the vapor was already alight, the flame spreading with explosive speed.

Chapter 44

"First, we've got loads of people trapped in elevators up here and probably in the North Tower too. So we need elevator technicians to get those elevators operating and help evacuate the wounded people from the seventy-eighth floor in the South Tower."

As he talked into the phone, he used a marker to scribble on a sheet of paper. "Can you please make fifty copies of that—real fast?" He handed the sheet to Sandi, who looked at it and gave him a thumbs-up.

A new ticker scrolled across the base of the screen: ELEVATOR TECHNICIANS NEEDED AT TWIN TOWERS.

Sandi came back while Nick was still on the phone to the news station and gave him a pile of photocopies. He riffled through them and handed them back. "Great! That's perfect. Now head straight for the stairs, and make sure you drop one of these on every landing you pass."

He looked back at the TV. They'd cut to a man in glasses. A subtitle said he was a defense expert.

"So there's a chance that, despite the wind and rising air around the North Tower—and it's going to be extremely hot up there on that roof—an expert pilot could touch a Chinook down there for just long enough to manage a rescue. But the real problem is that the nearest air force bases are Langley in Virginia and Otis in Massachusetts. Those are both over two hundred miles away. That's about an hour's flying time."

Nick looked at his watch and felt sick. On the TV, the commentator continued. "Plus, you still have to factor in the time for someone to authorize the mission . . . and the time to get the crews ready and on board. So possibly two hours to get here. And then, when they do, they'll have just about run out of fuel. And, finally, you have to factor in the time it'll take to clear the way to the rooftop door, break through the door, and get the people out, people weakened by smoke inhalation . . ."

Nick hurled the phone at the wall. Tash was screaming at him.

"Time's up, Nick, let's go, let's go!"

"You're right, you're right. Okay, let's go. Who else is up here?"

"It's just us, Nick, just us."

* * *

No one else was left on the stairs now—just Nick, Tash, and Kendra. "Anyone down there?" shouted Nick. Through all the other noise, they thought they heard a response. Or maybe it was just an echo. They kept going, sloshing through puddles of water and jet fuel, trying not to trip over the debris littering the steps.

Another landing. Another sheet of paper with a slashed-out scribble of a cigarette and a message: NO SMOKING—DANGER OF EXPLOSION. Another flight of stairs. Then a voice from below. "Hello? Anyone up there?"

"Yeah, up here!" Nick answered. "Three of us, one with a broken leg."

"Okay, coming up."

Seconds later, a gang of men in full FDNY gear climbed into view, panting under their load of helmets, fire axes, air canisters, ropes, a stretcher, and who knew what else.

"We got an elevator up to the seventy-fifth floor," said one. "Can you get her there on your own?"

Nick looked at Tash over his shoulder. She nodded.

"Okay," said the fireman. "There's guys there setting up a field hospital, they'll be able to treat her. We're going up to see who else is still up there."

"There are more survivors on the seventy-eighth floor," said Tash, "but I don't think there's anyone above that. But you're running out of time, this building's collapsing."

"Got it," said the fireman, and they charged past Nick and Tash.

263

"A field hospital?" Nick shook his head as they carried on down. "They need to get everyone in the elevator and go."

A minute later, another two firemen appeared, trudging up toward them. "You okay?" one asked. "They're waiting for you on the seventy-fifth floor, just one more flight down."

"We'll get there," Tash wheezed. "Seriously though, I don't think . . . I can carry this any farther."

"We've got it," said one of the firemen, taking her end of the stretcher. The other fireman took Nick's end and the two of them started back down at a furious pace. "Nice stretcher, by the way," called one over his shoulder.

"Can't believe how fast they move," said Tash, recovering suspiciously fast.

"Good thinking there," said Nick.

"If I hadn't pretended to be exhausted, they would never be coming down again. I only hope the other two don't spend too long up there."

They followed the firemen down the stairs and, seconds later, heard heavy footsteps behind them. They stood aside as the first two firemen rushed past with another unconscious woman on a stretcher, her face covered in blood.

"Thank God," said Tash.

At floor seventy-five, Nick pulled open the door and the firemen rushed through. The floor by the elevators was a sea of stretchers filled with medics getting ready for an invasion of injured. Oxygen for smoke inhalation, blankets for shock, drips on stands, and more things Nick didn't recognize at all.

"What do you want to do? Should we keep going down?"

"I'm exhausted. Got to get my breath back."

More firemen rushed in with more stretchers, most of their occupants looking more dead than alive. The floor quickly filled up.

"I hope they've got more than one elevator working."

Nick walked up to a fireman with a large mustache who appeared to be in charge.

"Sir! Please stand back!" said the fireman. "We need plenty of space to manage the injured."

"I understand," said Nick. "I just want to be sure you're aware the building has started to collapse."

"Sir, we're planning on evacuating everybody in the next ten minutes. Now if you don't mind—"

"How many elevators do you—"

"Just one so far, now please stand back."

Nick looked at the elevator bank just in time to watch the doors close on what had to be the only functional one. Ten minutes?

Tash was behind him. She looked stricken. "How long does this elevator take to go down?" Nick asked her.

"Never timed it. A minute or so?"

"So with the injured people having to get taken out at the bottom, maybe four minutes before it gets back up here."

"Then which of us is going to get in the elevator up here again? You can't fit all these people in at once."

"Let's hope to God they get more elevators working."

"This one's gone," said a medic quietly from just a few feet away. He took his hand away from a male patient's neck. "Pulse just stopped, not enough blood left. We just don't have enough plasma."

"Who could have planned for this?" said his colleague. "This is like wartime."

Tash leaned over. "You want blood, you can take some from me. I'm O-neg."

"Thanks, lady, but there's no time. I'm sure the hospitals could use some though."

Tash shrugged. She turned to Nick and murmured, "You know what I thought when that man died?"

"Exactly what I thought. One less person to fit in the elevator."

"What have we become?"

He squeezed her hand. "People. Just normal people."

The lead fireman—his colleagues referred to him as "Chief"—had been making and taking calls on his radio in a calm, controlled voice. But suddenly his voice changed. "You're where? Repeat, please."

A voice squawked back. "On the hundred and third floor, Chief. Just one person up here, she has a busted ankle and stayed behind. But the ceiling looks like it's coming down."

"Give me a moment to think, son." The fireman closed his eyes for a second.

"Chief!" called Nick.

The fireman turned back to him in exasperation. "Sir, did I not tell you—"

"Your man on the hundred and third floor—I know how he and that woman can stay alive. If you give me your radio, I'll explain to him."

The fireman looked skeptical but passed over the receiver. "You push this button here to talk. His name's Adams."

Nick pushed the button. "Adams, there's a way for you to save that injured woman—and yourself. You need to listen carefully though."

He released the button and heard, "Go ahead."

"Great. You need to find a big metal safe. That woman can point you in the right direction. You need to ask her . . ."

Tash had broken into a broad grin. The fire chief turned to her. "Is this for real?" he asked. "A safe?"

"I can assure you my colleague's tested it." Tash smiled. "If he says it'll work, it'll sure as hell work."

The elevator doors pinged open. It was empty.

"That was quick," said Tash. "Is that the same elevator?"

"Same elevator," said the fireman. "But we got another up to the forty-fourth floor. We're swapping people over down there, should give us just enough time. All right, come on, guys! Let's pack this elevator like your lives depend on it! Get people off the stretchers if they can take it. There's only time for one trip after this one!"

Seconds later, the elevator was jammed with sitting and prone injured people, plus a few firemen to help transfer them on floor forty-four. Anyone who could stand was ordered in too.

Nick was just handing back the radio. "You two!" said the fire chief. "Get in!"

Nick hesitated, but Tash simply grabbed him by the arm and dragged him. They found space for their feet and sagged against an elevator wall as a grim-faced man in coveralls punched the Door button. The doors closed. The elevator lurched. Everyone held their breath. Then the descent began.

"You got any more elevators working?" Nick asked the man in coveralls.

"Just a couple. The news is we've pulled out a whole lot of people who were trapped in them. But a lot more didn't survive when the plane went through the elevator cables." He swallowed. "Man, I've seen some things I will never forget."

"Well, a lot of us wouldn't have any chance at all without you," said Nick. He turned to Tash. "I'd forgotten all about that woman on one-oh-three. But the fireman and her are in the safe now."

"Just don't forget to tell someone to look for it," said Tash. "I'd hate to think of anyone locked up in it any longer than they need to be."

Nick closed his eyes briefly. "You can say that again," he said.

Tash touched his arm. "Wait. Us? Were we—"

"Sure were. Not such a bad experience, actually." He opened his eyes again and smiled. Tash stared at him openmouthed and blinking in disbelief until the elevator decelerated.

The doors opened and arms reached in to extract the wounded and transfer them across the floor to a waiting elevator. Nick and Tash grabbed a stretcher and dashed across with it. Another fireman was shouting: "You've got five seconds to empty that elevator and send it back! Move! Move!"

The injured packed the floor between the two operating elevators. The fireman reached into the now-empty elevator and punched 75, then the door button. The doors whooshed shut. "Elevator's on its way back up," he shouted into his radio.

"Roger that," came the voice of the fire chief.

The other elevator was already full. Someone hit a button and the doors closed. They could just hear the fireman outside: ". . . on its way down with more injured."

Nick checked his watch.

"How're we doing?" said Tash.

"Okay, I think. Don't know how far away we'll need to get to escape the collapse though. And we'll have to get everyone else away too. Hope there's enough people waiting down there."

"You told them though, didn't you?"

"Sure. Only hope they believed me."

Nick reran his earlier conversation with the news announcer and 911. He hoped he hadn't forgotten something vital . . . and that the emergency services people knew how urgent things had become.

The elevator slowed. Some of the injured groaned as the extra gravity weighed down on them. The elevator jerked to a stop, bobbing slightly. Nick looked up at the number display in a near panic. They were at the mezzanine level. Thank Christ.

The doors opened with their comforting just-another-working-day ping. Instantly, uniformed people were dragging out the stretchers and racing for the escalators. Nick put a hand on a stretcher and got barked at. "Leave that, sir, just follow those people—move, move!"

The mezzanine was deserted except for them and the people needed for this final desperate operation. A fireman was shouting and beckoning from the top of an escalator. They ran in between uniforms and stretchers. Down the escalator. More shouts and waving. They ran until they were outside in sunlight filtering through the blizzard of paper and dust and they were splashing through puddles of blood and jet fuel, some of them burning. A desk smashed out of the sky barely five yards from them, almost hitting a fireman.

Tash stopped, rooted in horror. A semicharred body lay in front of her with a scrap of pink tie sticking out to one side . . . and a multiknobbed watch on what was left of one wrist. The head looked like a botched papier-mâché experiment. Next to the body, almost intact, was a metal filing cabinet. Nick grabbed Tash's arm and tugged and they carried on running. "Seconds to go," gasped Nick.

"What about the other people we left behind up there?"

"Can't help them now."

They ran up the street and crossed at the first intersection. Police were holding back a mob of photographers and onlookers, herding them further and further back. A thousand sirens formed a deafening wall of sound.

They stopped for a moment and looked back, stepping backward every time a policeman shouted at them.

"Time's up," said Nick grimly, looking at his watch. A photographer looked at him curiously and took their photograph. A policeman walked up and pointed at Nick's shirt. He looked down. He'd forgotten he was drenched with blood. "I'm okay, it's not mine."

"Looks like you can use this though," said the policeman, handing over a water bottle. Nick took it and offered it to Tash. She took a swallow and handed it back. Nick tilted it back and drained it. "Sorry man, but Jesus, that was welcome," he apologized to the policeman.

The police officer shrugged. "You're welcome. It's weird, they seem to have switched off the water to the whole area."

Nick and Tash looked at each other, hardly daring to hope. Both towers stayed upright. Flames and smoke continued to billow out of them. A gush of white-hot liquid fell from the South Tower's impact zone, burning through the air until it hit the plaza, where it burst into separate fireballs.

"The aluminum," Nick breathed.

No one else was coming out. "Please, please, please," said Tash.

Nick swallowed. He took a step toward the tower, but Tash grabbed him. "No!"

"But—"

"Enough! Let it go!"

More uniforms holding stretchers erupted from the tower, running like hell was behind them. They crossed the plaza, then the street. The fire chief was among them, carrying an injured woman. Nick looked at his watch and shook it. Then he realized. "The water!" he screamed. "It worked! It fucking worked!"

Then his shoulders slumped. He turned to Tash, distraught. "Oh my God, what about those two people up on 103? They're probably still up there. If they wait too long in that safe, they'll run out of air."

"And if it does collapse?"

"I've got to do something—I sent them to that safe!" He took a step toward the South Tower, but Tash grabbed him and pulled him back.

"Don't you fucking dare! What would you even do in there?"

"Shit. You're right. Stay here, I'll find the fire chief." He ran off.

He was back two minutes later. "Thank Christ, they're coming down. The fireman found a special evacuation chair for the woman, it's got sled runners for the stairs."

"But that'll take forever!"

"No, they just have to get to the seventy-fifth floor—they can get an elevator from there."

"Let's pray they make it."

Nick looked at his watch. The South Tower had now stood for an extra twenty-four minutes. "I can't believe this, it's—"

"Oh my God, it's going!" someone screamed, pointing upward, and then everyone was screaming and turning around and running for their lives. A wind blasted through them, hurling debris, lashing their clothes and hair, covering them in grit, choking them with dust, filling their eyes so they could barely see their new monochrome world, an inhuman roar blotting out all other sound.

Nick and Tash ran and ran, doubling over with cramps and coughing but still stumbling on, and on, until they ducked into a doorway and held on to each other, shaking with adrenaline and relief. People staggered past, layered in grit. Firemen and EMTs ran past carrying stretchers filled with people who looked like they'd been dug from pits of ash.

"Oh God, those two people would still have been on the stairs! It's all my fault!"

"Nick! You can't save everyone on Earth. All those people—firemen and policemen and everyone—are alive right now because of you."

"But I talked to that fireman myself. I told him what to do."

"Listen! What's that?"

A stomach-buffeting bass thudding grew from behind them. People pointed up at the sky, shouting, but their voices were lost as a monstrous, double-rotored helicopter swept in over them, followed instantly by another. So ugly. And so stirringly beautiful.

"I've got to see this," shouted Nick, and they ran west to where they could just make out the top of the North Tower.

The first Chinook, barely visible through the churning dust and smoke, came to a stop just off the northwest corner of the tower and did a neat pirouette to aim its tail at the only clear space on the roof. With its two rotors lashing the smoke and dust into wild violence, it lowered its wide tail flap onto the edge of the roof.

A handful of men in military outfits and gas masks leapt out and disappeared into the smoke, the Chinook quickly moving to a safer hovering position.

A minute later, everyone flinched at a series of loud bangs. "It's coming down!" someone screamed over the helicopter din.

"No, they've just blown the door!" Nick shouted back.

For a while, nothing happened. Then the Chinook reversed back to the rooftop, touching its tail down again just as a stream of people, military and civilian, surged out of the smoke and up the ramp, some dragging or carrying others. As the last one ran up the ramp, the Chinook fled, beating its way to a nearby rooftop, and the second Chinook reversed into the vacated airspace.

Again, everyone watched and waited. As the second helicopter lowered its tail flap, two men in military gear charged out of the smoke, dragging a civilian between them. The tail flap hadn't even made contact with the roof before the two men hurled the third onto it, where he was instantly caught by two others. As the Chinook rocked in a raging updraft, the soldiers threw themselves across the gap just as the entire building dropped away from beneath them with another drawn-out, apocalyptic crash.

Tash clutched at Nick, collapsing slowly to the ground. "So . . . few!" she howled. Nick pulled her up and they half-ran, half-staggered away from the second engulfing tsunami of devastation.

"Nick! Nick!" Tash pointed at an apparition emerging from the murk. It was the fire chief, radio squawking on his shoulder.

He looked at them, clearly tired to the bone. "Can't seem to shake you two off," he said. "Did you see that helicopter rescue? God knows how they got here so fast. They got everyone out who they found alive. Smoke inhalation got the rest of them."

They looked at each other in mute resignation. Then the fire chief's face brightened. "You'll want to hear this though. We got a message from floor one-oh-three, just before your tower came down. They made it back to the safe again."

"Oh thank God," said Nick. "Thank God." He sat down.

The fire chief put a hand on his shoulder. "Take care of each other," he said to Tash and walked back into the storm.

* * *

Some while later, they stood on the Manhattan side of a bridge, silently looking at the ugly cloud of smoke and dirt that had replaced the towers. Helicopters still circled, but the Chinooks had long since left.

Finally, Nick turned to Tash. "Your humble employee awaits fresh orders, ma'am."

"Orders?"

"We're not even halfway through my workday, after all."

Tash wrapped her arms around Nick. "My orders are simple and highly inappropriate. Take me home."

He wrapped back. A minute later, they stepped onto the bridge together.

Epilogue

Thanks to the actions of Nick Sandini on the eleventh of September, 2001, over three hundred people caught in the World Trade Center above the impact zones evacuated safely: 287 from the South Tower and 26 from the North Tower. Of all the hundreds of firemen, law enforcement officers, paramedics, and elevator technicians who entered the towers that day, all but twenty-three emerged alive. Today, a plaque on the site of the collapsed Twin Towers commemorates the man credited with saving well over five hundred lives, including his own. During his appearance on the *Late Show with David Letterman* in October, 2001—after refusing two prior invitations—Sandini could not explain how he'd come up with his evacuation plans when he'd spent so little time in either tower before. He could only speculate that, as an insurance risk consultant, he had absorbed a variety of technical information on the Twin Towers, information which the shock of the plane impact must have "jolted" into his awareness, fully formed, as a detailed evacuation plan. Today, Nick Sandini lives with his wife, Natasha, in their single-story house in Omaha, Nebraska. Despite numerous invitations, he has not visited the World Trade Center Memorial or the plaque that bears his name.

Afterword

Let's be perfectly clear: responsibility for the tragedy of 9/11 lies with the terrorists who organized and carried out the hijackings, as well as the evil people who financed and supported them.

But we can't ignore the fact that so many of the systems in place to protect the public from harm simply didn't do their job. 9/11 was very much a multiple-failure tragedy. In a long chain of incidents and pressure points, few of the backstops, systems, and safety nets functioned the way they were designed to.

The simple explanation is that they were completely overwhelmed by an off-the-scale event, an event that "could not" have been anticipated or planned for.

But that explanation is a cop-out. This wasn't the first time a plane crashed into a building. In 1945, a B-25 bomber, lost in a thick fog, crashed into the Empire State Building. Neither was it the first time pilots had deliberately crashed their planes. Japan's WW2 kamikaze pilots became an archetype of horror. And in 1999, an EgyptAir pilot deliberately crashed his plane into the sea off New England, killing 217 people including his boss, who'd just demoted him.

It wasn't even the first time the World Trade Center had been endangered by an aircraft. In 1981, a Boeing 707 very narrowly missed crashing into the North Tower in thick fog and rain.

The concept of the vehicle bomber was well worn too.

In April 1983, Islamic jihadis demolished the USA's Beirut embassy with a truck laden with explosives, following that up by using the same tactic later the same year, again in Beirut, twice in the same day: at the US Marine barracks and at the barracks of a French paratrooper detachment. Then, in 2000, al-Qaeda terrorists drove a bomb-laden boat into the US Navy's guided-missile destroyer *USS Cole* in Yemen's Aden harbor.

Popular culture also contains numerous examples of passenger vehicles as missiles. Train bombs and runaway trains are a Hollywood staple: *Terror on a Train* dates back to 1953, *Silver Streak* to 1976, and *Runaway Train* to 1985. And in his 1982 novella, *The Running Man*, made into a film a few years later, horror writer Stephen King had a fugitive hijack an airliner and fly it into a skyscraper to settle a personal score.

The idea that 9/11 couldn't have been anticipated simply isn't true.

So what happened when safety experts got together to explore disaster scenarios at airlines, civil defense organizations, police forces, fire departments, etcetera, etcetera? Why had nobody come up with a plan to prevent suicide aircraft attacks, especially when a single, simple tactic would have made the whole tragedy almost impossible?

A couple of times, back in the free-and-easy days of air travel, I asked a flight attendant if I could visit the cockpit. Both times I was ushered in, greeted warmly by the flight crew, and spent a wonderful minute or two chatting with them while gazing at the fabulous views. Later, back in my seat, I couldn't help wondering what would have happened if I'd tried to seize control of the plane. I presumed I would have been overpowered or even shot. After all, they couldn't possibly have *no* security in the cockpits, could they?

Well, in 2001, we learned there wasn't. If, a long time ago, there'd been a ruling that the cockpit door had to be kept locked at all times and only visually identified personnel—and no members of the public whatsoever—could be allowed through, 9/11 simply wouldn't have happened.

That particular safety precaution would have cost peanuts to put in place. It's almost unbelievable that it hadn't been, considering people have been hijacking aircraft in midair since the 1940s.

That's the first failing: letting Joe Public into the cockpit so easily was a tragedy looking for a place to happen.

You could make a case about the failures of American foreign policy in Afghanistan back in the eighties or the failure to catch Osama bin Laden after his earlier terrorist activities, but it's not as if those issues were simply ignored at the time. The issues were visible and attempts were being made to resolve them.

Once the terrorists took control of American Airlines Flight 11, the fate of the North Tower was sealed. In a fictional world, a fighter jet would have been scrambled as soon as the airliner left its flight path and would have shot it down as soon as it headed for Manhattan. In reality, we give people the benefit of the doubt. The air traffic controller on duty naturally assumed there was a reasonable explanation for the deviation: an equipment malfunction or a medical emergency, rather than a supervillain outbreak. Nobody ever wants to make the first, second, or final move that gets a passenger plane shot down. Neither does anyone want to live in a world where mishap is automatically treated as misdemeanor punishable by mass death.

In the real world, once it was realized Flight 11 had been hijacked, there was also no chance a general alert would be put out soon enough to have been of any use. The idea that multiple hijackings could take place at the same time was unthinkable—that was the truly clever part of al-Qaeda's plan. Not one, not two, but four hijackings was utterly incomprehensible, and that disbelief was vital to al-Qaeda's success.

In the end, US airspace was shut down at 9:45 a.m., nearly ten minutes after the third hijacked plane had been crashed into the Pentagon and forty-two minutes after the second WTC impact. By this point, the passengers in the fourth hijacked plane knew what they were in for, and—heroically—took action. But this just highlights another institutional failing of passenger aircraft safety.

Before any passenger aircraft takes off, we get an elaborate safety lecture, including information on how to prepare for a water landing—something extremely few passenger airliners have ever achieved successfully. Surely they can spare ten seconds to ask passengers to report any suspicious behavior.

On the London Underground today, the public is expressly given permission to intervene. "See it, say it," we're told by posters and constant announcements. The announcements may not literally tell us to tackle terrorists ourselves, but they do make the point that as individuals, we have been given permission to take responsibility for our own safety.

In this day and age, it's a big step for a civilian to stand up and initiate action against an evildoer. Vigilante behavior is frowned on by the authorities. It also takes vital seconds to come up with a plan: do you charge the guy with the knife or throw something at him? Do you organize your neighbors and do it together? First, we're looking for permission, and second, we need a plan. But without permission, we're powerless.

Nobody would expect every member of the public to "go vigilante" if the opportunity arises. Today, more people would get out their phones and live broadcast the event on Facebook than get physically involved. But among any large group of people, whether in an aircraft or an office block, a small but useful percentage will have had formal training in some form of organized violence, whether that's martial arts, training by the police or armed forces, or even football or ice hockey.

Sitting on the second and third hijacked planes, many of the passengers already had a strong idea what they were in for but still hoped somebody else would "do something." It took three mass executions before the passengers on the final plane united to thwart the hijackers. By that time, they understood they were about to die, so there was no extra risk in tackling the terrorists. But, given more license to intervene, who knows how things would have panned out?

Once Flight 11 had been steered into the North Tower, everyone at and above the ninety-third floor was doomed. In theory and in hindsight, a handful could have been rescued by helicopter from the one corner of the rooftop that wasn't completely obliterated by smoke, or by descending below the impact zone in the window cleaning gondola. But either of those options would have required a preexisting plan, training, and luck. And how would you have decided who the lucky survivors should be?

But that left all the other people below the impact zone, plus all the people in the South Tower, none of whom need to have died that day. So what went wrong?

When Flight 11 hit the North Tower, everyone inside felt the blow. Up at the top, the building rocked ten to fifteen feet. It was obvious to them that something had gone horribly wrong. Few had actually seen the plane, but offices immediately started to fill up with smoke helped along by the ventilation system. Yet the message that went out on the public address system instructed them to "remain at your desks."

Granted, the people in the control center didn't know about the aircraft yet. But their assumption was that there'd been a bomb. Now, the last time a bomb had gone off in the WTC—the 1993 car bomb that exploded in the underground parking lot—the building came very close to collapsing. The forensic report concluded that if the car had been parked just a few yards from where it was, the bomb would have brought down a vital support column and that would have been that. Al-Qaeda was just as capable of learning from that report as the port authority. So, knowing the potential effect of a single bomb, why was the default announcement so wrong?

On the other hand, when people in the North Tower phoned the control center, they were told to evacuate immediately. But when the control center was told about their ongoing public announcement, they were unable to switch it off or change it. At the same time, people in the South Tower were being told to return to their desks. Again, the port authority knew the collapse of either tower would very likely have a knock-on domino effect on the other, as well as on the other buildings around them. So, again, this announcement made no sense at all. (In fact, the South Tower's collapse did indeed help to weaken the North Tower and probably helped bring it down sooner than it would have fallen otherwise. Jointly, the two collapses probably helped to weaken the burning 47-story 7 World Trade Center enough to bring it down sooner than fire alone.)

Finally, the word got out that it wasn't a bomb but an aircraft that had exploded. Yet for some reason, everyone assumed it was some sort of light aircraft—even though there was a gigantic gaping gash in the side of the building.

Lacking information, the New York Port Authority defaulted to a "manageable" version of reality, one they had a standing plan for. So yes, there'd been a plane crash, but it was a little plane. Yes, there was a fire, so sit tight until the fire department can put it out. As they had no plan in place for a worse disaster, they simply assumed or pretended one hadn't happened.

You'd think the priority would have been to go up in an elevator for a recon mission. There were actually around eighty elevator technicians in the WTC at the time of impact. Sure, we're always told not to use an elevator if there's a fire in the building because the flames can short-circuit the elevator call buttons and bring it straight to the floor with the fire. (Why hasn't that rather obvious design flaw been fixed by the elevator companies, you may well ask?) But an elevator technician would have been able to manually override the controls and stop at any floor they liked.

Instead, the eighty or so elevator technicians were told to go home. Remember the tower had been rocked sideways by ten to fifteen feet, so many of the over one hundred elevator shafts in the North Tower were presumably damaged at this point. In fact, many of the people who'd been in elevators at the time of impact were now trapped. No problem, the elevator technicians were on their way . . . home.

So while every fireman in New York, on duty or not, was now headed for the WTC, nobody was able to check which elevators were still functional or assess the situation upstairs. Evacuating via a working elevator meant risking your life because nobody was able to tell the people upstairs which elevators they could safely use. There wasn't even anyone who could listen to the emergency calls from the trapped elevators and tell them what to do or go and rescue them.

Unfortunately, there wasn't a lot most of the people trapped in the elevators could do, because most of the elevators had just been retrofitted with mechanisms that made their doors impossible to pull open by hand. Why? Because the elevators got stuck so regularly that passengers kept pulling the doors open, causing extra work for the elevator technicians. The solution was apparently to lock people in: that'll sort 'em.

To be fair, there had been some controversy about that decision—and there is some risk attached to enabling passengers to drag doors open manually and potentially step out into thin air—but on 9/11, the result was that over two hundred people remained stuck in elevators, with no way out, until the towers collapsed on top of them. Incredibly, some of the trapped elevators were actually at or near the ground floor at the time.

It was just another result of assuming the public can't be responsible for themselves and telling them to leave things to the authorities. But that only works if the authorities do take responsibility.

Some functioning elevators would certainly have helped the firemen. They charged into the building and up the stairs, each carrying around one hundred pounds of equipment. At least two made it as high as the seventy-eighth floor of the South Tower. And once they'd gotten that high, their deaths were sealed; although those in the North Tower were ordered to evacuate as soon as the South Tower came down, there wasn't time for all of them to get back down again.

In the South Tower, many had ignored the port authority's initial announcement and had evacuated before Flight 175 hit. But there were still many people waiting for elevators in the seventy-eighth floor Sky Lobby when the plane ploughed through it. If everyone had attempted to evacuate as soon as they could have, many more would have made it out alive, even though more may also have been in the Sky Lobby at the moment of impact.

But because nobody knew there was still one functional stairwell in the South Tower, everyone above the impact zone was doomed anyway—except for four lucky people who persisted in trying Stairwell A.

Again, had there been elevator technicians to test the different elevators, firemen could have gotten up to the impact zone earlier, discovered the one intact staircase, directed more people to it, and gotten them out of the tower sooner. They would also have been able to rescue some of the injured people from the Sky Lobby. As it was, it took four firemen fifty minutes to reach the impact zone or thereabouts, just in time to have the building come down on them.

Once they understood the towers had been hit by big passenger jets, should the port authority have known they were likely to collapse?

Yes. The towers' structural strength came from the 44 thick vertical steel beams in their cores and 240 thinner vertical steel beams all the way around their exteriors. In the North Tower, Flight 11 severed thirty-three of the external support beams and did God knows what immediate damage to the internal support beams. Then its nearly full load of jet fuel ignited, which may have weakened more of the core support beams.

In the South Tower, Flight 175 severed twenty-three of the external support beams and who knows what else inside (an MIT study estimated between seven and twenty core columns out of a total of forty-four were destroyed). Although a large percentage of its fuel erupted from the building and exploded in midair, there was still plenty more burning inside, with more and more furniture and fittings catching fire as time went by. (It's been strongly asserted that the core columns' concrete insulation would have prevented them from being weakened in the one- to two-hour timeframe of the day, although it's also been argued that much of the insulation would have been stripped off by the shredded airliners.)

With so much external support strength lost, the towers began to buckle, putting strain on bolts and joins that weren't designed to support that kind of leverage. The South Tower collapsed first because there was so much more weight above its impact zone, and its shock wave and flying debris helped to destabilize the North Tower even further, helping it to collapse as well. (The aluminum-explosion theory explains the detonations that seemed to precede the collapses and also explains why the towers collapsed so soon, but even if you disregard this theory, the buckling was still in progress at the time.)

The firemen who went into those buildings were very conscious that the buildings could collapse on them at any moment. It's unlikely that nobody at the port authority understood the danger. Still, if the FDNY chiefs had been alerted to the seriousness of the risk, would they have changed their tactics? As soon as they realized the South Tower had collapsed, they ordered all the firefighters and paramedics out of the North Tower, so possibly. It would have been a very tough call to make, anyway.

The firefighters and paramedics covered themselves in glory that day. But could the FDNY have done better by their employees? While risking firefighters' lives in the heat of the moment is what a fire department does, they sent more of their personnel back into Ground Zero after the buildings had collapsed, where they worked for days in highly toxic air with inadequate breathing masks. So far, over a thousand responders have developed cancer as a result of the air they couldn't avoid breathing. Many have more than one kind of cancer. The health effects didn't stop with the responders: tens of thousands more New York workers have been treated for 9/11-related respiratory problems, further unnecessary and usually uncounted victims of the attack.

It's clear that as far as the authorities were concerned, the WTC disaster was utterly unexpected, and their response was simply overwhelmed by the novelty and scale of the attack. Imagine a fire-breathing crocodile leaping out of the plughole in your bathtub—your defensive reaction would probably not be entirely effective.

It's the same rationale that gets pushed out every time a landmark disaster comes along. The *Titanic*. Pearl Harbor. Britney Spears. No one could have possibly predicted such a thing! So nobody is to blame for the results! Then the tedious process of fact-finding begins . . . and it becomes fairly obvious that the most dangerous parts of icebergs are underwater, that concentrating most of your Pacific naval fleet in one harbor and leaving it unguarded in the middle of an escalating war is actually insane, and that nobody can deal with relentless global adulation without constant, close support, preferably from their family.

But what about the next time? Can we expect terror and disaster response strategies to be more effective post-9/11? It doesn't look like it.

America hasn't suffered any major terror attack since 9/11, partly because it's more difficult for a radicalized Muslim to get through immigration nowadays, so let's turn to the UK for a test case. The UK lost sixty-seven citizens in the 9/11 attacks, has a significant number of radicalized Muslim citizens, and had also endured decades of terror attacks by the Irish Republican Army, so you'd expect them to be light-years ahead of the rest of the world in dealing with disasters, especially after seeing what went wrong at the WTC.

On the morning of July 7, 2005, that was put to the test when three al-Qaeda terrorists boarded three trains in the London Underground and blew themselves up. The public and the emergency services responded fast and heroically, yet the underground communications were dire, hampering the saving of lives. This had been a major issue on 9/11—it had actually meant some firefighters in the North Tower never received the order to evacuate and lost their lives as a result. Communication issues cost lives on 7/7 too.

Secondly, the fact that the terrorists targeted three trains simultaneously, at 8:49 a.m., had the authorities totally focused on the Underground. Unsurprisingly, they closed it down as soon as they realized it was under attack, but they inexplicably told commuters to finish their journeys by bus. They couldn't have told everyone to just wait for a while? As it happened, almost precisely an hour after the train bombings, a fourth terrorist triggered his device on a double-decker bus crammed with people who'd evacuated the Piccadilly Line. The bus was ripped apart, killing twelve and maiming many more.

Fortunately, a repeat attempt on the London Underground on July 21 failed due to faulty bombs, as did various other bomb plots since then, including a tenth anniversary bus bomb in 2015. But instead of giving up, the jihadis simply changed their tactics. In 2016, they unveiled their new modus operandi: mowing down pedestrians with trucks and cars. Again, it wasn't an entirely surprising tactic: Stephen King had once again prophesied it, in his 2014 novel, Mr. Mercedes. The first such attack killed 86 and injured another 434 on Nice's pedestrianized seafront in the south of France.

This was met with pure complacency in London—who could possibly have imagined that terrorists would try the same thing there?—and so over fifty pedestrians were mown down on Westminster Bridge in March 2017, five fatally. The terrorist responsible drove on to Parliament, where he stabbed the unarmed policeman on sentry duty with a knife, killing him. Where else could you find unarmed people guarding a nation's government?

Even then, the UK did nothing to make London's bridges safe from vehicle terror, so, in June 2017, three terrorists drove a rented van down the sidewalk of London Bridge before getting out and going on a stabbing spree, resulting in eight dead and forty-eight injured. Finally, steps were taken, and today there are barriers in all the obvious places.

The purpose of a terror attack is to sow a pervasive fear that an attack can come out of the blue, anywhere, any time, and there will be no effective response to it. You—or someone you love—can be alive one moment and dead the next, or in agony for hours without help.

The terrorists' task is to keep coming up with new "spectaculars": attacks that catch the public and the intelligence and emergency services completely unaware and seemingly powerless to prevent or reduce the damage. Consequently, it's the responsibility of our intelligence and emergency services to anticipate what kind of attacks the bad guys could conceive and figure out how to prevent them or respond to them. I'd imagine they've come up with plenty of chilling scenarios by now. Hopefully, they've cast an eye over Stephen King's back catalog too.

But no matter how many scenarios they come up with, it'll never be enough. Something will always slip through the net, and it's the response to the unexpected that makes the difference between a tragedy and the kind of nightmare that leaves a decades-long shadow.

The suicide bombing of the UK's Manchester Arena is a prime example. Bag searches are routine at any public event in the UK, and Ariana Grande's pop concert was no exception. What no one had realized, however, was that the unsecured atrium was as crowded as the actual concert arena just before or after an event.

So that's where a British-born Islamic terrorist blew himself up in May 2017, along with scores of young Grande fans and their relatives. A hideous attack. But it gets worse. Being a busy Saturday night, the emergency services struggled to get through the traffic. When they got there, the medics were ordered to wait outside a hypothetical blast perimeter until the many, many abandoned bags and backpacks could be checked for secondary devices: bags and backpacks owned by the victims, who were visibly pouring blood while the emergency personnel looked on helplessly.

The person who could have overturned this decision was stuck in traffic. There weren't enough trained people or dogs on the scene to check the bags for bombs, so it was up to members of the public—people who couldn't be fired for disobeying orders—to pitch in and do what they could.

It was nearly half an hour before the emergency personnel were allowed to start saving lives.

No doubt there was a plan in place to deal with this kind of emergency. But when the plan failed, no one on the scene had the authority to change it. Imagine being a critically injured victim, in agony and in shock, trying to make eye contact with a potential rescuer . . . and they're turning away.

In most military forces, it's understood that "no plan survives contact with the enemy,"—and combatants are expected to improvise. The most senior soldier on the spot takes charge, and everyone below them knows it. If the commanding officer dies or gets stuck in traffic, the person next in rank must pick up the ball and start making decisions based on current information. While soldiers train for all kinds of predictable situations, they expect actual conflict to be unpredictable; in any elite force, each individual is trained to make decisions in high-stress conditions.

On 9/11 and in Manchester, the response was to follow a script. Even when the 911 and port authority phone operators—and the Manchester paramedics—realized the script was no longer fit for purpose, they still tried to stick to it. But you can't necessarily blame them.

If you listen to the recordings of 911 phone operators from the day, it's clear they were emotionally overwhelmed. They quickly stopped receiving or transmitting any useful information. It's as if they stopped listening to the callers and simply tried to get them off the line as quickly as possible. And the information given to them by the callers didn't appear to go anywhere either. People trapped upstairs reported no water pressure, yet the firemen sent up the stairs were laden with firehoses. In fact, it was obvious to anyone on the ground that the fires were uncontrollable and the only priority should be to rescue people.

In both towers, there was a requirement for an elevator technician to get the elevators moving, firefighters with crowbars and stretchers to rescue trapped people, and paramedics to treat the injured. Instead, the elevators generally remained out of action—or full of trapped people—while the firemen had to climb eighty or more flights of stairs with fifty kilograms of equipment each.

It's natural to become overwhelmed by too much input, and the result is usually some level of anxiety. Fifteen minutes in IKEA is enough to set me off. If the input is threatening, the result is usually a surge of adrenaline and, often, panic. Most of us can remember our first solo foray onto a busy freeway, and just the thought of the Paris Périphérique gives me sweaty palms.

The extraordinary thing, though, is after you've been guided through a stress-inducing activity a few times and practice it regularly, the stress disappears. It's how commuters handle the freeway twice a day, how rugby players throw themselves into what look like suicidal tackles, and how underwater photographers happily swim among schools of razor-toothed sharks.

It's curious that desensitization to one form of stress doesn't necessarily help with another kind. Someone who's quite happy driving in London's rush hour might find LA's extremely daunting and panic instantly if caught in a riptide off the beach.

If you want to decrease the amount of stress you suffer in new and unexpected situations, you need to get used to doing new and unexpected things. It's why state-of-the-art military training now involves a wide range of activities, from night swims to ice climbing, from crawling through mud to white water swimming, all while still being subjected to merciless three a.m. wake-ups, full-kit cross-country runs, and severe mental and physical discomfort. At some point, the recruit learns adaptability, creativity, self-reliance, and that a dependable team will get them through pretty much any situation. The ultimate result is the superhuman SEALs and SAS members who'll parachute into the sea at night, fight their way through crazy odds, and come back alive.

The training doesn't only make individuals more proficient at dealing with extremely stressful situations, it exposes and disqualifies anyone who's not temperamentally suited to them.

But there's another problem. Even if the decision-makers in emergency services initially go through a range of stress-desensitization training, they do less and less of it as they become more senior. In the end, rather than adjust to new situations, it's much easier for them to simply impose a more comfortable view of reality on their colleagues, especially in a hierarchical system where candid feedback is strongly discouraged. It's also easier to reinterpret any outcomes in whatever way suits the top ranks best, justifying and perpetuating whatever status quo exists.

Of course, we can't expect middle-aged people to crawl though muddy trenches while being subjected to electric shocks, and they can no longer spare the time to stay fit enough to do dangerous activities without regular injuries. But in their positions, it's their mental agility that's important—and today, practicing instant decision-making in ever-changing, high-stress environments is simply a matter of firing up the Xbox.

Current immersive video games are spectacularly realistic, and the arrival of virtual reality makes them even more so. Video games like *Call of Duty* don't only sharpen your individual abilities to learn new skills and make quick decisions under stressful conditions, they also let the participants practice teamwork and joint decision-making.

While football players and race car drivers have long realized the value of video games, I'm willing to bet the people for whom regular game play would benefit society the most see them as toys for people who refuse to grow up.

But once you start thinking about the incredible strides game software has made in the last thirty years, it becomes tempting to suggest they take on more than just a training role. In fact, they could actually guide the decision-making process in crisis situations.

It's been some time now since a human could beat the best chess-playing computers. In chess, of course, there are a finite number of possible moves. But more recently, an artificial intelligence beat the world's best *Go* player—a feat which appeared to require some form of intuitive intelligence, as opposed to simply testing every possible move with brute-force number crunching.

Today, Google's DeepMind AI can quickly learn to outperform humans at any computer game, even when left to work out the rules for itself. The fact is that computers are massively better at analyzing and interpreting most forms of data than we are. So in fast-changing situations, when we humans instinctively close down many of our sensory inputs, why are we still in charge?

People who've been in life-threatening situations frequently report how "nonessential" senses like hearing simply shut down and their sight will narrow to the famous "tunnel vision." Sure, it leaves more brain power available to process whatever seems to be more important, but in fact it can often starve people of vital information.

You might think that, in the real world, the sensory stimuli we effortlessly process would make little sense to a computer. In a video game, after all, everything is already available in the form of data, but in the real world there's just a mass of colors and noise. And even once the computer has developed shape-recognition abilities, how will it know, for instance, how to differentiate between a real person and a picture of a person?

Yet you only have to look at the advance of self-driving cars to realize how effective computers have become at interpreting the real world—and how much better at it they are quickly becoming. Using a limited range of "senses," cars' onboard computers can distinguish between stationary and moving objects, figure out what the moving objects are going to do next, and even figure out whether stationary objects are likely to start moving (a child at a pedestrian crossing, for instance). There have been and will continue to be tragic exceptions, but what's learned from these exceptions makes the same mistakes less and less likely. While humans tend to repeat their mistakes, computers use them to design better behavior.

At the same time as artificial intelligences have blossomed in ability, the "Internet of Things" has mushroomed, with ever-cleverer and cheaper "things" to network. In the context of a large building, this can include video cameras, smoke detectors, temperature gauges, pressure sensors, water detectors, and seismographs, all wirelessly linked to an AI. The AI would be able to see an unusual object heading for it—like a plane or truck—sense the shock wave of an impact or bomb blast, and know exactly what's on fire and where, where the air quality is deteriorating, what doors are jammed, which elevators are and aren't operating, and how many people are trapped in them. It would know if the water pressure's been affected and could assess how successful the sprinklers or fireman's hoses would be. Room by room, floor by floor, it could tell people the best way to escape: take these stairs, take these elevators, break through this wall, remove this debris. It could even send elevators to the most appropriate floors and, if it's safe to do so, keep the doors open until the elevator is full before letting it proceed to ground level.

If it detected a significant change to the building's structural integrity, it would estimate the time remaining until its collapse and warn everyone accordingly. And if for any reason the AI found itself unable to assess the situation or make decisions, it would alert everyone to that fact, rather than mindlessly repeat some default message.

An even more exciting development is the growing ubiquity of drones of all shapes and sizes. In the very near future, a helicopter or medium-sized flying drone could deliver a collection of wheeled and smaller flying drones to an impacted area. Using a variety of sensors including infrared, laser-based LIDAR and chemical spectroscopy, the drones would attempt to detect secondary explosive devices and vital signs from the injured, then send a 3-D triage map to the emergency personnel to view on their augmented-reality goggles. They'd also provide emergency first aid kits and communications to people fit enough to use them.

It'll be interesting to see how fast some of these strategies and tactics are adopted to prevent and mitigate terrorism. Unfortunately, we can be sure the bad guys are thinking very carefully about how to use these new technologies to cause chaos and suffering.

Dear Reader

Thank you very much for reading *The South Tower.*

If the story moved you, I'd be enormously grateful if you could take a minute to leave a review on Amazon.

And if you'd like to find out more about me, the novel, and my research sources, please visit alexcanna.com

Yours,
  Alex Canna

Made in the USA
Middletown, DE
25 September 2023

39350626R00175